Soci

By Renee Daniel Flagler

BROWN GIRLS PUBLISHING

Houston, Texas * Washington, D.C.

Society Wives © 2014 by Renee Daniel Flagler
Brown Girls Publishing,
LLC www.browngirlspublishing.com
ISBN: 9781625175052 (Digital)
        9781625175069 (Print)

All rights reserved. No part of this book may be reproduced in any form or by any means including electronic, mechanical or photocopying or stored in a retrieval system without permission in writing from the publisher except by a reviewer who may quote brief passages to be included in a review.
First Brown Girls Publishing LLC trade printing

Manufactured and Printed in the United States of America

If you purchased this book without a cover, you should be aware that this book is stolen property. It is reported as "unsold and destroyed" to the publisher, and neither the author nor the publisher has received any payment for this "stripped" book.

Renee Daniel Flagler

Society Wives

Chapter 1

The Days

I *don't even like those women that much,* Pearson Day thought, taking another gulp of Merlot. Wincing, she put her wine glass down on the dressing table with a little too much force. The dark red liquid swirled over the top. While checking the bottom of the glass to make sure it didn't break, Pearson caught the smirk on her husband Niles' face through the reflection in the mirror. She snarled back. He shook his head and walked out of the bedroom.

She picked up her compact and dabbed concealer under her eyes. "You should be happy I'm still going tonight," she yelled after him.

"That's not the problem," Niles yelled back from the master bath.

"That's not the problem," Pearson scrunched her face and mocked.

"I heard that!"

Pearson snickered. The wine she'd been drinking while preparing for the evening started to warm her on the inside. She was finally feeling good—almost good enough to be bothered with 'the ladies' for the next few hours. Vonita wasn't so bad. In fact, she was quite grounded. Pearson liked her most. Ryan seemed to be in need of a nice, strong spine, but it was Nadalia's mouth and attitude that raked Pearson's nerves. Those women were a cast of characters and Niles wanted her to befriend them, ordering her to 'be nice' around them just because they were attached to his friends.

If it hadn't happened in all these years, why would it happen now?

Pearson had no problem with the guys and waved her thoughts of the women away. Truthfully, she knew she wasn't the easiest to get along with because she never had many friends. These women were the closest things to friends she'd had in a long time.

"Babe, you need to hurry up and get dressed. We're going to be late."

Pearson looked up at Niles' frustrated expression. He stared back at her through the mirror, pleading with his eyes.

He had been ready to go for a while—all decked out in a peach shirt, a brown velour sports jacket, and matching brown shoes. His naturally wavy crop was cut close to his head and a freshly-trimmed goatee framed his perfect lips. She was still sporting a brown lace bra and matching panties as she sat at her vanity applying make-up.

Pearson looked into his hazel eyes that matched his amber complexion and licked her lips. In response to her seductive gesture, Niles cast his eyes toward the ceiling and waved her off.

"Come on, woman. We have to go." He chuckled. "You're going to mess around and cause us to miss the whole evening with smiles like that."

Niles walked up behind her, connecting with Pearson's eyes in the vanity mirror. For a moment, he held her gaze and watched her pink lips. Pearson admired what she saw as her gaze swept over him from head to...waist.

"You're wearing jeans?" She raised her brow.

"It's casual night at the Beck even though a sports jacket is still required."

Pearson looked him up and down one last time, winked, and picked up her wine glass. Before she could get it to her lips, Niles pried it from her hand. A little spilled into her lap. She cut her eyes at him and Niles challenged her with his own look of defiance.

"You've had enough and we haven't even left the house. Can you please finish getting dressed?"

Pearson rolled her eyes, but she wasn't really upset. They had their issues, but after ten years of marriage, she was still giddy over him at times. He was the only human being for whom she'd curtail her razor-sharp tongue.

Pearson applied one last coat of gloss and lifted herself from the chair, holding onto the sides. "Oops!" she said and snickered at the fact that she nearly lost her footing. When she was steady, she turned to Niles. "I'm only doing this for you. I would never choose these women as friends."

"Just—"

Pearson put her hands up, stopping him mid-sentence. "And don't tell me to be nice."

She slipped on her strapless maxi dress with the airy layers of soft flowing chiffon, took one last look in the mirror, grabbed her evening purse, and headed downstairs.

Niles jogged down the steps and through the house at a brisk pace. Stopping at the front door, he turned to watch Pearson trailing behind. She could see the question he was itching to ask behind his eyes.

Pearson cast her eyes upward and sucked her teeth. "What?"

Niles took a deep breath. "Can you please take it easy tonight?" he asked, referring to her drinking.

"Sure, Niles," Pearson replied and waved him off once again.

Pearson reached for the doorknob and heard him sigh behind her. She knew he was annoyed and hoped he'd get over it during the ride.

Chapter 2

The Lees

Fully dressed and ready to go, Ryan Lee paced the length of her spacious foyer while waiting for her husband Anderson to come home. She hoped she had successfully applied enough make-up to hide the evidence that she had been crying. The heartbreak she felt the night before had numbed. The more she became familiar with these emotions, the less time she spent wallowing in them. When she woke, she'd been done with the crying. However, the underlying rage never left; it only revealed itself passively.

Anderson left the previous afternoon with nothing more than a simple, "I'll be right back. I need to run by Niles' house real quick." Ryan hadn't seen him since. All of her calls and texts went unanswered.

She knew he would return home soon because they had a dinner party to attend. It was Sage's birthday, and Anderson wouldn't miss dinner with the foursome at their favorite place. Ryan often felt like Sage, Niles, and Mike were more of a priority to Anderson than she was.

When she heard the tires of Anderson's Jaguar crackle against the gravel, moths took flight in her stomach. A fresh wave of anger enveloped her. She stopped pacing, stood rigidly still, and tried to tame her breathing.

As she continued rubbing her clammy palms together, Ryan flinched at the sound of the car door slamming. She envisioned each footstep, wondering what she would face when he walked through the door. She jumped again when she heard his keys in the lock. Shaking her hands, she tried to keep her trembling from making its way through her entire body. Her heart pounded as the locks tumbled, clicked and the doorknob turned. She convinced herself that she deserved an explanation and promised herself that she would stand her ground all the way through this time, no matter what he said.

Anderson pushed the door open and stepped in. They were face-to-face, Ryan's chest heaving. Anderson's expression showed no guilt. Ryan swallowed hard. So many words crowded her brain, pushing themselves to the tip of her tongue only to be held there. She didn't know what to say first.

"What's up, babe? You dressed already?" Anderson placed his hand on the small of her back and pecked her on the cheek.

Ryan's breathing increased. *How dare you walk up in here as if nothing happened? Where have you been*

since yesterday afternoon? Nothing is open all night but hotels, bars, and legs. So whose legs were you between?
"What happened to you?" she asked through tight teeth.

"I had some business to take care of," Anderson responded indifferently, then walked to the kitchen at the back of the house. He grabbed an apple off the table and walked back into the foyer, crunching obnoxiously. "What time is it? I don't want to be late."

Ryan stood straight, taller even, holding her breath for a moment. "Anderson!"

He turned and looked at her in a way that questioned what was wrong.

"Where. Were. You?"

"I told you I had to go by Niles," he said as if her question was ridiculous.

"You weren't there all night, Anderson. Who were you with?"

"Let's not do this now. I need to take a shower and get dressed so we can get to Sage's birthday dinner, remember?"

"No!"

Niles stopped chewing and held his apple in midair. He looked at Ryan as if she were crazy, then took slow steps in her direction. Ryan stepped back as he approached.

"No? Ryan…"

"You won't do this to me again. I'm your wife!" Her body defied her desire to stand firm and she trembled as she spoke. She felt her pale skin burn red hot. "You left here more than twenty-four hours ago. I called you...texted you. I deserve an explanation."

Anderson took another bite of his apple. Ryan imagined him choking on it. He stood silent, gnawing as if that apple was the best thing he'd ever tasted. As if Ryan wasn't standing in front of him. She felt like she would explode into a million pieces and wished she could do just that so the heat of her rage would set him on fire.

"Ryan…" He paused to take another bite. Juice from the apple shot from the sides of his mouth. He wiped it with the back of his hand. "We can talk about it after dinner. I don't feel like talking about this right now."

"Well, I do!"

Anderson narrowed his eyes.

She wanted to smack him, kick him, something.

"Ryan, I had things to take care of."

"All night?" She folded her arms, but looked away. "I won't put up with this much longer."

Anderson cocked his head to the side. "And just what are you going to do? Leave?"

He walked toward her, closing the space between them as he awaited her answer. Ryan said nothing.

"Where are you going? Back home to your alcoholic mother?" Ryan stared at him, eyes blinking, chest heaving, fighting back nasty words that were sure to bring on a full-fledged war she wasn't equipped to fight.

Anderson touched her arm gently. She jerked away, fire still shooting from her eyes. The things she really wanted to say taunted her lips. Things that if she were stronger, she'd say.

"Ryan," he called softly. "Can we deal with this later, please? I want to be able to enjoy my buddy's birthday dinner." Gently swiping away a wisp of her straight blonde hair from her forehead, Anderson kissed her cheek. "Now let's go upstairs and get dressed."

She watched Anderson turn around and take the stairs two at a time. Once he was out of sight, she let the tears fall and the trembling racked her body. She hated the fact that he was right. She had no place to go. She had nothing without him. She was lucky to have a man like him in the first place—a wealthy, well-known actor who was admired, desired, and gorgeous—on the outside. Someone who had given and shown her so much and had taken her far away from her more than modest beginnings.

Ryan vowed that one day she would have the courage to stand up to him. Until that time, she would stay until she got what she needed out of their union. How could she ever go back to having nothing when she'd become so used to having it all—almost?

Like he said, she went upstairs, but she didn't change her clothes. After all the effort she had put forth, it annoyed her that he hadn't even realized she was already dressed. Ryan went to her bedroom mirror and checked her make-up. She'd already done the best she could to mask the evidence of her discontentment. The only thing she added before leaving was her game face. She stood looking at her reflection in the hall mirror. *How did we get this way?*

Chapter 3

The Howards

Vonita and her husband, Mike Howard, waved at her sister, Nadine, as she drove off with their daughter, Noelle. Noelle was off to hang out with her auntie and cousins in Queens for the weekend. The moment the car disappeared from their view, Mike snatched Vonita, slammed the door shut, and pressed his body against hers, pinning her back to the wall.

"Mike! You had better stop. We're going to be late," she told him, giggling. Vonnie didn't offer any real resistance to his barrage of kisses.

"We've got a little bit of time," Mike said and raised his brows rapidly before licking his lips.

"Oh my goodness!" She laughed. "We don't have time." Vonnie tried not to melt under his influence.

"You hate being the first to arrive anyway. We can be fashionably late—and happy!"

Mike snuggled his face between her breasts. Vonnie threw her head back and laughed.

"Mike!" she crooned. "We have to go."

Mike pulled her top up to her neck and unsnapped her bra with a quick flick of his fingers. Vonnie didn't realize it until her ample breasts fell free.

"Yes!" Mike said with hunger in his eyes as he toyed with her breasts—shaking, squeezing, and then burying his face between them. "I love these girls."

As he took one of her pert nipples between his lips, desire overruled Vonnie's sense of control. Her hands roamed his chest and back as heat rose in her belly. They were definitely going to be late.

Vonnie's breath rushed through her nose and she licked her lips at the delicious way Mike made her feel. Releasing one nipple with a pop, he swooped down on the other. He looked up at her. They exchanged knowing seductive grins. Vonnie's smile soon faded when she groaned as Mike parted her legs and rubbed her warm center through her slacks. The friction made the temperature rise in the room.

"I don't hear you saying stop," Mike said breathlessly.

"Shut up!"

Mike laughed and lowered himself, unbuttoned her pants, slid them down her legs along with her lace panties, and thrust his lips between her core. Vonnie gushed and almost faltered, as her knees grew weak. She shoved her pelvis forward, giving him more access. Her head fell back against the wall. The slight pain dulled in comparison to the joy she experienced.

Mike pushed her pants down the rest of the way and helped her balance as she stepped out of them. Then he stood to shed his pants, as well, before lifting her up and sliding his erection inside. Vonnie winced at the sweet pain. She wrapped her legs around his waist, and he took her right there at the door until both of them had gleaned all they could stand.

Mike held Vonnie as she carefully unlocked her legs from around him. Once she was on her feet, he held on to her until she was able to stand steady. He smiled, proud of what he'd just accomplished.

"You're such a bad boy," she said, pulling her shirt down and leaning over to pick up her pants and underwear.

"Are you complaining?"

"Not at all! I hate goodie-two-shoes!"

Mike took her hand and led the way up the stairs to their master bedroom. He set his iPad to his R&B playlist, lip-synced the words to a song into the tube of toothpaste, and took her for a quick twirl as if they were on a ballroom floor.

After entering the shower together, they washed each other's bodies, taking special care in intricate places. Kissing under the spray of water caused desire to thump in Vonnie's core. As badly as she wanted to entangle herself with his body for a second round, she resisted in the interest of time.

Mike got out of the shower first. By the time Vonnie finished oiling her body, he was dressed in a perfectly-tailored black suit. She quickened her pace and slipped a royal blue, single-sleeved dress over her thick curvy frame. Unlike many women, she had no qualms about her body and never desired to be slim by society's definition. She enjoyed her curves and there was no doubt that Mike did, too. He often made her feel like she was the most beautiful woman in the world.

"Um um um! Turn around," Mike cajoled, shaking his head.

Vonnie twisted and turned, giving him an eyeful of her full breasts, indented waist, and ample hips. Easing up to her, he slid his hands around her waist and stared into her eyes.

"You are so beautiful."

Vonnie blushed and waved off his compliment as she tried to twist out of his arms so she could add the final touches to her outfit. Refusing to release her, Mike pulled her back in. At first, he just stared at her with a sly smile. Vonnie looked upwards and shook her head.

"I'm so into you. Even after all these years."

Vonnie thought her heart would stop. His words weren't paperback romance, but they penetrated deep. Lucky wasn't strong enough a word to describe how she felt to have a husband like Mike. Vonnie held his head between her hands and pulled him down for a kiss. Her passion poured out like lava. Then she released his tongue and planted several pecks all over his face.

"And I'm the luckiest woman in the world. I love you, baby."

"Now let's go." Mike grabbed her hand and tried to lead her out. "You're always making us late!" he teased.

"What!" She gasped and swatted his back. "Wait. I need to get my jewelry and finish putting on my make-up."

"You don't need make-up, woman. I like you just like that!"

Vonnie waved him off again and headed to the bathroom to apply a little eyeliner, mascara, and lipstick. The multi-colored platform pumps she put on served as a trendy contrast to her outfit, and the royal blue swirls strolling through them matched the dress exactly.

When she finally finished, Mike looked her up and down approvingly.

"Wait until I get you back home!"

Vonnie sashayed past him with a sexy stride, her hips swaying. Thoughts about how she couldn't wait to get back home filled her mind. With the house to themselves, she imagined all the things she would do to him and all the things she wanted him to do to her. Maybe she'd even pull out one of her wigs and become one of her alter egos.

Chapter 4

The Madisons

P acing anxiously, Nadalia Madison waited for her husband, Sage, to get in. She had already called him several times to see how close he was to home. Each time he would say he'd be there soon, but never divulged his exact location, which annoyed her. He hadn't followed her instructions to stay home from work. That way, he wouldn't be straining through rush-hour broods, traveling from New York City to Long Island on the railroad.

For that reason alone, Nadalia was glad she decided to open up an office and showroom in Long Island for Miso Custom Furriers, a company she helped run, which was started by her mother, Mina Sevan, and her sister, Sona.

Sage. Hearing a car pull up, Nadalia ran to the window closest to the door. Her mouth fell open at the sight of Sage getting out of a sports car with an enormous bow decorating the top of it. She was out of the door in a flash, meeting Sage by the time he could fully exit the car. The bold crimson leather interior stuck out against the slick silver of the car's exterior.

"Oh my goodness, babe!" Standing on her tippy toes, Nadalia reached up to give Sage a quick kiss. "A new car! Happy birthday to you," she sang as she traced the sleek lines.

"Actually," Sage held up the keys, "it's for you!"

"Me?" Nadalia squealed. "Really?" Her mouth dropped open. "But why?"

"Just for being you." Sage tossed her the keys.

Nadalia caught them and jumped into his arms. A former college lineman standing six feet, four inches and weighing two hundred and twenty-five pounds, Sage barely moved when Nadalia's slim, five feet and four-inch body landed on him.

"Go on. Take it for a ride."

Nadalia giggled and skipped back to the car. She jumped in and the engine purred so silently, she barely heard it.

"Is it on?" she asked.

Sage laughed. "Yes."

Nadalia noticed Sage hadn't gotten in the car yet. "Aren't you going to join me?"

"Ah, I really need a shower. It's been a long day."

"Awww, come on."

"Babe," Sage scrunched his face. "I'll take my joyride on the way to dinner tonight. How about that?"

"Cool!"

Sage didn't wait for Nadalia to get out of the car. Nadalia huffed, got out, and headed into the house behind him, skipping to catch up.

"Want me to join you?" she called after him as he trotted up the steps.

"No! I mean, I don't think you should."

Nadalia pouted.

"I mean, I don't think you want to. Let me just...freshen up first." Sage turned and continued trotting up the stairs.

Nadalia stood in the foyer and watched him until he disappeared into their bedroom. Lately, he always managed to leave her with a sense of longing that his extravagant gifts weren't able to fulfill. She hoped he wasn't getting bored with her. How could he? She was beautiful, successful, and she kept herself up. Nadalia wondered what else it would take to get her husband to pay her a little more attention.

She thought about the bold statement her aunt always made: *Men don't need much. If you feed and screw them, you can keep them happy.* Nadalia surely wasn't much of a cook, so she had to resort to being phenomenal in bed.

"Sage, honey!" she sang.

Nadalia decided to surprise him with a little special birthday attention before dinner as an appetizer. She slipped out of her clothes, tipped into the bathroom, and eased open the shower door. Sage stood under the stream of water with his head back and eyes closed. She stepped into the stall, which was large enough for six, and slid her arms around his waist. Sage jumped, startled by her presence.

"What's wrong?" Nadalia dropped her hands.

"Nothing, babe." Sage looked annoyed. "You just startled me. That's all."

"Oh...well, I think you've had enough time to freshen up on your own." She threw her arms back around him. "I just wanted to say happy birthday to my big teddy bear."

"Thanks, babe," he said, then leaned down and gave her a peck on her forehead.

Sage's kiss felt so distant and void of passion. She sighed inwardly, but wasn't ready to give up. Instead, Nadalia squatted, taking him into her mouth. She couldn't decipher if she heard him gasp from the anticipation of the pleasure she was about to give him or if he had huffed. Deciding this was not the time to question it, she worked on his shriveled manhood, trying to massage it to life. Every time she let it go, it fell limp against his leg. After several attempts, her ego couldn't take it anymore. She chucked it up to Sage having a long day.

Nadalia pressed her hand against the tiled shower wall and lifted herself up. She read the apology in Sage's eyes.

"I'm just a little tired, babe, but I'm sure I'll be better tonight after hanging out with the gang. All of the stress from today should be gone by the time we return home."

Nadalia thought about the 'gang'. She would have never chosen the women as friends. They were forcibly juxtaposed because their husbands were so close. She tolerated them at the very least.

She didn't really have an issue with any of them specifically. Well, maybe she did have a little bit of an issue with that Pearson. Her mouth was uncontrollable. That and the fact she could drink anyone under a table. Pearson's curt mouth didn't scare Nadalia. In fact, Nadalia always met her toe-to-toe.

Not wanting to waste another second thinking about Pearson, Nadalia turned her thoughts back to her husband and her inability to rouse him sexually. Sex had always been a strong point for her, but lately, their sex life was losing its luster. She had to do something, especially since she couldn't cook her way out of a paper bag.

"Okay." Nadalia all but pouted. *That's it—stress*, she convinced herself.

Together, they exited the shower and toweled off. Only cordial words passed between them as they dressed. Nadalia took her time putting on her clothes, adding extra effort into trying to be sexy as she did so—arching her back and extending her toned legs. Sage didn't seem to notice. Quietly, they finished dressing and headed out the door.

Chapter 5

Pearson

Pearson and Niles' ride to the Beckingham Country Club was silent, save for the soft jazz emanating from the radio. She gave Niles the space he needed to shake off his irritation with her for starting the party early. She had finished the entire bottle of wine while she was getting dressed. Pearson didn't mean to make him mad. She never meant to, yet she always did.

"If it bothers you this much, I promise I'll take it easy tonight. I just need to take the edge off when we get together," she said, referring to the wives.

Niles kept his eyes on the road, tucked in his bottom lip and nodded.

Halfway there, as a sign of a truce, Niles reached over and took her hand. He held it the rest of the way. Pearson looked out the passenger window wearing a small smile. At that moment they were fine, she couldn't speak for the rest of the night. All she knew was that he meant the world to her even if she didn't know how to show it.

Minutes later, they pulled into the circular drive at the members-only country club. The valet scurried over to Niles' side of the car, while another opened Pearson's side, extending his hand to help her exit.

"Mr. & Mrs. Day," the valet on Niles' side greeted them with a nod. "How are you this evening?" the lanky young man asked.

"Great! And you?"

"Wonderful, Sir. Now don't worry about this beauty," he said, patting the hood of the Porsche before hopping into the car. He fingered the steering wheel in admiration. "I'll take good care of her."

As Niles and Pearson turned toward the elegant dining room in one of Beckingham's several restaurants, Pearson spotted Anderson and Ryan Lee pull up in his latest toy—a Maserati.

"Pearson," Ryan called out in her small voice.

Pearson pretended not to hear her until Niles turned back. Still, Pearson didn't answer until Ryan called her a second time.

"Hi, Pearson," Ryan cooed. "You look lovely."

"Thanks." Pearson looked Ryan over, assessing her petite frame in a shapeless black dress. With her hair pulled back into a chignon, she looked like a little boy in girl's clothing.

Anderson on the other hand, being the A-list man that he was, looked debonair, even in jeans, a t-shirt and a sports jacket. A diamond sparkled from his left lobe and his bald head shone under the light. Ryan held on to his hand as if she wanted everyone to know he belonged to her.

"My man!" Anderson greeted Niles with a handshake, man-hug and a winning smile. His teeth glowed. "Pearson." Anderson nodded before kissing her hand.

Charm oozed from his aura. Anderson looked around, smiling and nodding at all the people gawking at him.

"Are we the first?" Anderson asked Niles.

"I'm not sure. We just got here."

The men stood talking while Pearson tapped her foot. She couldn't wait to get inside and get a drink. Just then, Mike and Vonita pulled up. Pearson released a breath. At least she could have a conversation with Vonita. She had a personality, unlike Ryan, who Pearson thought had as much character as spaghetti without sauce.

"Hey, Pearson," Vonita said as the women embraced while the men continued to chat.

"How's Noelle?"

"Great. She's home this weekend, but she's adjusting to boarding school very well. It's me who's having separation issues." Vonita released a hearty laugh. Everything about her was full bodied.

"That's good. Don't worry. I went away to school my whole life. She'll be fine and so will you."

"I sure hope so. Oh! Hey, Ryan," Vonita said turning her attention. "I didn't even see you." Vonita pulled her into an embrace. "How are you?"

"I'm great, Vonita. Thanks!"

Silence settled between the women as the men continued with laughter and easy banter.

Pearson was just about to suggest they go inside and get drinks when she heard Nadalia's whiny voice. They pulled up in a brand new Aston Martin. Pearson decided she wouldn't acknowledge the car, she'd see how long it would take for Nadalia to mention it.

"Hello everyone! Are we the last to arrive?" Nadalia asked as she exited the car in a lavender ruffled maxi dress and purple platforms. Her long jet black hair was parted in the middle and hung straight down the sides of her face.

The women said nothing.

Sage came around the car, kissed the women and fell right into the men's groove, shaking hands, offering hugs, and starting up with the jokes.

"Take care of my baby," Nadalia said to the valet as he drove off. She turned back to the woman. "Can you believe Sage surprised me with that car on *his* birthday?" She shook her head, beaming with joy.

The other woman just smiled. Pearson waved dismissively.

"Well, ladies and gentlemen, let's get this party started," Nadalia said, bouncing toward the entrance.

Pearson hung back with Vonita at her side. She looked at her watch, wondering how much longer she'd have to tolerate the crew.

The moment they were seated, Nadalia made sure the waiter knew it was her husband's birthday. Pearson immediately ordered a bottle of their finest Merlot and wondered what the others planned to drink.

The time passed easily for the men, while the conversation between the women didn't flow. Nadalia did most of the talking or bragging, as Pearson called it. With the Merlot flowing through her system, Pearson thought things were going well until Nadalia decided to toast her husband's birthday.

"Sage, sweetie! I just want to say how much I love my new car."

Pearson rolled her eyes and took a sip of wine. Niles squeezed her free hand under the table.

"Get to the birthday part," Pearson said.

Ryan lowered her head and snickered. Vonnie admonished her with a look, shook her head and chuckled. Nadalia twisted her lips before continuing.

"Sage, honey. Happy birthday and may we share many, many more together. This is for you." Nadalia pulled out a box. There were smiles around the table, except on Pearson's face.

Sage took the box and tore off the paper, revealing a Louis Moinet watch. Sage's eyes stretched and he stood to kiss his wife.

The couples cheered.

"Come on, baby. Put it on!" Nadalia took his hand, but paused for a quick moment before she helped him take off the watch he was wearing. Her smile faded in that moment, but she recovered quickly.

Pearson caught Nadalia's subtle leer. She took a sip and peered at Vonnie over her glass, noticing that she'd caught the slight change as well.

Pearson eased her hand from Niles' hold. He'd kept her pinned down for as long as he could.

"Okay, my turn." Pearson staggered to her feet. "Sage," she started, but felt Niles pulling on her hand again. "Ouch! Let go!" She yanked her hand from his grasp. He stood beside her. "Anyway, Sage. I just want to say happy birthday and next time, buy yourself something. Nadalia's got enough shit of her own."

"It's been a great evening." Niles jumped in before Pearson could say another word. "But it's time for us to go." He acknowledged the women with a nod. "Ladies," he said, then turned to the men. "Gentlemen, I'll see you on the green in the morning. Enjoy the rest of your night."

Niles practically pushed Pearson out of the restaurant and ordered the valet to bring his car. Pearson waited for him to scold her, but he kept quiet. She held on to her glass of wine until he snatched it and handed it to one of the other valets, causing the wine to tumble over the rim.

Niles side-stepped the spill, making sure it hadn't stained his shoes, and then shook his hand, trying to get rid of what had trickled on him. When the car arrived, Pearson flopped into the passenger seat. Niles slammed the door, slipped in on his side and sped off.

Pearson felt disoriented when Niles nudged her awake. She hardly remembered leaving the country club. Niles helped her out of the car and then held her weight as she leaned on him. Pearson giggled as she tripped up the three steps leading from the garage to the mud room, where she kicked off her shoes. One went flying into the kitchen. She heard Niles sigh.

"Come on. Let's get you to the room."

Pearson wanted to look at him, but felt as if she'd lost the strength in her neck. It lolled in his direction. One thing she was sure of was the love she felt as he held her by her waist and led her to their bedroom. As sketchy as things were, his care and gentle touch penetrated her altered state. She appreciated him so much, but her tongue was too heavy to put those feelings into words.

She felt herself smiling as Niles peeled off her dress and unclipped her bra, leaving her in the matching lace panties. After removing his clothes, he folded himself against her back and held her.

When Pearson woke the next morning, she didn't remember leaving the bedroom. Nor did she understand why she was lying across the dining room table—naked. She looked around and climbed down, and then held her palms against her throbbing temples.

Pearson went into the kitchen and she popped two aspirin, washing them down with a sip of water. A stiff drink could make her numb again and she wouldn't feel so low. Resisting the impulse, she tip-toed upstairs, hoping that Niles was still sleeping. He was and she released a thankful sigh. Silently, she pulled a gown from the drawer, slipped it on and looked back at Niles to make sure she didn't wake him.

Pearson headed back down to the great room, flopped on the couch and hugged her knees into her chest. She rocked as tears rolled down her cheeks. She wished she had more control over herself in the presence of liquor, but it had become her oxygen. Living without it frightened her. How else would she breathe?

Chapter 6

Nadalia

Nadalia squeezed her eyes against the morning sun pouring through her bedroom window. She stretched and reached for Sage, but found his side of the bed empty. Sitting up, she trained her ears toward the bathroom to see if she heard him in there. Hearing nothing, Nadalia pulled the covers back and tipped downstairs to find him in the kitchen standing over the toaster, sipping a steaming cup of coffee.

Pushing her long dark strands away from her face, Nadalia hugged herself against the slight chill and sat down at the breakfast nook.

"Morning," she said.

"Hey, babe. Morning. Want some coffee?"

"Sure." Nadalia yawned, still tired from the previous night's festivities and the fact that it was just after dawn. "You're up pretty early."

"The boys and I are hitting the green, remember?"

"Oh!" She nodded. "I forgot."

"I was just making myself some toast. Want some?"

"No. I'll just have the coffee for now. I may even get back in the bed. What time do you think you'll be home?"

"Probably around noon."

"Okay." Nadalia paused, trying to think of how to position her next question. She wanted to know where the watch he wore to his birthday dinner came from, but she also didn't want him to think it was a big deal. "That was a nice watch you had on last night. Of course the one I bought you blew that one out of the water." She chuckled attempting to take the edge off her question.

He placed a cup of coffee in front of her. Light and sweet, just the way she preferred. She took a sip before continuing. "I don't remember seeing that one before. Was it new?"

"Yeah. I'd been looking at that watch for a while. I picked it up yesterday as a present to myself. Had I known you were going to buy me a Moinet, I could have saved my money."

"Yeah!" Nadalia felt a little relieved. "You never mentioned it. I could have gotten it for you." There had been an awkward air between them for some reason and she wanted to make sure no other woman was trying to get between her and her husband by buying him expensive gifts. Not that he would admit it, but if she paid close enough attention to his response, it could clue her in on if another woman had been involved.

Sage had never given her reason to believe that he was cheating, but being undeniably handsome, a former NFL player who maintained his athletic build, and the owner of a successful sports marketing business, he was fair game to some, despite the platinum ring on his finger.

"So how's work?" Nadalia wanted to stir up more conversation.

"Busy, but promising."

"I've missed you around here."

"I know, babe. You know how busy things get every year around this time. Everyone wants to take advantage of getting in front of sports fans during basketball and football season. People spend more during this season than they do all year and that's why they come to us."

"I know." She dragged her words out and sighed. "Things are pretty busy for us, too. We have so many custom orders for the holidays. Now that I'm overseeing design, my schedule is even crazier than before. We're doing a beautiful mink and cashmere poncho for Coach Tate's wife. It's coming along beautifully. And," Nadalia clapped her hands, "our new line of faux vests will be launching in boutiques across Los Angeles, Atlanta, Miami, Toronto and New York in time for the holidays. We're in negotiations to release the line in London right after the New Year!"

Sage finished his coffee and toast in silence, which gave Nadalia's mind space to wander. The holidays and the impending Super Bowl were always a trying time, but she didn't like the distance she felt growing between them.

Sage brushed the toast crumbs into the trash can, gulped his last sip of coffee and placed the mug in the sink before looking at his watch.

Nadalia slid down from the stool at the breakfast nook and stepped behind Sage, hugging him. Sage turned around and looked down into Nadalia's eyes. His looming frame dwarfed her five foot six inch body by nearly a foot.

"What would you like to do when you get back this afternoon?"

Sage flashed a naughty smile. "How about a little more of what we did last night?" A second later, Sage sucked in air and said, "Ah man!"

"What?" Nadalia stood back a tad and looked alarmed.

"I forgot. Coffey is in town on business and he wanted to treat me to a few drinks for my birthday."

Nadalia's hopes were dashed. The well-known sports commentator and host of the Coffey Davis Sports Hour had been Sage's best friend since college. They even played for the same team during Sage's brief stint in the NFL before his injury. There was no telling what time Sage would be coming home if he hung out with Coffey.

"Did Angela come with him?" Nadalia's face scrunched. She figured if Angela was coming to town, she certainly would have called her so they could do lunch and perhaps a little shopping.

"Not this time. Like I said, he's here on business. I gotta run. I don't want to get to the golf course late. The last one to arrive has to pick up the bar tab. I have to at least beat Anderson there. No one ever beats Niles or

Mike." Sage gave Nadalia a quick peck on the lips. "I'll call to let you know if I'm definitely going to meet Coffey this afternoon."

Nadalia folded her arms and pouted.

"Aww babe! I'm sorry."

Nadalia waved him off knowing that she probably wouldn't see him again until possibly well into the night, which meant she wouldn't get to spend much time with him during his birthday weekend at all. Sunday, he'd be at the football game, partly for work and partly because he was simply a fanatic who held season tickets.

All this time away from him didn't help to close the gap between them. On the other hand, it did give her some time to conjure up ways to end the negative currents flowing in their relationship.

There was a time when they couldn't keep their hands off each other. Nadalia didn't buy the fact that they were settling into a 'comfortable' space that couples experienced when sex became lackluster. She didn't want to fall into a groove that felt worn and familiar. They had always been adventurous lovers. She needed the excitement and enjoyed the sparks that flew between them.

Nadalia took sad steps back to her room and crawled into bed. She needed to plan a romantic vacation for them. Maybe they could embark on a quick excursion between the holidays. With their workload, both of them could use the break. One way or another, she'd find her way back to her husband before it was too late.

Chapter 7

Ryan

T he cramping in Ryan's stomach that kept her awake half the night, now had her crawling from her bed to the bathroom. The pain stabbed at the insides of her stomach like a timed jackhammer. Assuming it was something she'd eaten at the restaurant, Ryan took antacids in search of relief.

This time she had a real reason to refuse Anderson's advances before he left to go golfing with the guys. She was sick, but still upset at him for his disappearance, which he had yet to explain. Holding out when he finally got around to wanting to make love to her was her way of getting back at him.

When Ryan made it to the bathroom, she noticed a crimson trail leading back to the bed. She reached between her legs and pulled back a blood-covered hand.

"No!" she screamed and scampered to the bathroom on her hands and knees.

Leaning her weight against the tub, she tried to stand and a pain shot through her. Ryan howled, folded her arms at her stomach and crumpled back onto the floor. The pain stabbed at her again, this time taking her breath. Beads of sweat rolled along her face, then dripped onto the blood spotted tile.

She needed to call someone, but couldn't move. Mustering up strength, Ryan dragged herself from the bathroom to the nightstand. The tile and carpet resembled a brutal crime scene after a massacre.

With bloodied hands, she pulled the phone down and dialed her mother. Ryan cried out when she had dialed a third time and couldn't get her. Who else was there to call? She wouldn't call Anderson.

Feeling a panic attack emerging, Ryan took deep breaths. She needed to call 911, but she didn't want to go alone. She tried her mother one last time, still no answer. Ryan knew she was losing time. Her breath was growing faint and her hands were shaking. She couldn't keep calling her mother. Chances were she was in an alcohol induced sleep.

As an only child, estranged from the rest of her family because of her mother's drinking problem, she had no one else to call. And she'd never been any good at making and keeping friends.

Another pain shot through her abdomen and she cried out and then panted. She needed help fast.

The closest people to her were the wives. Calling Pearson was out of the question. She wasn't sure Nadalia had the ability to push herself out of the way to run to anyone else's need. Vonita only lived ten minutes away and she was also a doctor. The fact that she was actually a pediatrician didn't matter.

She dialed the number and thankfully, Vonnie she answered.

"Hey Ryan. I was just about to call you. I——"

"Vonita!" Ryan yelled, gasping for air. "I need you!" Her voice squeaked and she panted out short spurts of breath.

"Ryan! Oh my goodness! Are you okay? Do you want me to call Andy?"

"No!" Ryan spat as her skin grew hot. She released another wail as another pain shot through her belly. They were lasting longer now.

"What's wrong, sweetie?"

"I'm having a miscarriage. I'm here by myself, can you come please!"

"Did you call 911?"

"I just don't want to be alone," she cried. *Why did Vonita have to ask so many questions?* "Can you come, please?"

"Oh Lord! Honey, I'll be right there. It shouldn't take more than ten minutes. Do you want me to get Andy on the phone while I'm on my way?"

Ryan wouldn't say to Vonnie that calling Andy would be a waste of time.

"Please don't call anyone," Ryan cried out again. "Just. Come. Now!"

"On my way!"

"Vonnie!" Ryan caught her just before she disconnected the call. "I'm upstairs in my bedroom.

There's a key under the potted shrub by the door. Please hurry."

"I'll be there as fast as I can."

Ryan dropped the phone and slumped over. Before she grew too weak, she dialed 911 and panted out her issue to the operator. After, she dropped the phone and tried to summon what little strength she could as she waited for Vonnie. When she felt like she would pass out, she started praying the way her grandmother had taught her.

"Ryan!" Vonnie's voice carried as she barreled up the stairs. She had made it in no time.

Ryan winched, squeezed her eyes shut and took several quick breaths. She couldn't get any words past her dry mouth.

"Ryan!" she yelled again just before busting through the bedroom door. Once inside, she froze.

Ryan read the horror on her face as she looked around the room. "Oh my goodness, Ryan. There's so much blood!" Vonnie covered her mouth and blinked fast.

"Help me, Vonnie." Her voice sounded like it was fading.

Shaking off the shock, the doctor in Vonnie jumped into action. She ran to the bathroom. Ryan heard her slamming the medicine cabinet and vanity doors, rummaging through their things.

Vonnie reemerged with wet towels and a thermometer. She stuck the thermometer in Ryan's mouth, and then grabbed her wrist in search of a pulse. She looked at her watch and counted under her breath.

When she was done with that, she read the thermometer and placed her hand across Ryan's forehead.

The blaring sounds of the police and ambulance sirens pierced the air. Vonnie ran downstairs to let them in. Her return along with the harried footsteps of the ,s sounded like a herd of stallions. They were communicating in a medical language that Ryan didn't understand. She tried hard to focus, but their voices were fading in her ears.

The EMT's took her blood pressure, then slapped an oxygen mask on her, wrapped her in a blanket, slid her onto a gurney, and rushed her to the ambulance.

Hours later when Ryan woke, Vonnie was sitting beside her bed in the recovery area. Vonnie took Ryan's hand and rubbed her thumbs across her small fingers.

"How are you doing?"

"I'm not pregnant anymore, am I?"

Tears filled the wells of Vonnie's eyes and then spilled over the rim. "No honey. I'm so sorry," she said, squeezing Ryan's hand.

"Don't be." Ryan turned her head. She didn't have any more tears for miscarriages.

"You're going to be okay." Vonnie wiped her tears. "This wasn't the first time, was it?"

"No!" Ryan kept her head turned away. "How'd you know?"

"Women know these things and so do doctors."

Ryan snorted. "Yeah."

Vonnie lifted her finger like she just remembered something and then rummaged through her bag.

"I have your cell phone. You've missed a few calls," she said, handing the phone to Ryan.

Just as she suspected, her mother had called several times. Nothing from Anderson.

"Have you spoken to anyone?" Ryan winced, trying to reposition herself on the narrow hospital bed. Vonnie tried to assist her, but Ryan held her hand up. "I've got it."

She was afraid for Vonnie to touch her. Every muscle and limb felt sore. Her pelvic area felt hollow, making her feel less than a woman. That reality made her breathing heavy, like boulders had been placed on her lungs.

She couldn't break down in front of Vonnie. She'd seen enough of her life for one day.

"Are the men finished golfing?"

"Yeah. Don't worry. I didn't say anything. I told Mike that you and I were having lunch." Vonnie sniffed out a small laugh. "Those men get so excited when we get together without them."

"I know." Ryan shifted again and grimaced. "I should call my mother back."

"I'll give you some privacy. If you need me, I'll be right outside. I want to talk to the doctor again before I leave anyway."

Ryan grabbed Vonnie's arm before she walked away. "Thank you."

Vonnie smiled. "No problem at all."

Ryan called her mom once Vonnie was out of sight. Bracing herself, she took a deep breath, pulling strength from the depth of her core. She counted the rings as she slowly exhaled. No answer. She ended the call and dialed again. This time she left a lengthy message. As soon as her mother got it, she'd be at the hospital in no time, ready to do her part. They'd done this dance several times before.

Chapter 8

Vonnie

V onnie yelled out to Mike louder than she had the moment before.

Frantically, she shook a fragrant mix of seasonings over the ground turkey and sausage, mixed with garlic, onions and peppers. She pushed the ingredients to her infamous turkey lasagna around in the large pot while opening the oven with a gloved hand to peek in on the stuffing.

"Coming!"

"You said that ten minutes ago! I need you now!" Vonnie rolled her eyes.

"I'm coming now!" Mike screamed back.

Another few minutes passed and Mike was still a no-show. Vonnie tossed her apron onto the center island, armed herself with the rolling pin she used to flatten the crust for her sweet potato pies, and charged through the halls of their expansive ranch home toward the bedroom.

"Mike!" As she suspected, he was still lying in the bed.

Mike peeked over the covers; Vonnie raised the rolling pin high in the air and Mike scurried back under the covers.

"Okay! You got me!" He laughed, trying to avoid Vonnie's strikes with the rolling pin.

"You're such a liar! Get up! You're supposed to be helping me."

Mike threw the covers back and grabbed Vonnie's hand before she could hit him again. He pulled her down and positioned himself on top. Vonnie giggled and squirmed beneath him.

"Get off of me!"

Mike grabbed her hands, held them out and kissed her neck.   "No!" Vonnie jerked and squealed as he pinned his mouth between her neck and chin. She hated being tickled.

Mike released her, rolled over and jumped to his feet. Vonnie tossed the rolling pin at him, which he swatted and squatted into a karate stance. "Waaa!"

Vonnie didn't want to, but she laughed anyway. His ability to put a smile on her face and a laugh in her heart was her kryptonite.

"Ouch." Mike held on to his lower back.

"That's what you get," she said as she peeled herself up from the bed. "Your old behind!"

"Whatchu talkin' bout!" Mike said, mimicking his uncle's country lilt and broken tongue.

"The hangover. All that drinking you and the boys did last night. Now you can't get out of bed. You can't handle it like you used to."

Mike puffed his chest and flexed his muscles. Vonnie knew he was about to protest or perhaps do something silly to prove he still had it.

Mike released the air he was holding in a rush and deflated his stance. "You're right. My ass *is* getting old." He leaned on the armoire and held his back, then pretended to walk with a cane.

"Silly behind." Vonnie threw a pillow at him. "Get your old ass in the kitchen and open those cans of tomatoes for me. This house is going to be full of people in less than two hours."

"Yes Ma'am!" When Vonnie looked back at Mike, he was standing at attention saluting her.

Vonnie shook her head and walked out of the bedroom. She returned to the kitchen, checked her pots, took the stuffing out of the oven and headed to the formal dining room to finish setting the table. Mike swooped in on her and hugged her from behind.

"Do you know how beautiful you are when you're working hard?"

"Mike!"

"I'm serious. You get that intense look on your face." Mike squeezed her. "And nothing or no one better get in your way because you're on a mission."

"You're right. I'm on a mission to get everything done before people start showing up and you're not helping."

"Okay, okay! I opened the cans." Mike turned her around to face him. "I keep telling you, I dig you, baby."

Vonnie thought she would melt right in his arms. Mike still dug her and showed it every chance he got. She counted that as a blessing and said a silent thank you to God. She wrapped her arms around him and showed her appreciation with a deep, long kiss. Welcoming her, Mike held her tighter and matched her passion.

The bell rang and at first they wouldn't release each other. After the second ring, they reluctantly pulled away. Vonnie pressed imaginary wrinkles out of her apron while she caught her breath. When she looked up at Mike, he was staring at her with hunger in his eyes.

"Go get the door, fool!" she yelled and then laughed as she made her way back to the kitchen, knowing Mike would be watching her as she walked out. She heard him grunt and then listened as he made tracks toward the door.

"Daddy!" their daughter, Noelle screamed and hugged Mike. "Mommy!" She ran through the house at top speed toward the kitchen and began telling her story to Vonnie before she was even in there. "This old fat man in the supermarket by auntie's house tried to hit on Lena. It was so funny. He was like, 'Hey suga! What you cookin' ta'day. Can I ha some?'" she said in her version of an old man's voice. She barely got the rest of her words out before she started cracking up.

Vonnie's niece, Lena, walked into the kitchen behind her carrying bags and rolling her eyes. "Hush, Noelle. That wasn't funny. That man was gross! We should have gone to the supermarket over here. That kind of stuff never happens in this neighborhood."

"Who's messing with my niece?" Mike said walking in the kitchen behind her.

Vonnie laughed and waved him away. "Noelle, go make sure your room is clean. Lena, do me a favor and finish setting the table in the dining room, and then do the one in the kitchen. The adults will eat in the dining room and the kids can eat here. That should be enough room for everyone."

"Okay, Auntie," Lena said and got to work.

Vonnie smiled at Lena's unwavering obedience and thought about how proud she was of her only niece, whom she treated like her daughter.

When Mike's data preservation business, Cyber Vault, took off, becoming successful beyond what they ever imagined, Vonnie made sure that her niece had the best of everything.

Coming from very humble beginnings, growing up in Jamaica, Queens, Vonnie and her sister, Nadine didn't have much, especially after losing their parents. Vonnie did everything she could to help her sister provide for Lena.

Vonnie was too proud when Lena received a scholarship to Columbia University and when she announced that she wanted to become a doctor. Vonnie made sure she had nothing to worry about but her studies, providing her with a car and condo near school.

Vonnie shook away thoughts from the past and for the next hour everyone sunk knee deep into getting ready for Thanksgiving dinner as holiday music flowed through each room from the intercom speakers. Mike had managed to shake off the rest of his hangover and was now finely dressed and ready to entertain.

Vonnie was used to hosting her family and friends for the holidays, but the thought of having the Days, the Lees and the Madisons joining them for the first time made her anxious. As she dressed, she wasn't sure how her friends would take to her down home family. She was by no means embarrassed by them, but she knew how pretentious the wives were and imagined them giggling behind her back.

She took a deep breath, twisted in the mirror and assessed her clothing, a comfortable knee-length sweater dress that careened her curves and displayed a rich collage of fall colors. She patted her bob, which she just had cut a little lower on one side on her last visit to the hairdresser.

"I will not let Nadine get on my nerves today, even if she comes late. I will not cry about my mother not being able to be here. I will not get annoyed at Uncle Eddie for trying to dig in the food before it's time," she said to her reflection.

Despite how long ago her mother had passed, the void of her absence loomed over every holiday. She also thought about keeping a watchful eye on Mike, knowing he'd try to hide the pain of his mother not being able to attend Thanksgiving dinner for the first time. He had to put her in a nursing home a few months back.

Vonnie took a deep breath and turned from the mirror. "Come on, people," she said and clapped when she heard the doorbell. "Our guests are arriving. It's go time!" Vonnie headed to the door.

"Hey Ryan!" Vonnie kissed her before leaning toward Andy for a snug hug.

"Hey Vonnie," Ryan said, holding her eyes on Vonnie a little longer than normal. Vonnie nodded. She got the message. Andy still didn't know about the miscarriage.

"Uh hmm." Frannie, Ryan's overly tanned mother cleared her throat.

Vonnie greeted the woman with the hard facial lines, limp blond hair and thin lips with deep creases. "How are you, Ms. Stemson?"

Before Frannie could respond, Andy excused himself in search of Mike.

"Don't mind him." Frannie waved her hand dismissively. "Nice to see you again and call me Frannie," she croaked out with a thick Brooklyn accent. Her voice sounded like she'd been drinking hard liquor and smoking cigarettes since infancy. "This is a beautiful home you have here," Frannie said loudly. She looked around in wonder. "I swear Ryan sure managed to snag her some fancy friends. This is beautiful!" she yelled.

"Nice to see you too, Frannie." Vonnie extended her hand for a shake as Ryan cast another warning glance. Vonnie smiled inwardly. Ryan would soon find out that their families were similar in many ways. "Make yourselves at home," Vonnie said, waving them in.

Just then, Lena approached with flutes of champagne, with a strawberry settled at the bottom of the bubbly.

"Ooo. Nice!" Frannie took her and Ryan's glass. "You don't really drink, Rye, so I'll take yours."

Vonnie tried to keep from laughing aloud.

Within the next half hour, all the guests had arrived except for Vonnie's sister, Nadine.

Lena eased up beside her and touched her arm. "Mom's not here yet. Are you okay?"

"I'm fine. And we're not waiting for her, either," she said, giving her a reassuring wink.

Vonnie looked out the window one last time before calling their guests to the dining room to say grace. As she suspected, Uncle Eddie was making his way around the room, flirting with all the women, young and old while Aunt Bobbi discredited every wild claim he made.

"Those women don't want your old butt. We all know at your age, things don't work the way they used to," Bobbi said.

"I got Viagra!" Eddie said as if that was the answer to every problem in the world.

"Don't pay my brother any mind, y'all hear?"

"That's all I need in this world. That and a Benz. We would drive all the ladies wild."

"You ain't got no Benz," Bobbi chided with a hand on her hip.

"I didn't say I got a Benz. I said I could drive a Benz—and would look damn good doing it, too. Shoot! I had a lil young thang with a Benz once. I even drove it a few times—gave her a hell of a ride, too, if you know what I mean!" Eddie cackled and slapped his knee. "I could have a Benz if I wanted. My nephew would buy it for me. Right, Mike?"

"Sure," Mike said sarcastically.

The antics continued around the table throughout the evening. Nadine showed up just before dessert was presented.

"Hey! The party has officially started! Nadine's here!" she announced.

Vonnie could tell she had already started drinking. The other obvious drunks, Frannie and Pearson, laughed the loudest.   "And who is this here?" Uncle Eddie asked, standing and looking over Nadine's flavor of the week, while shaking his whiskey on the rocks.

"Oh!" Nadine giggled. "This is Tony."

Tony wore a half-cocked smile.

"Well, looka here! How long you been 'round, boy? Two...three weeks?" Uncle Eddie asked.

"Eddie!" Aunt Bobbi scolded.

"I'm just checking to see how much time he got left. Y'all know Nadine change men like she change shoes!" Eddie cracked himself up.

Vonnie caught Nadalia stretch her eyes and grab Sage's hand while the others laughed.

"Don't mind my uncle," Nadine said to her date and pulled him along as she dropped her bag. "Oh yes! We're just in time for dessert."

Mike eased beside Vonnie and held her hand. "You okay?"

Vonnie laughed. "I'm fine. I knew she'd be late."

The men disappeared into the den to watch the game, the young people made their way downstairs to watch movies, and the women were left to gather in the travel-themed sitting room, donned with comfortable chairs, art and other collectibles from their trysts across the world.

Nadalia finally loosened up and chatted with Ryan, who seemed to shrink in her presence. Pearson was chopping it up with Aunt Bobbi, laughing and having a grand ole time. Nadine said goodbye to her 'friend' and within a half hour, another showed up. She introduced Kevin to everyone as if they hadn't just broken bread with Tony.

Vonnie sailed around the house checking on everyone, and then realized that Ryan's mother and Uncle Eddie were missing. Discreetly, she called Mike out of the den. They went in search of the two. She had to say something to Ryan. Surely she'd realized her mother had gone missing, too.

Before she could say something, Aunt Bobbi asked, "Is Eddie watching the game with the guys? I want to get ready to head back to Queens and he drove."

"No," Vonnie said offering no speculation.

Ryan looked up.

"I was just looking for him so I can introduce him to Kevin. I can't find him anywhere," Nadine said.

"Maybe he's in the bathroom," Aunt Bobbi said dismissively.

"I checked all three of them. He's not in any of them, but somebody dropped a load in the one downstairs. Um!" Nadine waved her hand in front of her nose.

Ryan fidgeted, pulled out her phone and started texting. Vonnie knew she suspected the same thing.

"Wait!" Nadine looked around at the women in the room. "Where's that cool white lady?" She looked at Ryan, whose face was turning red. "Oh. No offense." She pardoned herself before continuing. "Did Uncle Eddie run off with the white woman?"

Vonnie closed her eyes and took another deep breath.

"Lord, please tell me Eddie didn't run off with that girl's mama!" Aunt Bobbi sighed.

Pearson giggled, took a sip of wine and sat up as if she didn't want to miss the action. Nadalia looked like she was embarrassed for Ryan, who was texting frantically, her fingers flashing across the screen at lightning speed.

After a moment she stood up, straightened her pencil skirt, which made her look even more narrow, and headed toward the den. Vonnie followed behind and watched her engage in a quick, but discreet discussion with Andy.

"Vonnie," Ryan said with a nervous chuckle, "thanks for inviting us. I'm going to head home. Andy will catch a ride with Nadalia and Sage."

All the women watched as Ryan put on her coat, grabbed her purse and keys and rushed out.

Minutes later, Uncle Eddie waltzed through the front door, humming and patting his pot belly as an unlit cigar hung from his mouth. He smiled through lipstick stains.

Now Vonnie was more connected to Ryan than she'd ever imagined.

Chapter 9

Nadalia

The wind whirled as a car whipped down the street. Again—it wasn't Sage. Nadalia stood in the window of her boudoir in a silk nightie and glanced back toward that clock. It was now after ten and she hadn't heard from her husband since around lunchtime. He'd been working late for weeks while Nadalia was at home longing for even a smidgen of his attention.

Fur season was here and business was booming for her too, but at least she managed to make it home at a reasonable time each night. She moved from the window—tore herself away from anticipating his arrival. When he did get home, he was usually too tired to bother anyway. Coming home, jumping in the shower, and passing out on the bed in boxers had become his routine. Back up at dawn, he'd shower again, splash a peck across her cheek on his way out and then, close the door on her loneliness. Nadalia would be lucky to get in a 10 minute phone conversation during the day, without hearing, "I'm running into a meeting," or the emptiness of, "Can I call you back, babe?"

It was the same each year, but this time she had trouble dealing.

"I'm not going to cry!" she coached herself, holding her head high as she climbed into the bed that had grown cold. Unable to fall asleep, Nadalia pulled back the covers, sat up and looked around: The soft lighting, French linens, sheers hanging alongside the custom bed, and the painting of her in a white flowing nightie with Sage positioned behind her, topless wearing silk lounge pants as he stared into her eyes—all seemed for naught.

Nadalia pushed the covers aside, stood up, and with her arms folded across her chest, she paced.

"Think, Dali." She referred to herself by her mother's pet name for her. "You can control anything— even the direction of your marriage." She paced more before an idea struck her and settled her angst enough for her to get back to bed.

Another car pushed through the night air and slowed. This time she knew it was Sage. The garage door groaned, and then shut its mouth. She scooted under the covers, closed her eyes and pretended to be asleep.

Minutes later, she heard his muffled steps as he ascended the stairs and entered their bedroom. She could feel him standing over her for a moment, then, he walked into the bathroom.

Nadalia lay awake and listened to him shower until his phone rang. The caller tried again. She lifted her head, listening for the shower water; Sage didn't seem to hear the phone.

Nadalia looked at the clock — it was almost midnight. Who would be calling at this time? Tipping toward the items he'd just discarded, Nadalia fumbled through the dark and pulled his cell phone from his pants.

Coffey Davis lit up the screen and Nadalia released the breath that she was holding as her hand went to her heart. Alarm struck her again, assuming that if Coffey was calling at this time, there might be an emergency. Nadalia ran with the phone and burst into the bathroom, startling Sage.

"Babe. Coffey's calling. He called more than once. It woke me up," she stammered. "I thought it might be important."

Sage sighed with relief. "I thought something had happened." He waved his hand dismissively. "I can call Coffey back when I get out of the shower."

"It's late. Something could be wrong."

"I just left him. He's probably just calling to make sure I got in okay."

Nadalia stood stark straight. "I was sitting here waiting on you all night, thinking you were working and you were out gallivanting with Coffey? You could have called or something." Nadalia stood with one hand on her hip and his phone dangling from the other. She felt like throwing it into the commode.

"I was working, babe." Sage turned the shower off and stepped out. "Coffey is being courted by some other networks so he's in town for negotiations." Toweling off, Sage headed back to the bedroom with Nadalia in tow. "My company is working with his team on his branding to get the best set up for him. We discussed the plans over dinner and had a few drinks. Not to mention, they shut down one of the tubes on the Midtown tunnel for overnight construction so traffic was horrendous. That's what took me so long to get home."

Nadalia narrowed her eyes. She wasn't sure she believed him.

"I was the only one who had to drive a distance, so I told them I'd call Coffey when I got in. He's probably wondering what happened."

Nadalia continued to eye him as he dried off and then stepped into his boxers. She looked for any signs that would indicate whether he was lying. "Well call him back and let him know you're fine," she said, holding out the phone.

Sage looked at her with creased brows, reached for the phone and dialed Coffey's number. "What's up, man?" He kept his eyes on Nadalia, standing with her hands on both hips. "Traffic was crazy…yeah." Sage laughed. "Yeah man…I know…" Nadalia was still staring in his face. "Well, Nadalia said to tell you hello…I will…cool…later, man." Sage ended the call, walked into the bedroom, and tossed the phone into the fluffy pile of covers on the bed. "You happy now?" he said to Nadalia.

Nadalia rolled her eyes and got in bed. Sage snuggled behind her and fell right off to sleep.

Chapter 10

Nadalia

As expected, Sage was gone before dawn. Again, Nadalia pretended to be sleeping when he kissed her goodbye. Between Sage's snoring and her mulling over their lack of romance, Nadalia had tossed the entire night. Her sleeplessness showed up in the deep crevices around her eyes. It had been years since she'd taken a day off, but today, she needed the break.

"Hey, Sweetie," her mother, Mina, sang into the phone when she called.

Mina had rid her tongue of her Armenian accent a long time ago when she started the company. Mina and her sister, Sona, wanted to be taken seriously when they launched their business rather than risk sounding like naïve immigrants.

"Hey, Mom! I'm exhausted I'm going to take a day off."

"Dali! Are you sick?"

"No." She thought about telling her mother more, but refrained. "Just tired. I've got a lot on my plate."

"Yeah. It gets so busy around the holidays. Get your rest. We will be fine. You know, some famous reverend is bringing his wife in today to be fitted for a coat. He heard about us through Sanders. You know, Dayton, who used to play for the Cowboys?" She didn't give Nadalia a chance to answer. "She loved the coat we did for Dayton's wife last winter, and now she wants something designed for herself."

"That's cool! I have the girls working on a coat for one of the wives for Christmas."

"Oh! Nice. Which one?"

"Ryan."

"That's the petite one, right? Her husband is that actor?"

"Yes. That's the one."

"Oh! He's a real looker."

Nadalia laughed. "Mom. No one says that anymore."

"Well, I still do!"

"Okay. I'll see you next week for the monthly meetings. I still think you and Aunt Sona should come to Long Island more often. That big ole house is just sitting there and Manhattan life can be brutal. When I come out there, I can't wait to get back to the Island."

"We love it here. It's convenient, close to the business and we have everything we need right around us. Don't worry about us, honey. You should be the one to get a place out here. You're all alone in that big house with no kids. With the long hours Sage works, it has to be lonely. You really should come to the city more."

"Okay. Okay! I need to call the office." Nadalia didn't want to hear anymore. She had to get off the phone before she revealed her true feelings. "Talk to you later, Mom."

Nadalia loved her big house. It was one of her trophies for the wealth and accomplishments she and Sage had garnered. One day she'd add a kid or two— maybe. Right now she needed to worry only about lighting a fire under her marriage.

Since she wasn't going into the office, she decided to take the time to come up with more ideas to usher the romance back into her bedroom.

Nadalia thought about Mike and Vonnie and how into each other they always appeared to be. Mike looked at Vonnie as if his heart would cease to beat if he took his eyes off her. Vonnie sucked in every bit of the lavish love he doused on her. They held hands, pecked for no reason and openly doted on each other. If she didn't know better, she would have thought they were newlyweds, yet, they had been married the longest out of the four couples. Nadalia had to find out their secret.

Nadalia didn't doubt that she was still desirable. As the product of an interracial union, her mixed ancestry blessed her with a full head of long, beautiful, jet black hair, supple olive skin and a slim, yet curvaceous body. Men confirmed that every day by the way they poured themselves all over her. The one man she desired most seemed oblivious to her beauty and charm. She wondered what it would take and questioned if children had anything to do with it. Did Mike appreciate Vonnie more because she was the mother of their child? Though she wasn't ready to have children, she needed answers.

Nadalia dialed Vonnie's number and was grateful that she picked up after a few short rings.

"Hey." That's all Vonnie said when she picked up.

Nadalia understood since she didn't usually call Vonnie. They never had casual conversations outside of the times they hung together with their husbands.

"Hi, Vonnie. Are you available for lunch today? I'd like to chat with you about something."

"Uh…sure!" Vonnie paused. "I'm sorry. Actually, I'm not free for lunch. I'm looking at my calendar now. What about this evening? I see my last patient at four-thirty."

"Okay!" Nadalia had been taken aback at first when Vonnie said yes and then no, but now she brightened up a little. "We can meet at the Beck around six?" Nadalia thought about her suggestion. "Better yet, do you mind coming here? I have wine!" she coaxed.

The Beck was her husband's thing. Besides, she knew that Sage wouldn't be home anytime soon and she preferred a more private setting for their discussion.

"Wine!" Vonnie joked. "You said the magic word. I'll be there at seven!"

Both ladies laughed.

"Perfect! See you then." Nadalia hung up feeling renewed. After speaking to Vonnie, she'd get her other efforts in motion.

There was only so much she would reveal to Vonnie. She certainly didn't want to leave her with the impression that there was serious trouble in her marriage. A little light girl talk and advice would do. One way or other, she'd get her marriage back on track—no matter what tactics she had to resort to.

Chapter 11

Vonnie

Vonnie couldn't shake the curiosity that rose in her after Nadalia's call. First Ryan, now Nadalia. Two people she had never received random calls from before.

As she finished with her last patient for the day, a little rosy cheek girl with a head full of blond curls that reminded her of Shirley Temple, Vonnie thought about whether she should go straight over to Nadalia's or stop at home to freshen up. Vonnie often felt like she was under the microscope in Nadalia's presence, so she decided to go home and at least change.

Vonnie checked her messages one last time and shut down her computer. Mike sent a new text asking if she had a boyfriend. She laughed and dialed him instead of texting him back.

"You didn't answer my question," he teased.

Vonnie shook her head. "No, I don't have a boyfriend." She went along. "But I am happily married to a crazy man and I don't think he'll take kindly to you texting me."

"Yeah, well wait until he sees what I send to you next time."

"Mike!"

Mike laughed that infectious laugh that always stole Vonnie's heart.

"You are such a fool. Listen, I was calling to see what you had planned for the evening. Nadalia asked if I could stop by to chat and have a drink."

"What?"

"That's what I said. She didn't say what she wanted, but I can only assume it must be important. I'm still wondering why she called me."

"Well, she wouldn't call Pearson, and Ryan doesn't seem like she makes for interesting conversation."

Vonnie snickered, then asked, "Are you going to be home?"

"Actually, I need to run to Queens," Mike said and Vonnie creased her brows. "I need to take care of something for Aunt Kat," he continued as if he could sense her pondering.

"Oh. Okay. I'll see you later tonight. I should't be long." Vonnie wondered what his trip to Queens was about since he rarely dealt with his family there. When they reached out to him, it was usually for money.

"Cool."

"Love you, babe."

"Love you more."

"She must have asked for money," Vonnie said aloud, after she hung up. "Good ole Mike to the rescue." She grabbed her keys and purse, and headed home.

As she drove, Vonnie focused her attention back on the matter at hand, finding something nice to wear to Nadalia's. Effortlessly cute was the look she was going for.

She pulled into their circular driveway and hit a remote, simultaneously disarming the house alarm and turning on lights. She smiled as she made her way up the walkway, leading to the opulent double wood doors, feeling like she had to pinch herself even though it had been years. As ambitious as she was, she never imagined herself living in a home like this. Their life together and the wealth they acquired far exceeded her most imaginative expectations. She knew they would be successful, but never anticipated Mike's company taking off the way that it had. A few years in, larger companies came knocking on his door with lucrative offers to buy him out and Mike refused them all.

They would have never been able to afford the lifestyle they enjoyed on her pediatrician's salary. She didn't need all these luxuries to be happy, but she sure did enjoy having them.

Once inside, Vonnie shuffled through the mail, and then wound her way through the halls to the master bedroom. Stepping into her walk-in closet, she sifted through the section with all of her shirts and pulled out a sheer violet one with bishop sleeves, then, she searched the drawers for black leggings before grabbing a pair of tall lace-up boots with comfortable cat heels.

Vonnie tossed the selection across the king-sized poster bed and headed to the bathroom for a shower. Within minutes, she was standing before the mirror fully dressed, applying a light coat of lip gloss. On the way out, she grabbed a bottle of Cabernet Sauvignon from the wine fridge. Even after stopping by the bakery for her favorite pecan pie, she managed to get to Nadalia's right on time.

"Welcome!" Nadalia sang and ushered Vonnie in with a wave of her hand. She closed the door and sauntered toward the back of the house into the family room where she had a quaint set-up of wine, cheese and a few other finger foods.

Vonnie took notice of the red dress hugging Nadalia's curves and wondered who dressed that sexy at home. She could only imagine what the outfit cost.

Vonnie still shopped the outlets and stores like Marshalls, Century 21, and TJ Maxx, making only occasional visits to places like Saks and Bergdorf Goodman. Great bargains sent adrenaline coursing through her veins.

Vonnie followed Nadalia and offered up the wine. She suddenly felt a little self-conscious about her choice as she handed it over to Nadalia, who glanced over the bottle and then forced a smile. It was a brand she and Mike enjoyed for around twenty bucks, not the three-hundred dollar bottles that Sage or Anderson often ordered at dinners. She shook off her discomfort, deciding she didn't care what Nadalia thought.

"I bought pie!" she said, holding it up sheepishly. "It's pecan. My favorite."

"Yummy! Sage's grandmother used to make a pecan pie that was sinfully divine."

"Well, I don't know if it will beat granny's pie, but it's damn good."

Nadalia lifted the box and sniffed the pie, then closed her eyes and drew in a deep breath. "Let me get a knife for this baby. I'll be right back."

When Nadalia left the room, Vonnie placed her purse down, but remained standing. Rubbing her hands together, she looked around, admiring the ornate décor, specifically the large flat-screen TV hanging over the fireplace, which was surrounded by a wall of windows.

"Don't be a stranger, girl. Sit down!" Nadalia said when she returned with two slices of pie on saucers. She handed Vonnie one of the saucers, then poured two glasses of wine.

Vonnie noticed that the wine Nadalia poured wasn't the one she brought with her.

"Sage home?" Vonnie tried to make small talk before the discomfort she felt made the moment more awkward.

"He's working late! As usual…well, football season is really busy for him. I never expect him before nine. He comes home and practically passes out."

"Oh yeah? Just like Mike! If I don't make him slow down, he'd work himself to death."

"I know, right. I mean, I run a company too, and I know what it's like to have to put in some hours, but the way these men work themselves, it's a wonder they haven't aged beyond their years."

"Tell me about it." Vonnie sipped her wine. The awkwardness was waning and she was sure the wine would also help chase away the edge.

"Speaking of which, that's one of the reasons I asked you over. We never really get to chat and also I want to do something special for Sage. You know…since he's been working so hard." Nadalia's noticeable pause put Vonnie on notice. "And I…uh…love the way you and Mike are together." Nadalia cleared her throat. "I figured you could help me come up with some ideas to get him to, uh, loosen up. So tell me, what's your secret?"

"Well…" *So Nadalia and Sage were having trouble at home.* Vonnie wasn't sure what to say. "People ask us that all the time and I'm never sure how to respond." Vonnie thought some more. "Personally, I love the way he treats me. It may sound selfish, but it encourages me to be the best wife and friend I can be to him. We talk a lot, hang out together, have date nights. He's…" Vonnie thought for a moment. "He's just my best friend."

"Well that sounds pretty simple. I—"

"Oh and we have a lot of sex!" Vonnie interjected. She punctuated her statement by holding up her wine glass to toast her declaration. She glanced at Nadalia, who looked as though she didn't know whether to laugh or not.

Nadalia released the snicker she held behind her pursed red lips with a slight snort and both of them fell out laughing.

"I guess that will do the trick," Nadalia said, holding one hand over her heart. They laughed some more before Nadalia continued, "I guess we could do more dating, too."

Silence cushioned between them as they ate and sipped. Vonnie swore she saw a sadness settle in Nadalia's eyes. She wanted to ask, but didn't want to pry.

Placing her unfinished pie on the ottoman, she repositioned herself on the sofa and faced Nadalia. "I don't know if I helped much."

"Well…you did, but I'm still thinking that I need to figure out a way to just spark things up a little."

"How long have you been married?"

"We were engaged forever, but we're coming up on five years of marriage next summer. You and Mike have been married much longer, right?"

"Yeah. We were high school sweethearts. Separated during our college years, but we got married right after we graduated. We were still babies, but we made it. It's been twelve years."

"Wow!" Nadalia took a sip of her wine. "That's like a freaking eternity. And you still have a lot of sex? Geesh!"

Vonnie shook her head at Nadalia's reaction.

"I can only hope that Sage and I last that long." She stopped talking and appeared to be in deep thought. "He'll probably want some babies by that time. How will I get out of that?"

Vonnie reared her head back, shocked by Nadalia's statement. "Don't you want children?"

"Not particularly."

"Oh…okay."

"It sounds a little harsh I know, but right now I'm not ready and I'm not sure when I will be. It's so much responsibility. And poop and snotty noses have never been appealing to me."

Vonnie chuckled and shook her head.

"At the rate we've been going, I won't have to worry about babies. He's been working so many hours, my Sally hasn't even seen his Peter in weeks." Then she paused with an inquisitive grimace planted on her face. "You know what?"

"What?" Vonnie said.

"Well, I'll be damned. I haven't had sex with my husband in a month."

Vonnie raised her brows and then gulped the remainder of her wine. That was her cue to wrap up their conversation because she wasn't sure she wanted to hear much more. Nadalia had become more comfortable and she already knew Nadalia was one for blurting out interesting statements in the presence of the entire group. Vonnie could imagine the things she was capable of saying behind closed doors.

Vonnie placed the glass down on the coffee table. "Maybe it's time for a spontaneous excursion."

"What kind of spontaneous excursion?" Nadalia asked.

"Mike and I sometimes sneak off to different places just to get away for a night or two. It's a great way to reignite the spark every now and then. Maybe both of you can get some much needed R and R—or not!" Vonnie hooted and Nadalia's eyes widened like she'd just gotten a bright idea. "It might be good to help rekindle your fire and get Sally and Peter reacquainted."

Nadalia looked at her sideways before laughing herself.

Vonnie enjoyed Nadalia's company and after a while, they were talking like old friends. Vonnie looked at her watch and couldn't believe that two hours had past.

"Well, it's been nice, but tomorrow's my early day at the office so I really need to get going."

She gathered her purse and coat and Nadalia walked her out.

"Thanks for coming," Nadalia said as they reached the door, "and thanks for the advice. I think a little excursion is just what we need."

They exchanged a quick hug and as Vonnie started out of the door, Nadalia called out to her.

"Uh…Vonnie."

"Yes." She turned back.

"Do you mind keeping our little conversation to yourself?"

"Sure," Vonnie said slowly. "Take care." She exited knowing that Nadalia's request had more to do with keeping up appearances than confidentiality.

Chapter 12

Pearson

P earson hated the holidays. Everyone walked around all happy and full of glee and the whole scene made her sick. As much as she loved Niles' family, even they annoyed her with all of their cheer. She felt like she was stuck in a bad version of one of those happy-go-lucky Christmas movies, wishing she could bust through the screen and be the Grinch. She could relate more to "A Christmas Carol," but with a more painful past.

As she sat in her home office handling business for her foundation's benefit gala this coming spring, she did her best to at least match the upbeat tone of the photographer that worked the event for the past five years. As always, he was excited to get the contract signed because it gave him exclusive access to the Who's Who across New York City and Long Island.

"I'll be sure to get a couple of great shots of you and Niles to add to your collection of family photos."

"Sure…I gotta run, Kenny. I'll have my assistant drop the contract and deposit in the mail first thing Monday morning."

"Wonderful! Have a Merry Christmas and a Happy New Year, Mrs. Day."

"Yeah…thanks." She stopped herself from saying, 'Bah humbug.'

It was still early in the day, but she had a lengthy list of tasks she had to complete. Handling business for the foundation, which meant the world to her, topped that list.

Pearson started G-Day to support organizations with serious missions to influence the lives of young girls, especially those who'd suffered the loss of a parent—or at least felt like they did. The $500-ticketed gala was the marquee event, where the foundation received the majority of their funds, presented awards and scholarships and announced the names of young women who were selected to participate in the G-Day Summer Camp and the coveted G-Day Abroad Experience.

Pearson wanted to make sure girls felt valued and worthy, unlike she did growing up as a teen under her mother's detached thumb. She also wanted to be a part of giving them an experience beyond their wildest imaginations.

After that, she needed to get ready for the gathering at Nadalia's house later that evening. There were lots more crappy merry-happy greetings to push through before the holidays were over. All this time did for her was conjure unhappy memories to the forefront, along with emotions that she had to wrestle with. It was during this season that her life took a devastating turn all those years ago.

Pearson had been a daddy's girl from the moment she took her first breath. Her father, Alston Chambers was smitten with Pearson at first sight and happily cared for her every need the way a nurturing mother would. He had to, because for Candice, that mothering instinct that kicked in after a woman gave birth, never quite fell into place.

Christmas Eve, when Pearson was twelve, Alston went shopping, filling his car with all the dolls and gifts a pre-teen could ever want, but he never made it home. A massive stroke caused him to steer the car off the road, nearly splitting it in two. The impact killed him instantly.

On Christmas, instead of opening gifts, Pearson and Candice spent the day mourning: Pearson in her room, and her mother camped out in a darkened den while she drank several bottles of scotch. The gifts under the tree remained unopened.

New Year's Eve was spent sending her father off in the most opulent way imaginable. From that day, Pearson's life had never been the same.

Pearson shook those awful memories away and stood so abruptly, she knocked her chair over. The pain of her father's loss rushed her as if it had just happened. She doubled over and wept, crying for him and all the other losses that his death generated.

Pearson reached for the wine cooler; she couldn't deal with this agony in her own strength. Deciding that wine wouldn't cut it, she dug beyond the files in her bottom drawer and pulled out a fifth of vodka. She drank straight from the bottle, wiped her mouth with the back of her hand, and sat on the floor.

After a few more sips, Pearson put the liquor back in its place. She still had a few hours to put in even though it was the Saturday before Christmas.

Pearson got back to work, but not before grabbing a bottle of red wine, a glass, and an aerator. She uncorked the bottle and filled her glass to the rim, letting the crimson liquid pass through the aerator first. Bringing the glass to her mouth with trembling hands, Pearson took a long sip. She had to catch her breath when she finished.

After tapping out a few emails to her assistant and warning her not to act on them until Monday, she shut down her PC. Just because she was a workaholic who drowned her revulsion for the holidays in long, vigorous hours and expensive spirits, that didn't mean her employees had to.

Saving the rest of her work and errands for another day, Pearson decided to start preparing for the party, starting with a long soak in their colossal Jacuzzi spa. She'd hoped that the soothing rhythm from the jets and the velvety bubbles would wash away some of the feelings of grief and that threatened to consume her.

The sound of Niles' rich deep voice bellowed though the master bedroom and into the bath. Pearson's eyes fluttered open and she realized she'd fallen asleep in the tub. Niles called her name again and this time it sounded less distant. She sat up in the water and took a moment to clear her disorientation.

"I'm in here!" She heard Niles' footsteps growing closer.

He appeared in the door and grinned. Pearson smiled back as a sliver of heat swirled in her core, brought on by the sexiness her husband exuded by simply standing there. His handsome teeth, resembling ivory, were lined up like tall soldiers. She could tell that lustful considerations were brewing behind the smoldering look he gave her. As he stood taking her in, he never said a word.

"Wanna join me?" Pearson curled her finger, inviting him in.

Niles sauntered over, crouched at the edge of the tub and pushed his tongue into Pearson's mouth. She put wet arms around him, pulling him in and soaking his clothes.

When they managed to pull themselves apart, Niles answered breathlessly, "I wish I could." He looked at his watch. "But that would make us very late."

Pearson scrunched her brows. "What time is it?"

"A little after five."

Pearson jumped up, splashing water all over Niles.

"Whoa!" he said, stepping back.

"Oh my goodness!" she said, grabbing her cloth and soap. More than two hours had passed. Her fingers had shriveled like raisins and she shook her head. Quickly, she washed in the cool water, toweled off, and ran to the adjacent room, which she had turned into a huge walk-in closet. She had wanted to run out to her favorite boutique and find a cute shirt to wear, but it was too late for that. She threw on a mocha-colored knit dress that stopped just before her knees and then double wrapped a long silk, leopard print scarf around her neck.

By the time she emerged from her dressing room, Niles was just making it out of the shower. Nadalia's Holiday Pot Luck dinner was starting in less than an hour and Pearson hadn't cooked a thing.

"What are we bringing?" Niles asked as he buttoned his crisp yellow shirt.

"I was just thinking about that."

Niles dropped his hands to his side, looking puzzled. "I thought you were making that delicious pasta with the shrimp scampi sauce."

"Yeah…well…a thing happened and now that dish is not going to happen." As she slipped a sizable pair of pearls into her ears, she said. "I'll call DiMaggio's and ask for a pan of pasta."

Niles raised his brows like he didn't think that was a good idea.

"I know it's out of the way, but it's my only option right now."

"What happened to…you know what? Never mind."

Pearson was glad that Niles thought better of asking her why she hadn't made the dish. She didn't want to answer him anyway.

"I'll grab a bottle of wine out of our reserve. That will be one less stop we'll have to make. We shouldn't be too late."

Pearson walked over to Niles as he adjusted his cuff links and planted a sloppy kiss on his lips. "I appreciate you." She meant it. Besides her father, Niles had been the only one who genuinely showed her love, satisfying some of the voids that her mother left when she shipped her off to boarding school.

After her father's death, Candice treated Pearson more like a bothersome roommate than a daughter. She still craved Candice's devotion, but soon learned how to fill her empty places with vices that made her longings fade away.

"How about you show me how much when we get back from Sage and Nadalia's tonight," he said, slipping his arm around the small of her back.

"I guess I could do that." She pulled away. "Now come on."

As Pearson stepped into her shoes, she felt Niles looking at her. When she turned toward him, she drew in a deep breath. He wore a pensive look and his lips were twisted.

"What?"

"Could you please take it easy tonight?"

Pearson cut her eyes, grabbed her purse and walked out the room. Just like that, he had caused the edge that she'd managed to wash down the drain to return and cling to her like slime. If she got drunk tonight, it would be his fault for annoying her.

Chapter 13

Nadalia

N adalia ordered the lead maid to finish setting the table before her guests arrived.

She pushed the back onto the post of her cultured pearl earring and snapped at the maid. "Just give me the damn napkins!" she yelled, snatching them from her grasp. "I don't understand what's so hard. Just fold them like this and stuff it inside the ring." Nadalia demonstrated, and then tossed the napkin on the table.

"How's it going in here, babe?" Sage stepped in looking rather dapper as he fastened his cuff links. His red button down shirt was fitting for the holiday festivities.

"Look at you, handsome." Nadalia wiped the shoulders of his shirt and ran her hand down his chest. "All is well. I just need to light a damn fire under these girl's behinds. They're moving slower and slower these days. The last crew we hired was so much better."

Nadalia cast her eyes upward as if she just remembered something that irritated her. "Give me a minute, babe," she said to Sage and turned back toward the kitchen. "Ladies! Where are the favors I told you to place on the console in the foyer?"

"I'll get them right away, ma'am," one of the hired hands said and scurried past Nadalia with her head down.

"And make sure the girls are all dressed and ready to work. My guests will begin arriving any minute." Nadalia looked around. "I need someone at the door now to greet people!"

"Yes. Ma'am," one of them said.

"Hey! Where are you going?" Nadalia yelled at a women passing by. "I said put the favors out."

"But, ma'am. You asked me to check on the girls to make sure they were ready."

Nadalia parked her hands on her hips and glared. "Do what I ask in the order that I ask."

"Take it easy on those ladies," Sage said.

"I pay them very good money. The least I could ask for is efficient work."

Nadalia locked eyes with Sage and smiled. He seemed relaxed for the first time in weeks and she applauded herself for deciding to have this party, even though she thought of it at the last minute. She called it their Holiday Pot Luck dinner and determined that if things went well tonight, she was going to make it a permanent part of her holidays. She knew that getting together with his friends and their wives would lift his spirits. Maybe she could even get him to make love to her after their guests were gone. She'd been longing for his touch for far too long and with their sexual appetites, they had never gone weeks without having sex. She looked forward to the end of football season so she could have her husband back.

"Come with me." Nadalia grabbed Sage's hand and led him through the foyer. They passed the sitting room and headed into the kitchen where rows of chafing dishes lined the counters, all complements of a renowned local chef.

Nadalia paused, closed her eyes and inhaled, taking in the symphony of delectable aromas. "Smells divine, doesn't it?" She led Sage to the counter like a little boy being dragged by his mother. "There's lobster bisque, blackened prawns over arugula, shrimp scampi, made the Italian way, not the bootleg Red Lobster way, steamed mussels...mmm." Nadalia leaned over the dish she held open and relished the fragrant delicacies.

"Nice spread!"

"You mean mine or the food?" she said, poking her protruding bottom at him. Before he could respond, Nadalia burst out laughing. Sage joined her.

"Actually both. Let me get a good look at you." Sage spun her around admiring the red and ivory knit dress traveling around her hourglass figure. "Mmmm. You look as delicious as the feast you've laid out."

Nadalia giggled, loving the girly way she felt after his compliment.

"I have a question. I thought pot luck meant that you actually cooked the food yourself."

"Our guests are bringing food they cooked themselves. That's good enough." Nadalia laughed and the bell rang. "How do I look?" she said spinning around.

"Like I said." Sage smiled. "Delicious."

Nadalia winked, turned on her platform pumps and headed for the door. "Girls! Guests are arriving! I need you and one of the other girls at the door," she said pointing at one of the women. "The favors had better be in the foyer. Everyone else get in to place," she said, clapping her hands as she snapped out orders.

One of them met Nadalia at the door, balancing a tray of champagne flutes filled with eggnog cocktails, and cinnamon sticks. Nadalia checked her reflection in the foyer's mirror, puckering her bright red lips and moving her head from side to side to check her hair. Her jet black tresses cascaded down the sides of her face from a centered part ending just past her shoulders. Satisfied, Nadalia assessed her dress once again, took a deep breath and reached for the doorknob.

"Merry Christmas!" Nadalia welcomed Vonita and Mike with air kisses and stepped aside. She took Vonita's dish and handed it to one of the girls who were perfectly lined straight like soldiers along the foyer. A young plump girl with a pretty face stepped up and took the Howards' coats while another handed them glasses of eggnog.

The entire wait staff was dressed in stark white shirts, black knee-length skirts and red bow ties. Based on Nadalia's orders, each wore their hair in a tight bun at the base of their neck. Details were extremely important.

Nadalia noticed Vonnie raise a quick approving brow at Mike. They were obviously impressed.

"Nadalia, your decorations are beautiful!"

"I hired a designer to decorate for me. Who has time for that these days?"

"Hey! My main man."

Nadalia turned around at the sound of Sage's voice.

"Vonnie." Sage greeted her with a peck on her cheek. "Looking lovely as always."

"Not too bad yourself, Sage," Vonnie teased.

Sage gave Mike a firm shake and hug before taking his flute of eggnog and replacing it with a crystal snifter of Louis XIII.

"That's a girl's drink," Sage whispered loud enough for the women to hear.

Mike gladly took the glass, took a sip, popped his lips and said, "Ahhhh! Now it's a party!" The men cracked up while the women twisted their lips, shook their heads, and walked off.

"Oh, yeah, Nadalia."

Nadalia turned back. "Yes, Mike."

"You said this was a pot luck dinner, right?"

"Yes. Why?" Both she and Vonnie looked confused.

"So who's bringing the pot? Get it?"

The women snickered and walked off talking about Vonnie's great-smelling Paella, leaving Mike to laugh at his joke.

"Be sure to take care of the arriving guests and send them to the living room," Nadalia yelled back at the maid manning the door. She then led Mike and Vonnie down the few steps into the sunken room where art adorned the walls, and antique furnishings resided. Trays of canapés were placed around the room and a tall, slim member of the wait staff stood in her polished penguin uniform.

"So," Nadalia sat down next to Vonnie and turned to face her. "I decided to have this get together after our conversation. I thought about how much Sage loves hanging with his buddies and I thought it would be nice for all of us to relax and have some fun. I think Sage really needed it."

"Great idea." Vonnie looked around the living room. "I love the artwork. I minored in art during undergrad."

"Nice—"

The bell rang again and seconds later, Ryan and Anderson appeared in the entrance of the living room. Ryan wore a gold wrap dress and nude shoes with her hair pulled back in a chignon. Anderson outshined her completely in his simple black but perfectly tailored suit and emerald green shirt. His polished appearance made Ryan fade into his shadow.

"What's up pretty-boy?" Mike teased greeting him with a slap on the back.

"It's all good," Anderson replied to the men. "Ladies," he continued with a nod before giving each wife a kiss on the cheek.

Ryan waved and sat near Vonnie. Anderson fell right into the men's conversation, each boasting about their latest material conquests, and opinions about who were the best and worst on and off the field and court.

Within the next half hour all the guests had arrived. Eventually eggnog cocktails gave way to glasses of vintage wines. The men had already downed nearly two bottles of Louis XIII. Sage offered them each a single shot of an expensive prized 40 year old single malt whiskey.

Anderson insisted he'd tasted one better while filming overseas last year and promised to let them try some from his collection the next time he and Ryan hosted a gathering. Ryan sat more quietly that usual, mustering up the occasional smile, chuckle or outright laugh at Mike's antics.

Nadalia didn't miss the many times Anderson's eyes clung to her body as she moved about. It almost seemed as if he couldn't help himself. She wondered if Ryan noticed too, but she wouldn't dare look at her while Anderson was ogling her curves. Nadalia didn't want to embarrass the poor girl and almost pitied her for being so small in his presence.

The more Anderson drank, the more hunger appeared in his eyes as he watched her. The gesture didn't faze Nadalia. He would never act on any impulses that would put his friendship with Sage in jeopardy. Besides, she was used to men looking at her like she was a delectable meal.

Vonnie was the consummate cool girl who got along with everybody. Nadalia thought about spending more time with her one-on-one.

Pearson was doing what she did best, drinking like a fish until her head bobbed and her words slurred. As brilliantly smart and pretty as she was, Nadalia felt like the drinking took something from her.

All seemed to be going well around the table as everyone enjoyed the dinner and desserts Nadalia's friend, an award-winning pastry chef, prepared for the evening.

Then, Pearson slammed her glass down and closed her eyes briefly before saying, "I know I'm not the only one who sees Andy's prying eyes ogling Nadalia's Kim-Kardashian-ass every time she moves."

Silence arrested the room. Ryan looked aside and tightened her lips. Vonnie and Nadalia's mouths fell open. The men were still.

Anderson creased his brows. Sage narrowed his gaze at no one in particular.

The pause in the room swelled.

Niles placed his hands on Pearson's shoulder. "Pearson!" Niles admonished, but that didn't stop the next explosion.

"No! You're not the only one who sees it," Ryan said.

If there were a deeper level of silence possible, the room achieved it at that moment. "And it's making me sick to my stomach. I may not have a 'fat ass,' but I'm still a good woman." She directed her attention to Anderson. "And I'm still you're frigging wife!"

"Ryan, you're drunk," Anderson said.

"Not drunk enough," she spat back.

Pearson laughed, breaking the heavy quietness of the room and then reached over, picked up a bottle of wine and filled Ryan's glass to the rim. "Have some more," she said and laughed again.

Niles looked at her and stretched his eyes.

"Okay people. We've been having a great time so far. Let's not spoil it," Nadalia said, holding up her hands. We've all had a lot to drink. No one means any harm." Nadalia looked at Sage to gauge his expression.

Anderson also looked at Sage, whose face now bordered between confusion and disbelief. "I'd never disrespect you, man. You have a beautiful wife, but we're friends. I'd never cross any lines with you."

"Ryan, did you hear that shit? You want another drink?" Pearson said and giggled.

Anderson stood and tugged on his jacket. "No! She's had enough." He spoke to Pearson, but glared at Ryan.

"I'll have some more. Thanks," Ryan said with her eyes locked on Anderson.

Filling her own glass, Pearson squinted as she looked over the bottle. "Nadalia, what kind is this?"

"Pearson!" Niles admonished again.

Pearson cut her eyes at him, and then snickered. She reached over to refill Ryan's glass.

"I said no!" Anderson addressed Ryan through gritted teeth.

"You don't tell me what to do." Her words were slow and deliberate and her sneer was impressive.

Anderson dropped his head and chuckled, dismissing her irritation like she was his subordinate.

"You've had enough, Ryan." A slick smile veered across his lips.

Ryan picked up the wine and drank, glaring at Anderson over her glass. Everyone's head shifted in Anderson's direction as if they were witnessing a tennis match.

Anderson's small huff released into another smile. His restraint showed in the veins that protruded from his neck and his tight lips.

"Andy," Sage tugged on his arm, "just sit down, man. As a matter of fact, gentlemen, let's go into the den."

The men stood, but didn't move. Ryan finished her wine, turned the glass upside down, and let the remainder drip on her tongue. Then she plopped the glass down in front of Pearson, letting on that she wanted more while never taking her eyes off Anderson.

Nadalia wanted to stop the situation from ending explosively, but a part of her wanted to see just how this would play out. She'd been waiting to see Ryan grow a backbone.

"Ryan. You don't want to do this in front of everyone."

"Do what, Anderson? Go ahead and show your friends who you really are. I won't sit here and let you treat me like this anymore. Like… something you can toss aside when you see a nice piece of ass. I won't tolerate it. I'm tired."

Anderson moved like he would pounce on Ryan, but Mike jumped in his path, while Sage pulled his suit jacket from behind.

"Wait one minute! You will *not* do this here!" Nadalia ordered.

"Watch yourself, Ryan. Don't say anything that you know you'll regret," Anderson warned with a pointed finger.

"I'm done with regrets," she shot back.

Anderson moved toward her again and Sage, Niles and Mike blocked him.

Nadalia stepped up behind Ryan's back as a show of support, but also to be in position to get Ryan out of the way in case Anderson leapt over the table.

Fury danced in his eyes as he scowled at her. She stood her ground, staring him back down.

He straightened his suit, he tugged the cuffs of his shirts. "Done with regrets, huh? I don't care how much wine you drank. You had better think about what you're doing, disrespecting me. You're nothing without me. You hear me? Nothing!" He jabbed a finger in her direction, punctuating his statement.

Anderson stepped around Sage. "Excuse me you all. Nadalia, this was a great evening." Anderson drew into himself, standing a tad taller. He shot Ryan one last scathing look and walked out of the dining room, through the foyer, and straight out the door.

Everyone stood, looking from one to the other. The screech of Anderson's tires alerted them of his sharp departure.

Ryan grabbed the wine bottle and tried to pour herself another drink, but her hands trembled violently, threatening to send both the bottle and her glass crashing to the floor.   Vonnie gently took the wine from Ryan's shaking hands and hugged her.

Ryan pulled away, eyes glistening. "I'm fine. Thanks."

Slowly, everyone started to make themselves busy, clearing the table, and searching for their coats.

Ryan stood and turned toward Nadalia. "I'm sorry."

"Don't be," Nadalia snapped and cut her eyes at Pearson at the same time. "You didn't start this."

Either Pearson missed the comment or ignored it because she hadn't moved, nor did she stop drinking.

"Get the girls in here. It's time to clean up," she said to the help and then marched toward the kitchen shouting more orders.

"Ryan, Mike and I can drop you off if you want," Vonnie offered.

"Thanks."

Sage and the men moved to the foyer and huddled in a discussion.

Nadalia was pissed at Ryan, Anderson, and Pearson. Not only was her lovely party ruined, but also she knew that Sage was all wound up.

"Well!" she said, snatching everyone's attention with her sharp tone and a hand clap. "It's been a lovely evening," she sneered. "I do hope you enjoy the rest of your holiday, people! Good night!" Nadalia spun on her heels and left the room without bothering to see her guests out.

Chapter 14

Ryan

R yan folded her small frame into the back seat of Vonnie and Mike's sports car and wished she could have been completely absorbed by the buttery soft leather. Vonnie and Mike were kind enough to leave her out of their minimal conversation.

She couldn't believe how she stood up to Anderson in front of everyone, but when Pearson made Anderson's ogling known, she had to do something. She had noticed it long before, but kept her mouth shut. She was used to it. What she wasn't used to was other people witnessing what she often let pass.

As they pulled to a dreaded stop in front of the impressive home Anderson had built to her specifications, she hoped that this was one of the nights Anderson chose to run off to who knew where.

It hurt that somehow he'd got wind of her truth—that she was lucky to have a man like him. He shared the screen with Hollywood's most beautiful actresses, and that reality only fueled her insecurities. *Why had he chosen to marry her anyway?*

Ryan peaked out of the car window and her heart rate quickened at the sight of his fiery red Porsche in the driveway. It was posted haphazardly and dangerously close to the back of her Range Rover. She forced a hard swallow and summoned all of her inner strength just to push her leg out. Mike held her hand to help her exit.

She forced a weak smile. "Thanks again." Her mouth was dry and her voice croaked. "I have my key. No need to wait. I'll be fine." Ryan didn't want them to see the impending fire storm in case it started at the door.

"Are you sure?" Vonnie asked.

"I'll be fine," she said with strained confidence and waved off Vonnie's concerns. "Get home safe and text me to let me know you've made it. Thanks again for the ride." She pretended as if everything was okay, hoping her performance was convincing enough.

"Okay," Vonnie said, reaching for a quick kiss on her cheek. "If you need me, call me," she whispered during their embrace.

"I will," Ryan lied. Vonnie had already been exposed to far too much of her dysfunctional existence.

Ryan waved them off, watching their car retreat down the street past the mouth of their cul-de-sac. Once they were out of sight, she turned toward her home. Standing at the edge of her gate in the dark, she looked around and for a moment and thought of spending the night in their cottage behind the house. Then, she lifted her chest and drew in a deep cold breath before taking pointed steps toward her front door.

Lights were on all over the first floor and a few on the second level. Still a little surprised that he was home, she figured maybe he was preparing to go out. She hoped so.

Ryan slid her key in the lock and turned slowly. The door creaked as she pushed it open, and peered inside. When she saw no sign of Anderson, she tipped in and quietly closed it behind her.

The flicker of changing lights and colors indicated that the television was on in the family room. She could visualize Anderson sprawled across his recliner with a drink in his hand. If she was lucky, he'd be asleep.

Tipping further inside, she figured she could make a run for her bedroom, grab a nightie and head to one of the guest rooms to sleep. She preferred to deal with him after they both had some rest. She made it to the first step.

"Ryan!"

She flinched and froze. He was right behind her and his voice sounded colder than the ice he swirled around in his glass. Ryan closed her eyes and sighed before turning to face him.

He stood arrogantly, though he looked disheveled. His feet were bare, his belt was unbuckled, and his shirt was half buttoned with the bottom only halfway inside his slacks. Holding a snifter of scotch, Anderson peered at her over the rim as he drank.

"Bring your ass over here."

Ryan didn't move. Where was all of that courage she exhibited back at Nadalia's house?

The group had been her safety net. They'd never let him strike her or even go too far with his piercing words. But now, it was just the two of them.

Until now, he'd only struck her with his callous tongue. The scars he inflicted were invisible, but lasted longer and cut deeper than any physical ones. However, after her courageous outburst, she didn't know if tonight, he'd stop with just his words.

"I said—"

Her instincts told her to run and she tried to shoot up the steps, but Anderson grabbed her leg and dragged her back down. In one swift movement, he lifted her by her armpits, still holding his glass in the other hand.

"No! Anderson!"

Once she was on her feet, Anderson was in her face. The smell of the liquor assaulted her, stinging the insides of her nostrils. He pulled her in, gathering a handful of the front of her dress.

"What the hell did you think you were doing back there?"

"Let go of me," she pleaded, squinting to protect her eyes from the spit that flew from his mouth.

"How dare you talk to me like that in front of my friends?" Anderson grabbed her arm.

Ryan winced. "You kept looking at her. I wouldn't have said anything if Pearson hadn't. It was embarrassing."

"Embarrassing?" Anderson released her hard, causing her to fly backwards and stumble over her own feet.

"Anderson!" she yelled, just keeping herself from hitting the floor.

"Don't you ever…" Anderson paused, placed his glass down on the console and paced. "Everything you have is because of me. I had this house built for you. And you dare to disrespect me in front of my friends."

"What was I supposed to do?" Tears streamed down Ryan's face. If she just had a small dose of the courage she displayed earlier, she would say so much back to him. She would tell him she made sacrifices too—like giving up her dreams to become a bored, lonely housewife. What about all the nights she spent waiting on him to come home, the embarrassment she felt when she did accompany him to industry events, or the times she watched him flirt with other actresses. What about how he disregarded her feelings, opinions and constantly reminded her of her meager past? What about the pain of all of the babies she tried to have for him and failed? Ryan crumbled into her hands and cried harder.

For a while, Anderson just stood over her, watching her.

"Get up!"

"No."

"Ryan!" Anderson reached down and pulled at her. "I said get up."

Ryan was weary. She was almost afraid to get up because she didn't know if he would knock her back down. She hated this and was tired of living under

Anderson's thumb, but what choice did she have? She couldn't leave. He was right, without him she had nothing. His prenuptial agreement made sure of that.

Drooping like a rag doll, Ryan lay limp, offering no assistance as Anderson pulled her to her feet. Ryan knew she looked a mess, imagining the deep circles surrounding her red swollen eyes.

Holding her up by her arms, Anderson drew Ryan closer to him. She held her head down, refusing to look in his eyes as he bent over trying to force her to look at him.

Why did he want her to look at him? Why didn't he just go somewhere and crawl into bed with one of his lovers?

He shook her and her neck flopped. "Look at me!" he demanded.

Slowly Ryan lifted her head until they were eye to eye. She didn't know what was in the look he trained on her. He pulled her closer and she felt the rigidness of his erection poke her stomach. Ryan's brow creased in confusion. Did all of this arouse him?

Anderson covered her mouth hard with his, answering her unasked question. At first Ryan refused to kiss him back, but he forced her mouth open, pushing his tongue inside. He tasted of whiskey. He pulled in closer as if it were possible, squeezing her in his embrace. The kiss was wet, sloppy. His hands plundered her body and he pressed himself against her harder.

To her surprise, she felt a sliver of heat rise inside. The mix of adrenaline and the lust expanding in her made her dizzy. The feeling was foreign, but intense. The same sick intensity must have taken over Anderson's senses.

Without parting from her lips, he tore her dress off, backed her against the staircase, and laid her down. He set his body over hers and then dragged her underwear down her legs.

Ryan helped him, wiggling as he pulled them down. She kicked off her shoes and Anderson released his erection. When Ryan felt it against her, she lifted her legs. Anderson found her entrance and was drawn in by the muscles of her warm, moist canal.

Ryan screamed when he entered her fully and met him thrust for thrust right there on the steps. She slammed all of her frustration against him.

They stared at each other as if they were strangers who happened into this compromising position. His face contorted, as the intensity of their connection threatened to take him over the edge. The look of lustful desperation he held in his gaze caused heat to surge through Ryan. The walls of her center clenched and she squeezed, milking him until he yelled out.

Ryan thrust harder, lifting her back up off the stairs. Moments later, another shot of heat radiated throughout her body, causing the edges of her skin to sting deliciously.

Together, they cried out, riding out their releases by plowing into one another. Coming hard and fast, neither would let up as if they had something to prove.

Depleted, Anderson fell on top of her. She dug her fingers into his back and the rest of her peak rippled through her. Panting and trembling, they held each other until their breathing came under control.

Anderson peeled himself from her sweaty body and stood. Without even retrieving his pants, he grabbed the railing and helped himself up the stairs.

Ryan remained on the steps listening to his footsteps until she heard the bathroom door close and wondered what had come over her. What had come over them?

Chapter 15

Vonnie

Vonnie and Mike made it home just past midnight and Vonnie was so worried about Ryan. She knew something was up with them after the miscarriage situation, and tonight put all of the pieces of the puzzle together.

Anderson was abusive. Vonnie just wasn't sure how abusive or what kinds of abuse and she wondered if he had ever put his hands on her.

The thought of Anderson striking Ryan nearly made Vonnie cry. Ryan wouldn't be able to handle a punch from a fit man like Anderson.

Vonnie thought about trying to find out more about their situation for Ryan's sake. She wanted Ryan to know that if she needed someone, she'd be there for her and would never tell her secrets.

Or, maybe she should just mind her business. Ryan was pretty introverted and probably wouldn't take too kindly to Vonnie prying.

Mike came into the bedroom and fell asleep as soon as his head hit the pillow. But for Vonnie, sleep wouldn't come easy. Mike choked back a snore and Vonnie shoved him just enough for him to roll over onto his side. That would give him a few minutes of quiet breathing before he started snoring again.

Pushing the covers away, Vonnie got out of the bed and stepped quietly from the bedroom. She didn't know what to do with herself. It had been years since she'd suffered from sleepless nights.

Vonnie walked to Noelle's room. Lena had come to hang out with her while they went to Nadalia's house. When she peeked in, both Noelle and Lena were sprawled across her bed sleeping, with both the TV and the iPod on. The sight made Vonnie shake her head and smile. She'd closed the door, leaving it open just a crack and headed down to the kitchen.

Vonnie opened the fridge, then closed it, opened the door to the pantry and closed that. She wasn't hungry. She was worried. She tipped back to her room, retrieved her cell phone, then once she was back in the kitchen, she texted Ryan.

Hey. You awake?

Vonnie took a seat at the breakfast bar. She stared at the phone, waiting for Ryan's reply.

"Come on, Ryan. Give me something." She had hoped that Ryan hadn't fallen asleep, because if she had, Vonnie imagined herself staying up all night worrying. She didn't have to be the best of friends with someone to worry about their well-being and as fragile as Ryan appeared, Vonnie felt like she needed someone.

Vonnie's phone buzzed and she grabbed it so fast it almost fumbled out of her hand. She placed her hand across her heart and breathed a sigh of relief.

Yes. Can't sleep.

Me neither. Just checking on you to make sure you're okay.

I'm fine. Thanks.

Okay. Well I'm here for you if you ever need to talk.

Vonnie hesitated to hit send on that last text. She didn't want to run Ryan away by pushing too hard. Vonnie exhaled, hit send and then waited. She'd opened the door. If Ryan needed or wanted to confide in her, she was letting her know that she was there.

Ryan never replied. Maybe she did need to mind her own business.

Chapter 16

Pearson

Pearson woke with a headache the size of Texas. Even the soft morning light filtering through her blinds made her eyes hurt. It would have been worse if not for the rain and dense fog.

Her head felt like it was filled with bricks as she tried to sit up. She groaned and lay back down. Covering her eyes to shield the light with one hand, Pearson took her other and felt for Niles. His side of the bed was empty. She sat up quickly, jolting the pain in her head.

Pearson looked at the digital clock on her night stand. It was almost noon. She had missed church—probably for the better. Trying to listen to a sermon through a hangover would be sacrilegious. Pearson swung her legs to the side of the bed and noticed the bottles of Tylenol and water. Niles always came to her rescue. She popped two pills and downed half the bottle.

Pearson dragged herself from the bed and headed to the bathroom. That's when she caught the scent of bacon wafting through the air.

The sight she saw in the mirror was pitiful. Her eyes were red and encircled with deep creases. Her hair sat on top of her head like a tangled mess. She gasped and her breath was atrocious. Pearson brushed her teeth and washed her face. Before going downstairs, she covered her naked body with a nightie, and then slipped her feet into a pair of animal print slippers.

The scent of bacon grew stronger as she approached the kitchen and her mouth watered. Niles had always been a great cook. His family owned a chain of soul food restaurants, named after his grandmother, Clara Mae, who loved to listen to jazz as she prepared meals. At ninety-three, Clara Mae was still kicking and running the Day clan like a mob boss runs his family.

Pearson stepped into the kitchen, stopped and sniffed, taking in the delicious mixture flavoring the air. She smiled when she exhaled and then opened her eyes to Niles' back as he stirred a pot of grits.

"Morning, honey!" she said and climbed up on a stool.

Niles didn't respond.

"Morning, honey!" She spoke louder, trying to be heard above the noise of the frying pan.

"Hey," Niles replied without turning away from the stove.

Pearson frowned, slid down from her stool and went to Niles' side.

"What's up with you?"

Niles put down the spoon, drew in a sharp breath and blew it out.

Pearson put her hand on her hip. It was evident that he was mad so she braced herself with her own attitude.

"Let me finish making breakfast and we'll talk."

"Talk about what?"

"Pearson!" Niles threw his hands up. "Just. Let. Me. Finish."

Pearson grunted. "I don't see what the big deal is. If you have something to say, then just come out and say it."

"Give me a minute." He was exasperated.

"Why can't we just talk now? What's the difference between now and a minute from now?" Pearson crowded him, waiting for an answer. When she was tired of being ignored, she sucked her teeth and then walked out of the kitchen.

Pearson didn't go far. She folded her arms across her chest, paced for a moment and then came right back. When he continued to ignore her, she grabbed the spoon from his hand and tossed it onto the counter. Clumps of grits flew across the stove. "What is it already!" she yelled.

"Dammit, Pearson. I asked you to give me a minute, but since you can't wait. Here it is. I'm tired!"

Pearson's heart dropped. *Tired?* She clamped her teeth together to keep from reacting to soon. "Of what?"

"Your drinking!"

Pearson tried to push down the lump that formed in her throat. Niles had made comments about her drinking, but she'd never seen him react like this. "What?"

"You don't enjoy a drink like normal people. No! You can't just have one or two glasses of wine and have a good time. You have to keep going, and going, and going until there's nothing left in the bottle. You go overboard every single time. Once you get drunk… whoa!" He punctuated his expression by raising both hands. "You embarrass me like you did last night!"

Pearson's mouth fell open. "What do you mean like last night?"

"Oh, that's another problem." He hesitated. "The blackouts."

Niles' pause was calculated. Pearson sensed that he opted against using stronger language to make his point.

"What happened?" She wished he would just say it.

"You don't recall starting that whole thing between Anderson and Ryan? You asked everyone if you were the only person who saw Anderson ogling Nadalia's ass." Niles went on to recount the incident. "Clearly you owe Sage and Nadalia an apology for ruining their party."

Pearson tried hard to stir her memory.

"You were out of line."

"Anderson shouldn't have been ogling her ass in front of his wife anyway." Pearson knew that wasn't the right thing to say, but she couldn't bring herself to admit the truth. Niles shot a bewildered glance in her direction. She looked away.

"That's none of your business. If his wife didn't say anything, what gave you the right to?" He was in Pearson's face. She stepped back. "You start drinking before we even get to where we're going. By the time we arrive, you're already halfway drunk. You talk loud, you're obnoxious and you're crass!" Niles walked away. Pearson watched him. She hadn't realized how deeply he was affected before now.

"Life hasn't been the same," he continued and Pearson wished he would stop. "I don't know what happened to you, but I want my wife back." Niles walked back over to the stove and pulled out a pan of shrimp wrapped in bacon. "It's ready, let's eat." Niles tossed the plates and food on the table. "Get the glasses and the juice," he said.

Pearson closed her eyes for a moment, attempting to get her emotions in order. They sat down and ate in silence. The food was delicious, but she couldn't bring herself to enjoy it. Part of it was due to the hangover, but the other part had everything to do with the unsettling feelings that whirled in her stomach. Taking only small forkfuls, both of them pushed their food around on their plates, leaving most of it scattered. Pearson's headache still thumped. The Tylenol wasn't helping. She put her fork down and rubbed her temples.

"Eat the bacon, you'll feel better."

"What?"

"I said, eat the bacon. Greasy food helps you get over your hangover faster for some reason. I'm not sure why, but I know that it works."

"Oh." Pearson was grateful that Niles was at least talking to her in a more civilized manner. She reached for her bacon and nibbled, watching Niles while he ate. She wondered if she was even capable of fixing this.

Niles stared back for a moment. Pearson still had no words. At least she felt confident that Niles wasn't leaving. She knew she was a lot to handle at times, but what would she do without him.

Pearson had come into their union with piles of emotional baggage and he accepted her just the way she was. Apparently something shifted.

Yet, Niles was the only person in her life who didn't cause her pain. People always thought being rich solved life's problems. They didn't know that money couldn't buy attention from a mother. It couldn't keep her from feeling abandoned after her father's death. It surely didn't comfort her, un-break her heart or soothe her soul.

Until Niles appeared, she had forgotten what love even felt like. When she drank, it didn't matter. If she could give up all the money she had for a slightly dysfunctional, yet loving family of her own, she would do it without hesitating. Niles was the closest she came to having that.

"Pearse." Niles broke the silence and her heart fluttered. He'd called her by her pet name. "You really pissed me off last night. I'm concerned. I feel like I'm sitting back and watching you destroy yourself."

"Niles, I was drinking when you met me."

"Not like this. You used to have limits and your tolerance has changed. I remember when we could enjoy a glass or two of wine over dinner and that would be it. Now you can't control yourself."

"I—"

"No!" Niles held his hand up. "Let me finish. I've been waiting a long time to say this. I need you to see reality. You have a problem."

Pearson dropped her head and blinked back tears.

"I don't want to lose you. I meant it when I said until death do us part."

"Niles—"

"Promise me, Pearson!" he interjected.

She remained quiet. After a few beats she looked into his eyes. She could see his pain and hated that she caused it. The tears she held back, now rolled down her cheeks. "I promise," she said, wiping them away.

Niles got up, made his way around the table and embraced her.

"Thank you," he whispered.

Pearson laid her head on his chest and let the weight of her life fall on him. She wanted to stay there forever, coddled in his haven, unreachable by the rest of the world. She settled deeper into his arms and he kissed the top of her head.

The house phone rang, snatching them from the beauty of their moment.

"I'll get it," Niles said.

Pearson made herself busy clearing the table. She was serious when she said promised to work on her drinking. Niles always made her happy and she was going to return the favor.

"Pearse." The cautious tone of his voice alarmed her.

"What is it, babe?"

Niles held the phone out to her. "It's your mother."

Chapter 17

Nadalia

After all the effort she had put into making her party fabulous and making Sage happy, Pearson ruined it all. She couldn't shake the anger she felt for that woman.

Now Sage was walking around in a weird mood. She couldn't put her finger on just want it was. Anderson had called him first thing this morning to apologize. He'd accepted, but the whole thing still bothered him.

This was the weekend before Christmas and one of the first weekends that he'd been home in months. She was determined to make the best of it. They still hadn't had sex and not only was she starving for his touch, but her imagination had become overactive.

She found herself more and more wondering if he had been unfaithful, even though that was hard to believe. The two of them together were a match made in perfection. She was beautiful. He was handsome. They were rich. What more did they need?

But something was wrong and she had to warm things up before they got too cold. Her marriage wasn't going down without a fight. What would people think?

Nadalia went into the family room where Sage sat in his favorite chair, yelling at the television screen about how incompetent the coach was for the ridiculous plays he was calling.

"Did you see that crap?" he yelled into his phone. He laughed at whatever the person on the other line said. "Shut up, punk? Just wait until the fourth quarter. We got this, man. Don't count us out just yet. You'll see. What! You've got be kidding me." He directed that last comment at the television. "I need to focus. I'll call you back," he said. Sage ended the call, stuffed his cell phone between his leg and the chair, and then suddenly jumped to his feet holding his head in his hand, releasing a cry of agony. No!"

Nadalia smiled as she watched his usual Sunday afternoon football antics.

"Who's winning?" she said as she walked into the room.

"Not the damn Jets! Man!" He sat back down.

Nadalia came and sat on his lap. He kept his eyes on the television, looking around her. She grabbed his head, holding him by the sides of his face, made him look at her and laughed.

Sage laughed with her and she felt her heart beat.

"My Jets are screwing up bad, Dali."

"I can see that." She rolled off his lap and sat beside him. "Let's take a vacation."

"Okay," he said, only half listening.

"Let's take one now!"

"Now!" Sage reared his head back. "Babe, I can't leave work now. It's too busy. Besides, I…" Sage stopped talking.

"You what?"

"It's just not a good time."

"I know, but I'm talking about a quick excursion. Some place quiet, secluded and sexy."

"How about right after the Super Bowl?"

"No, Sage. We need this getaway now. I barely see you and by the time you get home at night, you're so exhausted you go right to sleep. We haven't made love in weeks. I miss you."

Sage sighed. "I'm sorry, babe. Work has been…crazy."

"I know. It's been crazy for me, too, which is why we could use this."

"Let me think about it."

Nadalia pouted. She was used to getting what she wanted from him. "Sage," she whined.

"The Super Bowl is just a few weeks away and then I'll take you somewhere for a quick getaway or maybe even a whole week."

Annoyed, Nadalia stood, blocking the TV with her hands on her hips.

"Are you cheating on me, Sage?"

"What?" Sage grabbed the remote, hit mute and looked at Nadalia with his entire face scrunched into a curious knot. "What would make you say that?"

Nadalia crossed her arms. "You love sex and you haven't touched me. If you're not screwing me, then who are you screwing?"

"Now you're just being ridiculous!" Sage shook his head and held Nadalia by the shoulders. "Babe. I'm not cheating on you!" Sage threw his hands up, exasperated."

Nadalia searched his eyes for any indication that he was lying. She surmised that her heart would cloud her judgment anyway and stomped off. If he was cheating, she'd need proof.

"Dali!" Sage called after her. "Jeez!" she heard him say behind her back. "Okay. Let's go somewhere."

Nadalia almost ran back to the room. "Really!"

"Yes. Put something together right after the New Year. Something quick."

Nadalia yelped. "Okay. I have the perfect getaway lined up." She kissed Sage. "It will be great." Nadalia headed out to make the plans. "I hope I don't have to wait until then to get some from my husband," she teased.

Nadalia took the stairs two at a time as she ran up to her bedroom to retrieve her iPad to book their getaway. She noticed she had missed a few calls on her cell phone and thumbed through her missed notifications. The one that surprised her was the missed call from Pearson. Curious to see what she had to say after her less than becoming behavior the night before, Nadalia dialed her back and stood with her hand on one hip as she waited for her to answer.

"Nadalia," Pearson said when she answered.

"What do you want?"

"You're mad, of course. I just called to apologize for last night. I didn't mean to raise a ruckus."

"Pearson. You always mean to raise a ruckus. You ruined my party."

"Nadalia, please…" She heard Pearson sigh. "I'll make it up to you. In fact, I'll make it up to all of you. Dinner. My treat—over at Monty's by the pier. When would you like to go?"

Nadalia didn't answer right away. She thought about it for a minute. Did she really want to go to dinner with Pearson? " Fine, but not Monty's. I'll choose the place."

"Whatever."

"Pearson!"

Pearson laughed. "I'm kidding, geesh. Loosen your panty straps. Relax."

Nadalia found herself chuckling, too. When Pearson wasn't getting on her nerves, she did manage to make her laugh. She was the only wife besides her who had the courage to speak her mind, although she didn't doubt the Vonnie had it in her. Ryan didn't. "How about this Friday, right after Christmas. I'll let you know which restaurant I choose. Does seven o'clock work for you?"

"Works just fine. I'll call the other girls to invite them."

Nadalia thought about it. In all the years that their husbands had been friends, this would be the first time that the wives would be hanging out without them. She wasn't sure how she felt about having Ryan come after last night, but if the men were fine, then she'd be fine.

"See you then," she told Pearson and ended the call without another thought.

Nadalia planned to find the most expensive restaurant along the gold coast and enjoy every morsel on Pearson's dime.

Chapter 18

Ryan

C hristmas had finally come and this time, Ryan was particularly anxious as she prepared for the evening. Anderson told her that his parents had flown in to spend the holidays in New York this year and would be joining them for dinner. His mother especially enjoyed the lively vibe that electrified her home town during this time of the year. They were to spend a few days in their condo down in Battery Park, and a few days at their home in the Hamptons before flying back to LA right after the New Year.

She was under tremendous pressure to cook or have an impressive meal catered, as well as serve as a referee between Frannie and Anderson's mother. From the moment those two met, they were enemies, exchanging snarls instead of smiles. They were polar opposites in terms of their upbringings. Phoebe, who was brought up under the bright lights of Hollywood, was cultured and had traveled the world by the time she was ten. Frannie on the other hand, hadn't seen an airplane up close until after Ryan had married Anderson. As far as Frannie was concerned, all that fancy talk and fancy clothes didn't make Phoebe any better than anyone else.

Ryan was still on a little bit of a high since this morning when Anderson showered her with lavish gifts for Christmas. He'd done better this year than in the past and that made Ryan both happy and nervous. She was happy about the beautiful tennis bracelet, diamond earrings and custom designed fur coat from Miso Furriers, but it also made her question his motives. After their intense sex the other night following the blow up at Nadalia's house, Ryan woke up the next morning to find the house empty. Anderson showed up later that night without an explanation of his whereabouts. She gave no resistance other than a cold shoulder. Everything had returned to normal until he surprised her with all those great gifts earlier.

The doorbell sent a jazzy tune reverberating throughout the house and Ryan ran to the door to let in who she thought were the caterers.

"Merry Christmas, honey," Frannie choked out with her raspy voice. "I came early to help with dinner." She walked past Ryan. "Where's that husband of yours?" she said, heading to the kitchen with bags.

Ryan stood, still holding the doorknob, willing her insides to stop twirling. She was already anxious and her mother's early presence would only add to that.

"Merry Christmas, Ma." Ryan closed the door and sighed. "Anderson is upstairs taking a nap."

"A nap!" Frannie looked at her watch—the Rolex that Ryan had purchased for her birthday last summer. "At this time of the day? He should be down here helping, making merry with you over some fresh baked bread as it wafts through the corridors of this big old house. It's Christmas for Christ's sake." Frannie stopped and sniffed the air. "How come I don't smell anything? Aren't we supposed to be having dinner here this evening? Did I make these desserts for nothing?"

"I catered. I thought I told you that I didn't need you to come over early. I've got everything under control."

"Oh you do?" Frannie looked her up and down. "Then why do you look like you just ran through a field of poison oak?"

Ryan gasped and touched her face. She looked in the mirror in the vestibule and almost cried when she saw the red blotches. The stress had made a physical appearance.

"Oh no!"

"Relax! Something told me you needed me." Frannie went into the powder room and came back with a wet hand towel. "Come on in here and sit down for a moment." She still had her purse hanging off her arm. "Here." She placed the cool towel over Ryan's face.

Ryan cried, letting the towel absorb her tears. Anderson's parents' impending visit was getting to her more than she realized.

"Hold that." Frannie took Ryan's hand and placed it over the towel. "It's a little cold, but keep it there. Do you have any allergy medication here—some fresh ginger, maybe?"

"I have allergy pills in the medicine cabinet in my bathroom upstairs," Ryan said.

"Good, go get some while I boil this ginger. I'm half Jewish you know, and we have lots of remedies for stuff like this."

"I know, Ma," Ryan said as she headed upstairs for the pills. When she returned, her mother was at the door letting the caterer in. "Merry Christmas. You can bring that right over here," Ryan said leading the handlers to the formal dining area, and then she ran into the kitchen to get the envelope that contained their pay.

Frannie peeked inside the chafing dishes. "So much food! Who else is coming to dinner?"

Ryan didn't want to say their names. "Um."

"Um? We're having dinner with someone named Um?"

Ryan rolled her eyes. "Anderson's parents are in town. They're coming for dinner."

Frannie stood silent for a few moments. "If that woman says one word to me other than hello, I'm going to—"

"Ma!"

"Well she better watch it."

"Just help me set the table," Ryan huffed. If her mother kept it up, she'd never get rid of the nervous blotches.

In the midst of their preparations, Anderson came down the steps in all of his Hollywood glamour. His descent resembled something from a movie.

Ryan's heart skipped a beat when he rounded the bottom of the staircase and headed toward her in the dining room. He had freshened up and even smelled handsome.

"Afternoon, Frannie," he said in his deep, debonair tone.

"What's up, Andy? You're looking dapper. Is it because momma and daddy are coming for a visit?"

Anderson ignored her.

"How was your nap?" Ryan asked.

"Good." He kissed her. Ryan was surprised. "What happened to your face?" he asked.

"I just got a little too stressed out over preparing for dinner."

"Well relax. There's no need to be stressed. They're not spending the night." He chuckled.

Anderson leaned over and sniffed the pans lining the antique buffet table. "Clara Mae's, I suspect."

"Yes. I wanted to make sure we had delicious soul food your mother could appreciate."

"Niles' family does it best. It smells great. Well, they called just before I got in the shower to say they were on their way. They should be here soon. I'll get a few bottles of wine from the cellar. Maybe you should put a little make up on. Is that what you're wearing?"

Ryan touched her face. "I haven't gotten dressed yet, Anderson," she said.

"Go ahead and get yourself ready, honey. I'll be happy to greet your in-laws for you when they arrive." Frannie's Cheshire cat smile spread across the length of her thin face.

"I'll take care of that," Anderson said, admonishing Frannie with his eyes.

She tossed him an innocent look and followed Ryan upstairs.

Ryan heard the doorbell as she dressed.

"They're here!" Frannie sang as she sat on the side of their bed.

Ryan examined herself in the full length mirror. The red dress hugged her waif frame and she added a white belt to add the illusion of definition to her waist. She wore the bracelets and matching earrings that Anderson had given her earlier. She pulled her blond tresses into a roll and quickly curled the edges into spirals.

"You look fine," Frannie said. "Now let's go greet the beast!" She pulled Ryan's arm, dragging her along and calling her on her obvious attempt to prolong the inevitable.

Frannie lifted her chin as she drew closer to Phoebe and Sheldon. Ryan watched the women look down their noses at one another as they entered the sitting room.

Phoebe looked gorgeous as always with her salt and pepper spiral curls cascading down the sides of her flawless caramel face. Her lips were painted her signature red and her opulent jewels and winter white pants suit spoke of her elegance. In contrast, Frannie wore skinny jeans that clung to her wiry legs a red, white and green Christmas sweater with riding boots.

"Frannie," Phoebe said and nodded.

"Phoebe," Frannie said and turned to Anderson's dad. They engaged in a quick, but genuine embrace. "Hey Chuck, how ya doin'?"

"Couldn't be better, Frannie and yourself?"

"Like you, I couldn't be better."

"Ryan. You look lovely as always," Sheldon said.

She heard Phoebe suck her teeth as she hugged her father-in-law. Anderson had inherited his mean streak directly from her, Ryan had always surmised.

Anderson was the darker version of his distinguished looking dad. Both were tall and handsome, but Anderson inherited his mother's caramel complexion, which was several shades darker than his fair-skinned father.

"Phoebe." Ryan offered a polite nod in her direction.

"Ryan." Phoebe nodded back.

"I'm starving. Let's get started," Anderson said, placing his hand on his dad's back as they walked into the formal dining room.

"It smells great in here. Ryan, did you cook all of this?"

"Of course she didn't," Phoebe answered for her.

Frannie cut a quick glance at Ryan. She didn't want her mother to fall into Pheobe's trap.

"We called in a favor," Anderson said to his dad and smiled.

"Hmm." Sheldon sniffed. "Good ole Clara Mae's. I can tell. I swear that food reminds me of my days back in South Carolina as a child. My grandma—the little woman that she was—would wring a chicken's neck and snap it so fast. Next thing you know we had dinner. I tell you, those were the good ole days."

"Oh Sheldon, please!" Phoebe said. She couldn't stand for him to speak of his modest days before becoming a celebrated actor and producer.

"Well I hope you enjoy it Mr. Lee," Ryan said.

"I'm sure I will."

"I assume we will say grace. I mean it is Jesus' birthday," Phoebe said and looked over at Frannie. "If you don't mind me saying that."

"I know who Jesus is. I'm surprised that you do?" Frannie countered.

Phoebe's mouth fell open and Frannie laughed. Sheldon snickered and Phoebe narrowed her eyes at him.

"Mr. Lee. Would you do us the honor?" Ryan asked.

"It would be my pleasure." Sheldon said a brief, but beautiful grace and ended with how grateful he was to be able to spend Christmas with his son and daughter-in-law.

"Just beautiful, Sheldon! Sounds like you really do know who Jesus is," Frannie howled, her laugh making everyone else at the table burst into laughter—everyone except Phoebe.

"So…still no babies, I see," Phoebe interjected.

Ryan assumed that Phoebe's goal was to suck the joy out of the atmosphere.

"Not yet, Ma! One day." Anderson looked at Ryan and smiled.

"Sweetheart, could you pass those great smelling yams?" Sheldon asked.

Phoebe handed Sheldon the yams and he dug in, piling them on his place along with the greens, rice and mac and cheese.

"Got any projects coming up, son?"

"As a matter of fact I do. I'll be heading out on an early flight tomorrow. I'll be back next week to celebrate the New Year, and then I'm off again for a few weeks of shooting."

Ryan tried her best to contain her annoyance. She knew Anderson would be leaving after the holidays to start shooting, but until he just said it moments ago, she didn't know that he was leaving the next day.

"What kind of movie?" Sheldon asked.

"It's an action flick. I'm surprised you didn't know. Everything gets around in this industry since it's so small."

"Yeah. Well, I've been taking it easy lately. I'm thinking about retiring. I've done my share."

"You're retiring!" Frannie said with a mouth full of turkey.

Phoebe rolled her eyes and turned away.

"Yep," he said pushing back from the table. "I think it's time."

"Congratulations, Mr. Lee. Are you excited?" Ryan asked.

"Actually, I am. You know how it is in this business. You never really retire. I wouldn't mind taking on a project here and there at my leisure."

"Nice! I tell ya. There's nothing like retirement," Frannie said. "Those years I gave up to the telephone company, answering those calls from all those angry people just sucked the life out of me. I still hate talking on the phone."

"Andy, dear. You're looking a little thin these days. Doesn't the wife cook anymore? You need to stay healthy and strong in your line of work," Phoebe said.

"Sheldon, you're looking a little thin, too. Does your wife ever cook?" Frannie countered and plastered a smile on her face as she stared Phoebe down.

"Ladies!" Sheldon admonished.

"Ma! Give Ryan a break."

Ryan looked at Anderson. He hadn't come to her defense much when his mother attacked. He and Sheldon mostly ignored Phoebe's snide remarks as if they never heard them.

"How about dessert?" Frannie suggested and stood. "I made my homemade apple pie. It's to die for. Have several pieces, Phoebe!"

"Ma!" Ryan chided.

"Just kidding, geesh!"

"I'll have a slice. I remember that pie," Sheldon said, holding his plate out.

Phoebe cut her eyes at him.

"I'll certainly have some, Frannie," Anderson said.

"Ryan, honey, want me to cut you a piece, too."

"Yes, please."

"Phoebe?" Frannie said, lowering her voice an octave lower to sound more serious and then laughed.

"I'll pass," Phoebe said dryly.

"I'm shocked," Frannie said.

Ryan placed her elbows on the table and rested her head in her hands. She couldn't wait until this dinner was over. Fortunately, the evening did end without many more hitches, though the exchange had drained Ryan. Frannie left after she helped Ryan in the kitchen.

Ryan dragged her tired bones upstairs to join Anderson in bed. She pondered asking him about his leaving the next morning, but Anderson had been pretty nice to her. She wanted things to stay that way. But she remembered how good it felt to actually speak her mind the other night—frightening, but good. Things didn't end as badly as she thought. She was still nervous about taking the chance, though.

Anderson rolled over and put his arms around her. She melded herself against him. The question swirled in her mind, just behind her lips.

"You didn't tell me about tomorrow." Her curiosity made her force the words out before she choked on them.

"I didn't?"

"No. Where are you going?"

"To take care of a little business." He kissed the back of her head. "Now go to sleep."

Ryan stared into the darkness as her body grew warm under the heat of her anger. The red blotches on her face started to itch.

Chapter 19

Vonnie

Mike slid his arms around Vonnie from behind as she stood in front of the vanity applying a touch of nude gloss.

"You sure you don't want to stay home with me tonight?"

Vonnie shook her head. "I thought you'd love the idea of me hanging with the girls."

"It's cool, but the girls are not what I'm thinking of right now." Mike ground his pelvis against her backside.

"You better stop it."

"Alright." Mike released her and took a seat on the side of the Jacuzzi tub. "I think it's cool that you ladies are finally connecting."

Vonnie switched her gloss for eye liner and framed her lids. "I don't have anything against them. They're pretty cool. I just don't think we have much in common."

"Why not? You're a smart professional woman. Hell! You're a doctor. You might even be smarter than them."

"Silly. You know what I mean. Pearson and Nadalia came from money. Ryan's just different. I can relate to her a little more."

"How so?" Mike lifted his chin and folded his arms in front of him.

"Well for one thing, they grew up attending the finest schools money could buy and riding their very own horses. We, on the other hand," she said, referring to her and Ryan, "grew up riding the city bus to our very own choice of public schools."

"So?"

"I'm just saying. That makes them a little different. Not better. Just different." Vonnie stuffed her make into its designated bag and continued, "Take Nadalia for instance. I think she squanders away too much money. Look at her party the other night. I can only imagine how much she paid for all those servants. Oh and those favors… they were fabulous, but engraved crystal ornaments? I put that sucker on the tree and it almost tipped over," she said and Mike laughed.

"Well, Pearson is actually the only one who grew up swimming laps of luxury. But Nadalia, she was a teenager when her mother's business took off."

"She's so over the top you'd never know. I thought she was born with a platinum spoon in her mouth." Vonnie twisted her head from side to side and nodded, approving her final look. "Oh I forgot to tell you, she snubbed the bottle of wine I brought with me the other week. I just laughed."

Mike followed her out of the bedroom. Vonnie knew he was probably staring at her backside, so she sashayed over to the closet to figure out which coat to wear.

"What do you and Noelle plan to do for the evening?"

"I need to run out to Queens really quick. I'm going to take her with me and then I'm going to take her to the new Asian fusion restaurant in Port Washington and catch a movie at the mall."

"How cute. A daddy-daughter date."

"Yeah. I'm hanging with my young gal tonight. Don't be jealous!"

"I'm hardly jealous," Vonnie said, still searching her walk-in closet. She was looking for something that went well with her jeans and cute green top. Finally she settled on a belted mink jacket that Mike surprised her with last winter. "You've been running out to Queens quite a bit lately." She pushed the words on her mind past her lips.

"Yeah," Mike said.

Vonnie frowned a bit, but didn't press the issue, assuming it was some family drama that she probably didn't want to hear about anyway. She pulled on her jacket, grabbed a sexy pair of high-heeled riding boots and grabbed her purse. She turned and Mike was right on her back. Vonnie, shook her head, planted a quick peck on his lips and headed out the room, summoning Noelle.

When Noelle didn't respond, she went to her room and pushed her door open to find her sitting in the center of her bed, lip-synching with her eyes closed, holding the jeweled headphones against her ears.

Vonnie walked in and snatched the headphones off Noelle's ears. "Girl, you didn't hear me calling you?"

Noelle shrunk sheepishly. "Sorry, Mom."

"I'm leaving now. Give me a kiss."

Noelle rose to her knees and kissed Vonnie. "Have fun, Mommy!"

"You too!"

"I always have fun when I'm hanging out with Daddy."

On her way out, Vonnie grabbed the keys to the sports car. After all, she was hanging with the rich girls. Although she qualified, Vonnie couldn't get used to calling herself rich.

The ride didn't take long, but once she arrived at the marina, it took a while to find the artsy restaurant. It was tucked deep into a pier filled with yachts big enough to hold small cars. Vonnie chose to walk along the waterside after parking. Lights from the pier reflected across the waves of the midnight blue water like a string of bouncing pearls. Vonnie pulled the neckline of her coat closer to shield her skin from the sharp cold air whipping against the boardwalk and looked up. Billions of stars twinkled against the dark velvet sky.

Vonnie entered the dim but cozy restaurant and was greeted by a mature gentleman with salt and pepper hair who reminded her of the Michelin man. For a moment, she thought that he was about to hug her, but he gently touched her elbow and asked, "How can I help you?" in a rich Italian accent.

"I'm with the Madison party."

"Oh yes!" the man said excitedly. "Right this way." He led her along as if he were bringing her to proudly meet his family. At the table, he presented her to Nadalia and Ryan.

"Your guests, ma'am."

"Thank you!" Nadalia nodded and smiled, politely dismissing the gentleman.

"Hello ladies," Vonnie greeted the girls as she looked around. The décor fit the wharf setting with wood-planked walls, boat wheels, and pictures of upright distinguished gentlemen in nautical attire.

"Hi Vonnie," Ryan squeaked out in a near whisper.

"How are you, darling?" Nadalia lifted halfway from her chair and planted air kisses on either side of Vonnie's cheek. "Pearson just sent me a text that she'll be here in a few minutes. How do you like the place? It's one of my favorites. The Chilean sea bass and the lobster scampi are amazing. I recommend you get one of those."

"It's so cozy. I love it."

Seconds later, Pearson blasted in like a wild wind. The plump man couldn't keep up with her step. Instead he nodded and turned back toward the front.

"I made it, ladies." Pearson swirled off her mink cape and placed it over the back of her chair. "Nadalia, how did you find this place? You won't believe how long I drove around looking for the address only to realize that I had passed it three times. The entrance is so dark and hidden that I thought I was walking into someone's secret lair." Pearson's loud laugh let everyone know that her party had already started.

"Waiter, I'll have what she's been drinking," Nadalia said and laughed.

"Very funny, Nadalia. Now hand me the wine list so you can get it right," Pearson said and howled. She laughed so hard, spit caught in her throat and she started coughing.

Ryan patted her back. "Are you okay?"

Pearson waved her off. "Girl, I'm fine." Pearson took a few seconds to get herself together and then cleared her throat. "Thanks for accepting my invitation, ladies. Again, I apologize for my behavior the other night. So eat, drink and be merry on me. Are we good?"

"Yes," Ryan said.

"I've been good," Nadalia said. "Now tell me what you were drinking before you joined us."

Pearson looked through the wine list. "It's not on here, but this will do." She pointed out another brand. Nadalia summoned the waiter and ordered a bottle for the table.

Ironically, Pearson's voluminous entrance shifted the dynamics and the girls fell into easy chatter. Nadalia wanted the pleasure of ordering for everyone, insisting that they would love their meals. After she ordered, she held her fork in Pearson's direction. "Listen Pearson. Don't drink too much because I'm not driving your ass home," Nadalia said. "Niles isn't here to be your designated driver."

"Aw shut up, Nadalia. I actually think you need to drink a little more. You wouldn't be so uptight."

"You really think I'm uptight?" Nadalia sat back with a look of wonder.

"Sometimes." Pearson dug into her plate half acknowledging Nadalia.

Ryan looked nervous as if she were afraid that the two would break out into a fight. Vonnie was enjoying herself more than she anticipated.

"You may be right." Nadalia's response shocked everyone. Forks fell onto plates, backs straightened. Everyone looked at her. "I haven't had sex in over a month!" Nadalia took a sip of her wine and continued eating as if nothing happened while everyone else's mouth hung open.

"Nadalia!" Ryan chided.

"What, girl? You and Anderson never had a dry spell?" She scrunched her brows at Ryan.

Ryan looked as if she pondered that thought for a moment and everyone fell into a fit of laughter.

"I told you to take him on a sexy, spontaneous excursion," Vonnie interjected.

"Don't worry. It's already been planned."

"Good," Vonnie said and held up her wine glass. Nadalia clinked glasses with her and winked.

"Date nights!" Vonnie yelled as if the words would vanish before she had a chance to say them. "Date nights are good, too. Mike and I go out on dates all the time."

"Niles and I used to do that. We need to start doing them again," Pearson said, taking another sip and clearing her throat.

"Okay…and about the other day," Nadalia looked at Ryan. "I don't know if I should be the one apologizing…" She then cut her eyes at Pearson who rolled her eyes toward the ceiling. "…but I'd never do anything inappropriate to entice any of your husbands. I only have eyes for Sage. I'm sorry that whole thing happened."

"I know!" Ryan cast her eyes down for a moment. "We're fine. He bought me these for Christmas." Ryan turned her neck and held out her wrists to show off her diamond earrings and tennis bracelet.

"Very pretty!" Vonnie said.

"Oh." Nadalia nodded. "He did good! And let's not forget the custom fur from Miso, right!" she said, taking the opportunity to plug her company's work. "Did you love it? I had one of our top designers create that for you. It's one of a kind."

Ryan nodded.

"Nice!" Pearson added.

"What about you, Pearson" Nadalia added. "How's things over at the Days?"

"Oh. Never better," she said with a mouth full of sea bass. "Mm. Nadalia. This was an excellent choice," she said, pointing at her meal with her fork.

"We don't have to ask Vonnie. She and Mike can't seem to keep their hands off each other. Even when they are not touching, Mike fondles her with his eyes," Nadalia said laughing.

"I know right!" Pearson said. "I love me some Niles Day but your kind of love just oozes out all over the damn place."

"It's the curves. Maybe you three should gain some weight. Pass me the rest of that fried calamari," Vonnie said, reaching for the crispy appetizer, surprised that she was having a good time with this bunch.

"Maybe we should do this again sometime soon," Pearson said and laughed. "Next time we'll get Ryan drunk and see how quiet she is then."

The laughter around the table continued through dessert, and their talk stayed light. None of them dared to reveal too much or venture too deep into their own issues.

Vonnie had been exposed to a glimpse of Nadalia and Ryan's lives. She didn't know much about Pearson's situation except the disappointing stares she caught Niles giving her at times when she was intoxicated.

No matter how funny it sounded, wives and husbands in healthy relationships should be having sex. Miscarried babies shouldn't be secrets.

Right now, Vonnie wondered if these women were oblivious to their issues or if they were just trying to pretend that their issues didn't exist.

Chapter 20

Pearson

P earson wore the Persian rug down in her office for two reasons. First, she was wondering if Niles would find out about the DUI that she narrowly escaped on her way home from having dinner with the girls. Fortunately her story about getting an emergency call about her sick mother worked. Instead of locking her up, the cop followed her home to make sure she arrived safely. There was no need to inform Niles.

As she held the phone in her hand, she thought about her second issue. She wasn't in the mood to talk with her mother. When Candice called the other day, Pearson lied and told her she was on her way out and would have to call her back. Pearson had even sent Candice a text to say Merry Christmas, figuring she'd done her job of reaching out.

Niles helped her get through the holidays. He stayed by her side, missing some of his family's traditional gatherings to nurture Person through her rough time. His family understood and encouraged him. The only outing she participated in was her time with the girls. That had been surprisingly enjoyable.

Niles seemed happy that she leaned on him as opposed to drowning her taste buds in a vat of full-bodied reds.

Pearson took a deep breath. She was ready to see what her mother had to say; her curiosity had been piqued when her mother pleaded with Ryan to call her back. She only hoped that their conversation didn't end in an argument as it usually did.

Pearson dialed the number before she lost her will. She counted the rings, hoping the call would go to voice mail. She could leave a message and that would show that she tried.

"Pearson! I'm glad you called."

Pearson let out the breath she'd been holding. "Hey, Mom. Sorry I didn't call back before now. I—"

"No problem. I need to see you. What's your schedule like this weekend? Come over for dinner?"

You want me to come for dinner? Pearson wondered if her mother realized whom she was speaking to. "This is Pearson, Ma."

"What?" Candice was confused. "I know who I'm talking to." She clucked her tongue. "Don't be silly."

"What's this about?"

"We need to talk. That's all."

"About what?" Pearson felt her patience waning and started pacing.

"I'll fill you in on everything when you get here. How's Sunday?"

"Hold on, let me see." Pearson checked the calendar on her phone. Her shoulders deflated when she saw that her schedule was clear, leaving her no real excuse to avoid Candice. "Sunday should be fine. I just have to check and see if Niles has anything to do."

"I need to speak with you...alone."

"Oh." Pearson went silent. Niles was always her buffer—the peacekeeper. She wondered what was so important and secretive. "Okay. I'll stop by after church."

"Good. See you then. Goodbye, Pearson."

"Goodbye, Ma." Just as Pearson pulled the phone away from her ear she, heard her mother say I love you. It sounded forced. Like her mouth wasn't used to framing those kinds of statements.

After a few awkward ticks, Pearson replied, "I love you, too." The words felt as foreign to her tongue as they did to her ears. "Goodbye, Ma." She ended the call and stood for several minutes without moving.

Pearson had always loved her mother. Somewhere inside of that shell of Candice's, Pearson assumed she had love for her too, but she couldn't remember ever hearing her voice it.

Pearson drifted through the rest of her work day in a haze. Candice's declaration affected her and made her even more curious. When the rest of her staff left for the day, she dragged to her car, wrapping her fur coat around her as a shield against the sharp winter winds. The icy temperatures had taken the color from the landscape, leaving the ground an ashen gray and the naked trees a dull brown. The wind whipped at Pearson, stinging her legs right through her tights. She picked up her pace, jumped into her car, and sat while the heat thawed her skin and heart.

She actually said she loved me.

Pearson didn't know how to take the comment. Should she be happy or leery?

Waving off her anxiety, she started on her fifteen minute commute from her office in Garden City to her house in Sands Point. She couldn't wait to get home and submerge herself in Niles' arms. She called him to make sure he would be home when she got there.

"What's up, beautiful?"

"Hey, hon."

"Are you okay?" She knew he would recognize the weariness in her voice despite her efforts to sound cheerful. "Did you have a hard day?"

"I finally called my mother back."

"Oh." He was silent for a moment. "What did she say?"

"She wants me to come over for dinner on Sunday…alone."

"Oh." Niles paused again. "Are you going?"

"Yes. It seems important." Pearson felt lighter having shed some of the burden by talking to Niles. "I'll be fine. You know she actually ended the call by saying she loved me."

"Uh…wow!"

"Yeah. I know."

For moments, Pearson drove along just listening to Niles breathe on the phone. Having him on the other end gave her comfort. He was truly her refuge.

"Are you bringing work home with you?"

"Not tonight."

"Good. Hurry up and get here. I just thought of something."

Pearson smiled as she ended the call through her car's Bluetooth. She wondered what Niles had planned and again thought about how blessed she was to have him. She sped up and tried to get home as fast as she could.

When Pearson got to the house, it was empty. She took a shower, put on a comfortable pair of lounge pants and tank top and then headed back downstairs.

Niles walked into the kitchen struggling with several bags.

"What did you get?" Pearson said, taking some of the bags from him and setting them on the counter.

"Crab legs!" Niles raised his brows. "Go turn on the TV in the family room and chill out while I get this ready."

"Okay!" Pearson smiled.

The TV was already on and frozen on the opening scene from her favorite movie, *Pretty Woman*. When it came to her relationship with Niles, she could relate to Julia Roberts' role. Like Richard Gere's character, Niles had been her knight, rescuing her from a hard existence. She may have been financially wealthy, but emotionally, she was destitute. Niles' love for her seeped deep into the lonely, neglected crevices of heart and filled her up at times.

"Crab legs and *Pretty Woman*." She laughed. The two together was like a salve.

Pearson retrieved two throws from the linen closet and curled up on the sofa. Once Niles got things settled, he joined her. She wished he had brought a bottle of wine with the crab legs, but she kept her mouth shut.

Pearson didn't see her drinking as a serious problem. She could handle her liquor. Those few inexplicable episodes and blackouts were random events as far as she was concerned. Unfortunately, Niles didn't see it that way.

Niles sat on the couch, pressed play on the remote, and the television came alive, filling the room with sights and sounds.

Pearson looked at him. "Thank you."

Niles kissed her and then settled into the couch. She wanted the wine, but drank in Niles' presence instead.

"This was perfect," she said to Niles and kissed his cheek. Pearson imagined the ways she would show Niles her appreciation once they got into bed. Thinking about the things she wanted to do with him made her heart flutter. A mischievous smirk spread across her lips.

The crab legs were all gone when the movie ended, and the warmth inside of her turned into a glowing heat. The look she gave him revealed her shameless thoughts. Niles looked at her and his eyes narrowed.

"Ready to go to bed?" Lust made his voice husky and he licked his lips.

"I'm ready," she said with a wink.

Niles pulled her into his arms and kissed her with a passion that ignited her senses. She felt the hairs on her arm stand up and her center lurched. When their lips parted, Niles gazed into her eyes. Pearson stared back with adoration. The heat of her desire still warmed her parts.

"Let's go make a baby."

A Baby. Pearson felt like someone had assaulted her with a bucket of cold water.

Chapter 21

Nadalia

N adalia walked into the kitchen as Sage sat at the breakfast nook sipping a steaming mug of coffee, swiping through the news on his iPad. She smiled at just the thought of seeing him there. It had literally been weeks since she'd gotten up on a Saturday morning and found her husband home.

Sage looked up at Nadalia standing in the doorway, staring at him and nodded as he blew into his cup, then took a sip. Wincing from the heat, he took his time swallowing, sipped again and placed the cup back down. "Morning," he said and winked.

Nadalia winked back, but didn't move.

He drew his brows together. "What's up?"

"Nothing." Nadalia smiled again. "I'm just happy to see you home." She began to make her way over to him. "Any plans for the day?"

Sage raised the side of his cheek to receive Nadalia's kiss. "Not really."

"That's rare." Nadalia went to pull her robe together, then, decided to leave it hanging, revealing her black lace night gown. "Let's do something."

"Like what?" Sage laid the iPad on the countertop and turned toward Nadalia.

She raised her brows and laid a seductive smile on him. Sage smiled and shook his head. Nadalia was slightly offended, expecting him to respond more enthusiastically to her advance. She checked her emotions and took a deep breath.   She had already planned their "spontaneous" excursion that had to wait until after the Super Bowl, but she figured a date night would be ideal for the evening.

Nadalia closed in on Sage and cozied up to him, snuggling against his arm. "How about you take me out on a date?"

"A date! We're already married?"

Nadalia took a moment to contain her annoyance before responding. "Sage...honey. Married people go out on dates, too."

"No, married people go out. You are no longer dating, once you get married."

"Then let's pretend we are not married!" Nadalia huffed and then lit up as an idea popped into her head. "Yes! Let's role play. We can go somewhere and meet up like we're going out on a real date and then come back home and make love all night long." Sage looked at her sideways. "Come on," she whined. "It will be fun. It will be like old times."

"You really want to do this?"

"Yes! We'll even take separate cars." Nadalia clapped her hands. "Come on." She pulled on his arms when she saw that he wasn't sold on her idea. "It's been so long since you've taken me out. We always go out with a bunch of other couples and by the time we get home, you're tipsy and tired and you ignore me." Nadalia didn't mean to sound like a whining child, but she was getting frustrated.

"Fine, where do you want to go?"

"Geesh, Sage. Could you at least sound like you actually want to take me out?"

"What's that supposed to mean?"

"Just forget it." Nadalia waved him off and got up from the stool.

"Wait! What's going on here?"

"You tell me!" She stood defiantly with her hands folded tightly across her chest.

"Tell you what, Dali?"

"Are you sleeping with another woman?"

Sage's eyes grew wide. "N…no! Why do you keep asking me that?"

"Because if you're not screwing me, then who are you screwing?"

"Whoa! Here we go again. Where's this coming from?"

"Sage! Think about it. When was the last time we had sex?"

Sage shrugged. "I don't know, a few days ago."

"Really, Sage!" Nadalia's chest heaved and the warmth of her anger settled over her. "Who did you have sex with a few days ago? Because it sure wasn't your wife."

"What are you talking about?" Sage asked with his shoulders drawn into his neck. He stared into Nadalia's reddening face and huffed, exhibiting his frustration before taking another deep breath and choosing a softer angle. "Babe. I'm not cheating on you."

"I want you to think back and tell me the last time you had sex with your wife."

Sage drew in a sharp breath. "I don't know. I've been extremely busy! What do you want from me?"

"It's been months!" Nadalia screamed and slammed her hand on the countertop. I've been trying to get your damn attention for months now. Walking around here half naked." She pulled her robe back revealing her sexy silk and lace gown. "And you've completely ignored me. If you're not screwing me, then someone else must be fulfilling your needs. What's wrong? You don't find me attractive anymore?" Tears fell from Nadalia's eyes before you she knew it. Her own words hurt as if Sage had declared them.

Sage's mouth fell open, but he appeared to be at a loss for words. After another beat, he walked over to her and pulled her into his arms. "Of course I find you attractive. Who wouldn't? You know how busy work gets."

"Yeah." Nadalia pulled back from him. "It makes you too busy to screw your own wife?"

Sage opened his mouth and again, nothing came out at first. "Baby, I'm sorry…I didn't realize." Sage reached for her again. Nadalia swiped at her tears and moved outside of his reach. Sage dropped his arms to the side. "Dali, I'll make it up to you." He tried again to embrace her. Once again, she stepped away from him.

Nadalia wanted to be in his arms. She wanted to feel the strength of him around her, but she was too upset to give in. She knew his schedule was hectic and he often came home exhausted, but she couldn't believe he had no idea they hadn't been intimate in months.

Suspicions took her imagination to unconscionable heights. What if there really was another woman? What if she were no longer desirable to him? What if he left her? Was she at risk of losing her husband and best friend? The pain of those possible realities was too much to bear.

The tears continued to roll. Nadalia felt like her heart was breaking already.

"Okay. Let's go on that date."

Nadalia looked at Sage and narrowed her eyes.

"I'm not patronizing you," he said, surrendering his hands in innocence. "I want to make this up to you. I guess I got so wrapped up in work I didn't notice how it was affecting you." He looked hopeful.

Nadalia didn't answer, but she wiped her tears and unfolded her arms before sitting on the nearby stool.

Sage approached her again, taking her into his arms. This time, she let him hug her but she didn't hug him back. Kissing the top of her head between words, Sage asked her to forgive him.

After holding her in his arms for a few minutes, Sage pulled back, cupped her face in his hands and lifted her chin to meet his gaze. "Can I take you out on a date?"

Nadalia stared into his penetrating eyes, hooded by thick brows and lush lashes and tried to keep the smile in her heart from spreading across her face. She didn't want to let him off the hook so easily.

"I'll be somewhat respectful," Sage said and smiled. Nadalia's face crumpled in confusion. "I'll have you in bed...I mean, home by midnight."

The smile that had been tickling the corners of her mouth slid across her face and she cut her eyes at him. "You better."

Still holding her face in his hands, Sage kissed her. Starting out with a few pecks, the kiss swelled into a passionate lock that left both of them pining for breath. Heat flickered in her core and her nipples grew tense.

Nadalia stood and pressed body against Sage's taut physique. His hands roamed her back and found refuge on her ample bottom. He squeezed those cheeks gently as he pushed his tongue into her mouth.

Nadalia didn't know what felt better, the mere fact that she finally had him in her arms or the white hot flickers of desire that made her tingle. What she did know was that if she didn't get him inside of her soon, she would spontaneously combust into a million tiny pieces of fire.

Nadalia's hands ravaged his body, feeling over every inch of him as if she had to prove to herself that he was real. She roamed, caressed and squeezed his back, chest, and behind.

Uninhibited lust surged through her, so when her hands found him limp, she was a little disappointed. She expected to find his erection straining against his sweat pants. She knew what to do to get his loins ablaze. Nadalia stooped down and released his soft manhood from his sweats and boxers and looked up at him seductively before gently taking him into her mouth. She'd work him up in no time.

After several minutes, Sage remained unresponsive while Nadalia struggled to keep her temperature from falling. She pushed his limpness around for a few minutes longer before lifting herself up.

Sage looked down and then back up at Nadalia apologetically. "I'm just tired."

"Let's go to the bedroom," she suggested and took him by the hand. He bunched his sweats with the other hand so he could climb the steps safely.

Once they got to the room, Nadalia took over. Backing him up against the bed, she pushed him back and mounted him. She took him into her warm mouth again. When he grew slightly rigid, they guided him inside of her canal. She was finally getting the response she wanted, but it didn't last.

Sage turned over and looked into her eyes seductively. "How about this. Let me take care of you." He buried his face between her legs and fondled her bud until her muscles convulsed uncontrollably.

Afterwards, Sage went to the bathroom and returned with a wet cloth. He wiped the left over juices from between Nadalia's legs before wrapping her in his arms.

Nadalia moved away from him, leaving him lying in bed. Even with the little slice of joy he stirred in her, she wasn't content. She wanted to make love to her husband. She wanted more.

Chapter 22

Pearson

Pearson paced, not sure of what to do next. Her nerves had taken control of her. Standing still had become impossible. She fidgeted as she tried to find something to wear. Nothing she retrieved from her expansive closet was fit for a meeting with her mother.

Pearson hadn't seen the woman in months and the fact that her mother reached out to her during her mourning season made Pearson even more uneasy. When Candice ended the call with a declaration of her love, Pearson's emotions became unexpectedly fragile. She hadn't heard those words since her father passed. Hearing them from her mother unearthed a fresh combination of battered emotions, confusion and suspicion.

Pearson stared at the black slacks and purple shirt she laid across her bed, snatched the shirt up and traipsed back toward the closet. As fashionable as she usually was, she felt like none of the ensembles she paired made sense. It wasn't just about choosing the right top, pants or skirt. Regardless of what she wore, she'd still feel exposed in her mother's presence. Candice always had the ability to pull the vulnerable little girl inside of Pearson to the forefront. Every tender piece of her character rose to the surface when Candice was involved and then once she was gone, anger would chase them all back into their hiding places.

Pearson's therapist once told her that was her inner child, crying out for her mother's love. "Love? *Pft*," Pearson mumbled aloud. "Whatever."

After shoving hanger after hanger of shirts aside, Pearson stopped at a simple cream shell with a beaded neckline. She walked down a few feet to where her pants hung neatly and flipped through a few pairs, choosing deep blue skinny jeans. Spinning on her heels, she walked a few more feet, past a lingerie chest, and headed to the side of her closet that housed coats, sweaters, and jackets. Pearson chose a floral blazer with bold colors and carried her new collaboration into the room. Taking a step back, Pearson looked it over one last time and nodded approvingly. This was it.

Pearson inhaled and exhaled slowly, hoping to push away all of the anxiety that caused her shoulders to tense. She could still smell the faint, but fragrant scent of the bacon that Niles prepared that morning before they went to church.

She took another deep breath and was able to hear the sounds of her home. Off in the distance, she heard the sweet appeal of Niles' tenor sax even though he was inside his studio all the way in the basement. Pearson closed her eyes and tried to let the shadowy sound penetrate her mind.

After a while, Pearson switched out of the dress she wore to church and put on the outfit she'd just selected. The jeans had some stretch in them. The tank was made of soft cotton, making her feel comfortable. That's just what she needed. Pearson put on the blazer and twisted her frame in the full length mirror inside her closet. She grabbed a pair of flat black boots that would serve well in the endless snow and headed down to let Niles know she was leaving.

The closer she got to the basement, the louder the horn crooned. Niles' talent was incredible. The way he fingered his instrument and toyed with the notes was almost sensual, as if he was in love. Pearson teased him about his 'relationship' with his sax often feigning jealousy, but in reality she'd been intrigued by his talent since they met.

He was playing at the family's restaurant and to Pearson it felt like he was playing just for her. Not simply because she was smitten by the incredible sound, but because he kept staring at her over the top of the sax and using it to reel her in. By the time he'd finished the set, she found herself at the end of the stage. He came straight to her.

Pearson brought her mind back to the present and walked into the studio. Niles smiled without sullying a single note. He finished the song with his eyes on her and then licked his lips. Pearson felt sexual tension rise in her, chasing away the little bit of tightness that had settled in her shoulders.

Niles put the sax on its stand and walked over to her, sliding his arms around her waist. He looked into her eyes. "Are you ready?"

Pearson gave him a small smile. "Yes."

Niles' expression told her that he wasn't convinced. She couldn't fool him. Pearson sighed and gave a firm, "Yes," and then followed it up with a bigger smile.

Niles kissed her forehead. "You're sure you don't want me to go with you?"

"I'll be fine." Niles stretched his eyes and looked at her sideways. "I will be fine," Pearson confirmed.

"All right." Niles kissed her again and released her. "I have a little something upstairs in the fridge for you to take with you."

"You made something?"

"You're going to dinner, right? It's rude to go empty handed. It's just a little dessert. It's one of your favorites so you'll be more comfortable."

Pearson went to the kitchen to see what Niles had made.

"That pie's staying here!" she said when Niles came up behind her.

"I knew you would try something like that so I made two."

Pearson laughed.

"What time are you supposed to be there?"

Pearson deflated. He brought her back to her reality. Several times over the past few hours, she considered canceling. But she knew she had to do this.

Chapter 23

Pearson

P earson arrived at her mother's house minutes before their scheduled dinner, but refused to leave the car until the digital clock on her dashboard hit the hour. Taking one last deep breath, she pushed the car door open with a rush, stepped out and made haste through the frigid air, up the expansive circular drive to her mother's enormous home—the same home where she'd grown up.

Pearson often wondered how her mother managed in that massive sixteen-room mansion all alone. She couldn't recall any mention of her mother dating, but imagined that she must have had some male companionship over the years. It had been nearly two decades since her father's passing. Surely Candice entertained herself somehow, despite that fact that Pearson believed she wasn't the friendliest person.

Candice swung the door open as Pearson approached, and Pearson looked up startled. She forced a smile at her mother who was grinning in the doorway with outstretched hands. Pearson didn't exactly know what to do and finally coaxed herself into stepping between her mother's arms.

"I'm glad you're here, darling."

Pearson looked at her mother. She bit back the curt remark that stung the tip of her tongue and responded based on what would be appropriate. "Thanks." Pearson continued through the door, stripping out of her heavy winter coat.

"Let's go out to the Florida room. It's comfortable there. My maid prepared a nice meal and she makes the best ceviche with shrimp and calamari. I'm sure you'll love it." Candice led the way, stopped and turned back to Pearson, "You're not allergic to shellfish, are you?"

"No. I'm not." Pearson decided that she could only take a little more of her mother's acting. Her niceties seemed foreign and forced. Not to mention it was ridiculous that her own mother didn't know whether or not her own daughter was allergic to shellfish.

"Good." Candice continued walking. "Please take Pearson's coat," she told the maid.

Pearson handed it over to her.

When they made it to the room, Candice flopped into an antique winged-back chair and sighed. "I've wanted to do this for so long."

The woman returned with a tray with two dirty Martinis.

How did she know? Pearson thought jokingly, but then really wondered as she took the glass and luxuriated in a long sip. She smiled her first real smile since she arrived at her mother's house.

"Like mother, like daughter," Candice said, taking a sip and smiling over her own glass.

"Pardon me?" Pearson asked, not sure if she liked being compared.

"I see you like a well-made martini." Candice grinned.

"Yeah. I like 'em stiff and extra dirty," Pearson said mischievously and she shared a genuine laugh with Candice.

"Dear! Make sure Pearson's next one is extra dirty. As a matter of fact, why don't you go ahead and prepare the next one? It looks like it won't be long before this one is finished."

Pearson rolled her eyes, not sure if her mother was being facetious or not. "Yeah. Please toss in a few more olives if you can."

As the warm liquid flowed through her body, she felt more at ease making small talk with her mother. By her third martini, she was ready to get to the point of the visit. The maid had just placed a colorful mixed green salad on the cafe table that sat between her and Candice's chair. Pearson pushed a few forkfuls in her mouth as she tried to put words together that would get her questions across without stinging or sounding too eager.

Swallowing hard, Pearson pushed down her last forkful and turned to her mother, who was eating like she was demonstrating proper etiquette to a class of potential debutantes.

"Why didn't you like me?" Pearson tried her best, but she was never one for tip-toeing around any matter. Straight forward came easy.

Candice stopped chewing. She looked at Pearson, sighed and then finished chewing before responding. "It's not that I never liked you."

"Then what is it?"

"I didn't know what to do with you," Candice simply stated as if she were talking about the weather.

"What the...hell is that supposed to mean?" Pearson looked at her mother sideways and pointed to her empty glass so the maid could bring her another martini.

"Do we really have to go there? I have some really important information I want to share with you. That's why I asked you over. Not for this."

"Yes. We have to go there because I honestly don't know when we will ever be in one another's presence this way again and be so...cordial."

"Oh, please, Pearson!" Pearson twisted her lips and Candice rolled her eyes. "Okay. We don't talk much, but don't make me out to be a bad person." Candice scrunched her shoulders. "I'm just not one for a lot of unnecessary conversation."

Pearson bit back the sting of her mother's comment. "Even with your own daughter?"

"You don't understand."

"Make me understand." Pearson felt herself getting emotional and knew that tears wouldn't be far behind. That last thing she wanted to do was cry in front of Candice so she could see how badly she was affected by her. She was just glad that she had the courage to finally ask her mother these questions.

She took the martini that was handed to her, settled in her seat and looked at her mother, waiting for her reply.

Candice put down her plate and turned toward Pearson." You want the truth?"

"The whole and nothing but," she said sarcastically. "What kind of question is that? You think I can't handle the truth? News flash old woman: I'm grown!"

"Your tongue has always been so unpolished. No amount of training or exposure was ever able to change that."

"Like mother, like daughter," Pearson said and flashed a smirk that complemented her sarcasm.

Candice rolled her eyes. "Touché." Candice sat quietly for a moment. "Okay. I never wanted children."

Pearson felt something in her chest plummet into her stomach. Though she suspected it, she didn't expect Candice to come out and admit it. Immediately a flesh cloak of abandonment shrouded her. She swallowed hard to keep her emotions in check.

"I had you to keep your father happy." Candice looked off into the distance. "God, I loved that man." She paused. "I wasn't good at that stuff. I didn't have a good mother and I thought for sure that I wouldn't be a good mother. But it didn't mean that I didn't like…love you."

Pearson bit the inside of her lip. "Well that's how it felt." Pearson paused, waiting for an apology to go along with the confession. There was none.

"Sweetie! Bring me another martini. Make it good and stiff." Candice turned her attention to Pearson. "Now can we get down to the reason I called you here?"

Pearson shrugged. "I guess so." She nodded for another martini.

"I'll be retiring soon and I want you to run the company."

"What?"

"Pearson! It was your father's joy. The thing he seemed to love the most, besides you of course." Candice appeared to have gone off in a distance somewhere in her mind. "I wouldn't want to leave it in just anyone's hands," she said, reaching for the freshly made martini.

"Ma—"

"Just think about it," Candice interrupted, waving off Pearson's potential comment with a toss of her hand. I'd hate to hand it off to someone outside of the family."

Pearson felt like a boulder had been dropped in her lap. "I don't know anything about the business."

"But you know how to run a business. You've had your foundation for what...almost ten years now?"

Pearson was surprised that Candice knew that bit of information. "Yes, but that's different."

"If you can run one company, you can run any company. Your father wanted this. He built this company to be a legacy for his family."

"Oh no! Don't try to guilt me into doing this."

"That's not what I'm doing." Candice cast her eyes at the ceiling as if she were searching for the right words there. "Listen." She twisted her body to face Pearson full on. "How about this? Come spend a few days in the office and see how things are done before you shoot down the opportunity. Make your decision after that. Let's say...one week. That would give you enough time to shadow me and see how we operate."

Candice turned away from their conversation as if all was settled. She nodded and the maid delivered their plates with an appealing presentation that could rival any upscale restaurant. Shortly after their meals of grilled sea bass with risotto and green beans arrived, Pearson dug in, hoping to soak up some of the liquor swimming in her belly. She was convinced that she needed those drinks to help bear this meeting with Candice. She had to make sure some of the effects of her martinis wore off before she got home.

After eating, Pearson was ready to leave. She'd done her duty and endured a few hours with Candice. It was a little better than what she expected, but she still felt the sting of her mother's unapologetic admission. She had more questions, but couldn't handle the answers just yet. She'd wait for their next bout of 'quality' time if she could subject herself to it.

Chapter 24

Ryan

The moment Ryan woke with that nauseating taste in her mouth, she knew she was pregnant—again. It happened every single time. She and Anderson didn't have sex that often so she attributed this most recent conception to the night of Nadalia's holiday party several weeks back. Getting pregnant wasn't a problem for Ryan. Staying pregnant was her issue.

Ryan pulled back the covers and a chill ran across her arms. She held herself and looked around the lonely room. Anderson had been gone for weeks now, filming in various cities across the country. The odd thing was that he'd been checking in more than usual. Something clicked the night she raised up at him at Nadalia's house. He'd been giving her just a little more respect. She liked the attention, but knew that she still didn't fully have her husband and never did. She wondered if she ever would.

Things hadn't always been that bad and she longed for the Anderson who had won her heart in the beginning.

Sliding her feet into a pair of tan lambskin slippers, Ryan stood, stretched, and made her way to the adjoining bath. She reached into the far back of the vanity and pulled out one of the pregnancy tests she hid in there. Ryan relieved herself and just as she had suspected, the test was positive. Ryan jumped in the shower and threw on a pair of jeans and a soft pink cashmere sweater and boots. For breakfast, she stuffed a few crackers in her mouth and washed them down with a small cup of ginger ale. Anything more would run the risk of coming up on her way to the city. She packed a few pieces of fruit and a few more crackers to take with her.

It was still rather early so she decided to call her doctor a little later. This time, she wasn't going to wait for a visit. She vowed to be sitting in front of her doctor within the next twenty-four hours talking about strategies for keeping this baby inside of her.

Maybe this would be the key to their marriage finally falling back into place. As the mother of his child, Anderson would have to respect her even more, she thought.

Ryan planned to keep it a secret from everyone, including her mother, until she knew if it would actually happen this time. Maybe she would tell Vonnie, since she was both a mother and a doctor. She might have tips to help her maintain a successful pregnancy. What could she lose by telling her?

Ryan stuffed a leotard, spandex shorts and shrug to keep her arms warm in her bag, but then took it out.

She'd still meet her old dance buddies at her friend's studio, but she wouldn't dance today or in the near future until she knew exactly what was going on inside of her body.

When Anderson was out of town for extended periods of time, Ryan took advantage of the time to reconnect with her dance community, using their rehearsals as workouts. She's even entertained going back to teach at the university, but Anderson didn't want her doing that, so she stayed home and played the rich wife role. She often argued that the wives of his friends all worked and even owned companies. Anderson didn't care and would retort that he wasn't married to them. *His* wife wasn't working and if Ryan wanted to remain as *his* wife, she'd have to comply or be threatened to be sent back to the rat hole he found her in—although she'd since upgraded her mother's small apartment to a modest three bedroom ranch home in Garden City Park.

Anderson's absence gave her an opportunity to indulge her passion just a little. He didn't know she kept ties with the artistic community she used to work with during her brief stint as a dancer on Broadway, where she'd met him after a performance. She'd try her best to get her fill while he was away, visiting studios, taking classes here and there to hone her craft, and checking out performances. Other times, she'd busy herself doing volunteer work, keeping house, hanging with her mother and doing yoga. He didn't want her getting involved with too much else because as he said, he didn't need people in his business and he needed to keep his circles tight.

Despite the cold, Ryan drove halfway to the city with her windows open until the rush of winds were too much to bear. After meeting up with the women, she planned to take in a musical and enjoy a nice lunch before returning to the Island. At some point she'd call and make an urgent care appointment with her GYN.

Ryan pulled her car into a lot on 43rd street, right in the heart of the theater district, and headed up to her friend's studio. The dancers were already on the floor stretching when she arrived. Catching her friend, Nadia's attention, she nodded and continued to instruct the group on the next move. Ryan pointed to a folding chair near the corner and Nadia frowned. Ryan frowned and rubbed her belly. Nadia nodded again and guided the group to the next movement without breaking her eight-count.

It was hard for Ryan to watch the dancers on the floor and not be able to join them. She longed for the days when she indulged her passion on a daily basis. Before Anderson came into her life, dance had been her knight in shining armor, promising her a life bigger than the one she had always known.

Nadia clapped her hands and the dancers stood awaiting their next set of directions. Nadia moved with grace even as she walked over to switch the song on her iPod, which was connected to the sound system. An upbeat classical rhythm filled the space with a mix of soft harmonies against an eclectic bass and Nadia snapped her fingers as she counted the dancers off.

"Five, six…five, six, seven, eight," she yelled, casting a stern glare across the sea of dancers, all donned in black leotards, tights, and ballet shoes. "And reach!

And up! Yes! Just like that, Talia. Do it just like she did next time. Keep going. And out…one, two, three, four, and hold." Nadia called out directives like a drill sergeant as she guided the dancers through several renditions. She moved about the room joining in on certain steps or snapping her fingers, and yelling to make sure they were hitting all of the accents.

Ryan allowed the rhythms to capture her. She made small movements from her seat, gliding her arms in the same fashion as the dancers on the floor. Then she closed her eyes and swayed to the beat until it reached a dramatic end.

"Okay. Take five. Get some water," Nadia yelled and the dancers filed out of the room. She directed her attention to Ryan as she wiped her neck with a hand towel. "Not dancing today? What's up with that?"

"I must have eaten something that didn't agree with me." Ryan held her stomach for affect. "My tummy is just not right."

"Aw! I was looking forward to you helping me work out a few kinks on a new dance I just choreographed."

Ryan formed her lips into a half frown and half pout. "I would have loved that."

Nadia raised her hands in excitement, startling Ryan. "Oh! Guess who was selected to choreograph the new musical that Leland Bogart is going to be starring in?"

"Are you serious?" Ryan jumped up. "You've got to be kidding me. That's great!" Ryan hugged her friend as a slight wave of jealously passed through her. She was happy for Nadia, but couldn't help but think that it could have been her had she continued on her desired path.

"I screamed down the house when I got the call. Well…after I hung up, of course. I couldn't believe it. This will be my first gig where I will actually be working with a Hollywood star." Nadia smiled as the exhilaration flickered in her eyes. "Broadway has its share of celebrities, but it's nothing like working with someone as rich, famous, and gorgeous as Leland Bogart. I can't wait."

Ryan laughed. "I bet."

"Honey, I'm still single and from what I know, so is Leland. I just might snag me an A-lister, too." Nadia threw her head back and cackled.

Ryan laughed with her, but didn't share Nadia's zeal. She knew that being married to someone like Leland couldn't be easy. As much as Nadia wanted what Ryan had in her union with Anderson, Ryan longed to be free to indulge her passion the way Nadia did.

"You're going to hang out a little longer, right?" Nadia asked as the dancers began returning to the studio.

Ryan looked down at her watch. "Actually, I have to run. I have a few more stops to make before heading back to Long Island." The morning had passed and she still hadn't called the doctor. She wanted to see if she could get that appointment.

"Okay. It was so good seeing you." Nadia hugged Ryan. "Next time, be ready to dance." Nadia wiggled her hips.

"I will. I promise."

"I'm going to hold you to that. Bye, hon." Nadia clapped her hands and directed her attention to the group before her. "Are we ready, people? We need to clean this up."

Ryan gathered her coat and purse and eased out of the studio. She could hear Nadia giving orders behind her. "We'll run it a few more times. And…five, six…"

Suddenly Ryan couldn't wait to get away. She dialed her doctor and was thankfully given an appointment for later that afternoon. That would leave her with just enough time to dine at one of her favorite restaurants before heading back. She'd have to catch a show another time.

Ryan decided to leave her car at the lot and hailed a cab. She didn't feel like tackling city traffic until she was ready to leave. Now that it was lunch time, it took a while to flag down a taxi. When one finally pulled over, she made the mistake of telling the driver that she was in a hurry and ended up with red knuckles by the end of her short ride. Several near misses had her shaking in her heels by the time he pulled up in front of Tao, one of the cities most frequented Asian fusion restaurants.

Ryan tossed the driver a twenty and got out in a rush, slamming the door behind her. She wanted to give the driver a piece of her mind, but wouldn't have been able to get the words past her thumping heart, which was now lodged in her throat.

Ryan shook off the dread of her ride and headed inside. She confirmed to the hostess that she was a party of one and was led toward the seating along the wall, a bit of distance from the enormous sitting Buddha statue.

From the quiet nook where Ryan was seated, she could see the majority of the restaurant. She looked around and what caught her eye caused the nausea she felt earlier to come rushing back. She slapped her hand over her mouth to keep from screaming or throwing up, whatever tried to come up first.

Ryan stood and rushed to the restroom, bursting through the door. Luckily no one was inside. She ran into the stall and stood over the toilet in case the churning in her stomach wanted to relieve itself. When she was sure she wasn't going to vomit, she came out and splashed water on her angry face. Red crooked lines trailed across the whites of her eyes and tears filled the wells, but didn't fall.

She wanted to approach Anderson and find out who that woman at his table was, but remembered she wasn't supposed to be in Manhattan in the first place.

She took several deep breaths and tried to reason with herself. She didn't see the woman's face, so it could just be a fellow actor, co-worker or even a reporter out for an innocent or working lunch. Nevertheless, what was he doing in New York when he was supposed to be in Los Angeles filming?

Ryan pulled her phone out and dialed his number. The first call went to voice mail and she dialed again. The second time, he picked up and she choked back a scream.

"Hey babe," Anderson said cheerfully.

"Hey!" she said. Her voice was as shaky as her hands. Then she was at a loss for words.

"Ryan?"

"Uh…yeah."

"Well, what's up?"

"Um. Where are you?"

"Having lunch right now. Why? Is everything okay?"

"Yes. I just wanted to know…when are you coming home?"

"I'll be home next week. Are you sure you're alright?"

"Yes. I'm fine. I just miss you. Hold on a sec." Ryan tipped out of the bathroom and peeked through the dimly lit restaurant. Anderson was still seated at the table with his phone to his ear. The woman was seated across from him giving her attention to her cell phone. "Andy."

"I'm still here."

"Okay. Well. I love you." Ryan continued watching him. She wanted to see how he'd react in front of his lady friend.

"Okay, babe. I'll see you soon."

"Tell me you love me."

"What?"

"I said I love you. Tell me you love me, too," Ryan insisted as she watched him through narrowed eyes.

Anderson turned slightly from his lady friend. "You know I love you too. What's this about?"

"Nothing. See you when you get home next week." Ryan ended the call.

Ryan took several deep breaths to keep from losing her composure. Intuitively, she placed her hand across her stomach as she observed him. He put his phone aside and continued his conversation without missing a beat. Ryan watched for a few minutes more to see if she could glean anything else from his maneuvers and when she couldn't take anymore, she slipped out the front door. Her heart pounded so loudly she felt like the thumping could be heard outside of herself.

Ryan had never seen that woman before, but would make it her business to find out who she was.

Chapter 25

Vonnie

A drenaline coursed through Vonnie's veins as if the news she had received earlier had just come in. She found it difficult to contain her excitement as she waited for Mike to come home from work. This was too good to tell in a phone call. She had to deliver it face-to-face so she could see the excitement in Mike's expression.

Vonnie still couldn't believe all of the notoriety she'd received after she delivered a speech on childhood obesity a few months ago. That twenty-minute talk placed her on a trajectory that she had never seen coming. A few weeks after she spoke, calls started coming in from magazine editors, and television producers asking her take on issues concerning the matter that meant so much to her. Vonnie had come across scores of children suffering from major conditions that normally affected adults, such as diabetes and high blood pressure. As a self-proclaimed 'former fat kid' she also knew firsthand how insensitive people could be toward an overweight child—from peers to parents. The subject was personal for her.

Today's call got her so excited she could hardly stand still. She'd been asked to appear on the infamous Rayne Medley's talk show to talk about the effects of childhood obesity and offer tips for parents to combat the issues, and to talk about her own experiences as an obese child who as they say 'beat the odds.'

Vonnie tried to release her nervous energy by tidying up the house. When she found herself cleaning the kitchen countertops for the third time, she put the cleaner away and took up pacing.

Mike called earlier and she almost spilled the news. Vonnie literally bit her lip to keep from ruining the surprise. Now, she sat in the great room nursing a glass of Merlot.

When she heard Mike's car pull into their circular driveway, she jumped up and raced through the front door. Vonnie accosted him before he could get out of the car. She laughed at the stunned look on his face.

"What the hell!"

Vonnie covered his face with kisses. "I've got great news!"

"Okay…" Mike just stared at her, which made Vonnie giggle even harder. "Well, are you going to tell me right here or can we take this inside where it's warm?"

Vonnie looked down and realized she didn't have on a coat, though she still didn't feel the cold sting of the twenty-something degree weather. Grabbing Mike by the hand, she pulled him inside, pushed the door closed and backed him up against it.

"Hmm! This news seems delicious," Mike said when Vonnie came so close that they could feel each other's breath.

Mike closed his eyes and kissed Vonnie and their passion was unleashed. By the time they pulled away from the kiss, both were breathing hard.

Breathlessly, she looked down at Mike's fingers unbuttoning her shirt and said, "I'm going to be on TV."

"What!" Mike's fingers paused.

Vonnie's proud smile spread clear across her face. She shook her head. "You heard me right. Your gal is going to be on TV."

Mike's mouth dropped open. "What? How? When?" How much are they paying you?"

Vonnie stepped away from Mike and spun around with her hands in the air. "Woo. This feels like a dream."

"I want details," Mike said. "My baby is going to be a star? What show? And how much do you get paid?"

"The Rayne Medley Show! Can you believe that?" Vonnie jumped up and down.

Mike took her in his arms and planted moist pecks on her lips and cheeks and then took over her mouth with his. The passion in the kiss he laid on her, pushed her excitement out of the way, replacing it with desire.

"Wow. But how much are they paying you?"

Vonnie waved him off. "Silly. It's a talk show. They don't pay you for that, but the publicity will be great for the practice and could lead to paid speaking gigs."

"Oh. Okay. Let's celebrate," Mike said, picking Vonnie up, attempting to carry her to the bedroom. After a few steps, he stopped and huffed and let Vonnie slip out of his arms. For exaggerated affect, he bent over holding his knees and then placed one hand on his back.

Vonnie slapped him playfully. "I'm not that heavy!"

"No, but I'm that old! How about I save that energy for when we get to bed?" Mike lifted himself as if it were straining him to straighten his back.

Vonnie laughed and shook her head.

"Seriously, I'm proud of you, babe." He slipped his arms around her waist. "I bet you already know what you're wearing."

"Right down to the bra and panties," she confirmed his suspicion. "Go ahead and get changed up and meet me in the kitchen. I've got dinner ready."

"Cool."

"Hurry. Because I want to call Noelle and tell her about it too."

Vonnie missed her daughter whenever she was away at boarding school and would find any reason to call her even if she'd already spoken to her several times in a day.

This would excite Noelle. Vonnie could picture her telling all of her school friends.

Vonnie removed her clothes, save her bra and panties. She pulled a pair of pumps out of the front closet, slipped them on and headed back to the kitchen to heat up their meals. By the time Mike changed and made his way to the kitchen, Vonnie was seated on the kitchen table along with their plates sipping from her glass of Merlot.

When Mike noticed her in lace panties and a matching bra, and his lips curled into a seductive grin. Mike always loved her body, despite the fact the she couldn't possibly be defined as thin by any stretch.

Rubbing his hands together, he said, "Yes. Dinner is gonna be delicious tonight!" and roared like a lion.

Vonnie nearly spit her wine out laughing. He danced to an imaginary tune as he made his way over to his wife. Vonnie moved with his melody as she welcomed him warmly.

Mike stopped suddenly. Vonnie sat straight, wondering what was wrong. Mike held his hand up as if to say, 'wait,' pulled his t-shirt over his head and stepped out of his pants and boxers. Vonnie covered her mouth to keep the sip of wine she'd just taken from spilling out as she laughed at him once again.

Mike started his dance up again and continued making his way over to her. Vonnie was nearly choking on her wine as she held in her laugh.

Choosing her luscious brown core over the meal, Mike laid her back on the table and feasted on her instead, treating her with extra care.

Vonnie fell into a trance under Mike's influence and lay sprawled across the table, barely able to move after Mike had taken her to a sexual peak so intense that her entire body shuddered. Still wanting more, Vonnie sat up and pulled Mike into her arms. She wanted to give him the same pleasure that he'd lavished on her.

Mike kissed her and stepped out of her reach. Vonnie's eyes narrowed.

"It's all about you, babe. Let's eat and then I'm going to take you to the room and show you how proud I really am."

Vonnie smiled and then squeezed her legs together trying to quell her desire. Sliding her panties back up, she hopped off the table, pulled a cloth and some cleaner from the pantry and sanitized the table before setting out their dinner. They sat, scantily clad, enjoying their meals and teasing each other with their eyes. By the time they were done, they'd drummed up a fresh batch of desire and raced to the room, locking lips and groping one another.

They lay wrapped in each other's arms reveling in the afterglow of their fiery love making.

Mike pushed a strand of hair from her eyes. "I'm proud of you."

"Thanks. I couldn't wait to tell you. I almost spilled the beans when I called you earlier today."

"So they really don't pay for these television appearances?"

Vonnie wondered why he kept asking. "No, Mike. They don't for the umpteenth time."

"Okay, okay. I was just asking. It would just be nice if you got paid for it, that's all."

His concern began to raise suspicion in Vonnie. "Why?"

"No reason," Mike said and yawned. "I'm exhausted. Night, babe." He turned his back and fell asleep, cutting their afterglow short.

Vonnie was left up alone, wondering about Mike's sudden concern about money.

Chapter 26

Nadalia

N adalia was having one of those days. She forgot to set the alarm on her phone and woke up at nine o'clock—the time she should have been walking into the office. She rushed to get dressed and seemed to have been behind every senior citizen driving through Long Island. A commute that should have taken no more than fifteen minutes on a bad day, stretched out to nearly thirty minutes due to detours and road work.

Slamming her fists against the wheel, she cursed the old man in front of her crawling toward the yellow light. "I could have gotten through that damn light five times. Jeez!" Nadalia pulled to a full stop behind him, sat back and groaned. The second the light turned, she laid on her horn. The blaring sound startled the old man. Nadalia could see him jerk and seconds later, he began his crawl once again.

Nadalia slapped her indicator, turning on her left blinker and whipped around the man as soon as she could. She tried to give the old man the evil eye as she passed, but his focus was trained on the road. He was barely tall enough to see over the dashboard and wore glasses as thick as the windshield itself. Nadalia gunned the gas, trying to at least shave off a few minutes of her drawn-out trip to work.

The phone rang and Nadalia pressed the information center on the car's dashboard activating the Bluetooth system. "Yeah," she said in frustration.

"Hey babe. Are you all right?" Sage's voice filed through the speakers filling the car.

"Why'd you ask?" she inquired even though she already knew the answer. Despite her mood, Nadalia was happy to hear from Sage.

After their epic fail at attempting to make love the other night, things had grown awkwardly distant between them. She'd gone into the bathroom to cry that night while her mind filled with thoughts of why her husband couldn't make love to her anymore. Her ego was battered and her heart was torn.

"You sound irritated."

"Bad morning. What time did you leave?"

"Around six-thirty. I needed to get in early to prepare for meetings. We've got clients coming in at the end of the week and we need to be ready."

"Oh."

"Listen, babe. About our trip—"

"Sage! No! I won't let you cancel on me. Ugh! We need this getaway, Sage! Don't—"

"I'm not canceling on you. Relax." Sage huffed this time. "I just need for you to email me all the details. I'm working on my schedule and I want to make sure I have that time blocked off. As a matter of fact, send it to Cindy so she can update my calendar."

"Really, Sage! I have to go through your secretary to secure quality time with my own husband."

"Dali. It's not like that."

"Then what's it like?" Nadalia sucked her teeth and swerved around a car that had pulled out into oncoming traffic. "Ugh!" She let the passenger side window down and slowed next to her assailant. "You idiot!"

"Dali!"

"This guy just cut me off," she grunted. "Listen I'll send the email. Let me call you back when I get to the office."

"You didn't get there yet?"

"Sage!"

"Okay! Call me back…and don't forget to send the email. I'll forward it to Cindy myself."

"Whatever!" Nadalia hit the display, releasing the call. She didn't mean to take out her frustration on Sage, but couldn't help herself.   The phone rang again. Nadalia muttered under her breath and jabbed her finger on the display. "What?" she groaned.

"Nadalia?"

Immediately she recognized Angela's voice. "Oh. Hey, Angela. Sorry about that."

"Bad day so far, huh?"

"You can tell?" Nadalia said sarcastically generating a light laugh between the two.

"Damn! I don't think what I have to say will help make it any better."

"Spit it out, Ang."

Angela waited a few moments before speaking. Nadalia wheeled into her designated parking spot in front of her office building and switched the audio from the car's Bluetooth system to the phone.

"Nadalia. I think…"

"Just say what you have to say!" she admonished, grabbing her purse and tote, slamming the car door, and taking rapid steps toward the entrance.

"Our husbands are cheating! There are two bimbos out there trying to take our husbands away from us."

Nadalia froze, almost losing her grip on the phone and the bags in her hand. Air circulated in her chest and she felt it tightening. "What did you say?"

"They are cheating on us."

"How do you know?" Nadalia turned her back to the door as if she could shield the people inside from hearing her conversation.

"I'm not one hundred percent sure of everything, but there have been a few things that have given me a pretty good indication that something is going on. Coffey has been using Sage as his alibi for all of his frequent trips."

"What have you found?"

"Hotel receipts. And it's always the same hotel."

"So! Coffey stays at a certain hotel when he comes here. Sage hangs out with him sometimes."

"These receipts include night after night of room service. Coffey usually eats out when he comes into town on business. He never stays in his room. So if he's having dinner in his room, he's not there alone."

"So what makes you think Sage is cheating?" Nadalia asked hoping, that she didn't have any proof involving Sage. She'd already had so many of her own doubts about her husband. "Sage may just be covering for Coffey. You know how those two are."

"You know how good I am with computers, right?"

"Yeah. So…"

"I found a few email messages talking about them meeting up at that hotel. I checked them against his trips and they show ridiculous charges for his hotel on his company card. The amount that's being charged just doesn't jive with business trips and regular business expenses."

To Nadalia, this didn't sound like much of anything. Angela was clearly overreacting to her speculations. "Angela."

"Don't patronize me, Nadalia. I know you don't think I have much, but I know what I'm talking about. Because I know my husband and something isn't right. And you may not want to believe it, but I also know that Sage is in on it."

Nadalia grunted. "Okay, Angela, but I can't approach Sage with any of this without some kind of proof. I need more than what you've said."

"You want proof? Check your messages in ten minutes and then call me back."

Nadalia rolled her eyes. "Okay."

Angela ended the call.

Nadalia shook her head, straightened her posture and headed into the building. When she got to her floor, she waltzed through the office with a no-nonsense scowl on her face. She could sense the atmosphere become tense. She nodded in response to several "G'mornings" from her employees and from their wide eye stares, she knew that her staff would be walking on egg shells.

Stepping into her office, Nadalia pushed the door closed and locked it, before tossing her coat and bags onto the sofa. She walked to the windowed wall and looked out. Her phone dinged, indicating that she had a text. Right after that, the phone chimed several more times. She knew it was Angela, but she wasn't ready to see what she called proof.

What if her accusations were true? Nadalia put her hand across her mouth to muffle her cry. She swallowed, threw her head back, shook her hair and got herself together. She couldn't break down here. Not yet. She hadn't even seen the so called proof. Sage may not even be guilty.

But when she thought about the fact that she hadn't had sex with her husband in months, how distant they had become, all the nights that she waited for him to get home when he claimed he was working late, and then, thought back to that disheartening attempt the other night, she was already starting to believe it was true.

Nadalia wiped the tears, marched to her office door and pulled it open just enough to bark out an order. "Kim, I need a latte." She shut the door without waiting for an answer and then sat at her custom designed glass desk. She pictured the staff outside of her door scurrying and whispering, wondering what could have gotten her so upset.

Nadalia powered on her computer, but instead of working, she opened up Facebook and sifted through her timeline. Then she opened her emails and skimmed the subjects, but she didn't really pay attention. Looking at her phone, she sighed again. She wanted to see the text, but she was afraid.

The cell phone dinged again. Nadalia grabbed it, held it tightly in her hands and looked at the ceiling. She put it back down, deciding to wait for her coffee before she faced whatever was there. She couldn't take bad news on an empty stomach, but then again, her stomach was churning and she wasn't sure she'd be able to keep any food down. The coffee would have to do.

Finally she heard a light tapping at her door. Nadalia opened it, trying to look as professional as possible. Through a narrow crack, Kim handed Nadalia a venti latte from the Starbucks in the lobby. Nadalia pushed the door closed and locked it again. She leaned against the wall and sipped, closing her eyes as the hot strong drink eased down her pipes. Nadalia sipped all the way back to her desk and then picked up her phone.

Taking a deep breath, she touched the message icon. Angela had included three images as well and the last message just said 'hello' with a question mark. The phone chimed again with a message. *"Call me back already."*

The first image was of a text exchange between Sage and Coffey about how crazy last night was. Nadalia figured they went to a strip club. That's what men do. She wasn't mad at that. It was the next two messages that set off her alarm. One about them setting up a time and date for round two and next was an exchange between the two where Coffey had texted, "That was some next level shit! This weekend is going to be off the hook."

Nadalia dropped her head. The phone rang and she jabbed the screen.

"Yeah."

"Now do you believe me?"

"How did you get that stuff?"

"Did you forget? I majored in computer engineering. I still dabble to stay abreast of new technologies."

"Oh. Yeah." Nadalia's voice was despondent.

"There is definitely something going on and I'm not going to lose my husband to some trick. We need to do something."

"What do you suggest?"

"Coffey is supposed to be heading back to New York by the end of this week."

"So come with him!" Nadalia perked up.

"No! That won't work." Nadalia frowned as Angela continued, "If I come, they will probably cancel their plans. He can't know I'm coming." After a few moments of silence. Angela's voice boomed on the lined, sounding renewed. "I know. I'll send the kids to my mother's for the weekend. I'll come and you meet me at the airport. They will probably be at the same hotel and we can catch them with the whores."

"That could work, but how do you know something will go down this weekend?"

"If Sage tells you he's working this weekend or meeting up with Coffey, we'll know."

"Okay." Nadalia prayed that Angela was wrong. "If Sage says anything suspicious, I'll let you know so you can make your arrangements. It's been a while, so it will be good to see you. I just wish it were under better circumstances."

"Me too." Sadness rang out in Angela's tone and for several moments the only sound on the line were the women breathing.

"Nadalia." Angela's voice sounded small.

"What's up?" she replied, fighting the urge to cry.

"I'm sorry, too."

"We aren't going down without a fight."

"No…we're not. G'bye Angela. I'll call you when I have something." Nadalia ended the call, buried her head in her hands and cried again.

After a little while, Nadalia stood, refusing to sit around crying prematurely. She walked back to the window and thought of how she could get the answers she wanted. Trotting back to her desk, she picked up her phone and called Sage.

"Hey, babe!" She tried her best to sound cheerful. "Sorry about earlier. My day started out crazy."

"Sounds like you're feeling better."

"A little."

"Good!"

"Listen, babe! I was thinking that we could check out that new Greek restaurant this Friday or Saturday. Work has been crazy for both of us and I think a nice date would do us both some good."

"Sounds good."

Nadalia smiled, relived. "Okay. I'll make reservations."

"No, I can't!"

"What!" Her heart rate quickened and a tight ball formed in her stomach.

"Can't do this weekend. Coffey's coming in and we have to meet with clients Friday evening. I probably won't be in until late and I'll have to head back out early Saturday morning. This new venture looks like it's really going to happen, but we have to play our cards right. We are starting with breakfast and want to show them around New York, then, get this deal sealed. Wish me luck."

Nadalia sat in slow motion, afraid that her shaky legs would give out. She bit her bottom lip.

"Babe…babe."

She heard Sage calling out to her through the phone, but she didn't answer. She'd rather let him think the cell phone malfunctioned. When it was clear that he'd hung up, she turned the phone off, just in case he called back.

Chapter 27

Pearson

Pearson was in the Chamberlin and Associates offices, but handled business for the G-Day Foundation for the better part of the morning. She attempted to learn what she could about running her father's company, but with her own annual benefit being a few months away, she couldn't afford to push all of her duties aside without having to deal with major backlash once she got back to her own office.

Candice peeked into the spacious temporary office that had been issued to Pearson the day before. "Don't forget we have a new client to see at ten."

Pearson gazed over her laptop and nodded. Candice waited a moment and after Pearson didn't offer any response, she closed the door.

Being in the building and the company that her father had built played a nostalgic trick on her. Most of the time she was fine and felt the pride of his legacy as she roamed through the halls. Other times, sadness enveloped her and she found it hard to breathe. Pearson imagined that Candice's rigid, no-nonsense management style must have been a world of difference from that of her father. Even though she was young, she remembered how people adored him. He was so easy to like with his warm demeanor and that huge charming smile he always wore.

Pearson's phone rang and a number from her office lit up her display. "Hello."

"Morning, Mrs. Day." It was Pearson's assistant. "We just received the manifesto that you wanted to air at the benefit from the videographer. He also sent a link for us to view the trailer. When you have a moment to view it, let me know and I'll get any changes that you might require back to him ASAP."

"Thanks, Natalie. I'll be in after lunch. We can view it together."

"Okay. I have a few things for you to sign and I emailed you a couple of schedule changes to approve."

"No problem."

"Oh! The printer said we will have the printed invitations in the office today, right? If you want I can go ahead and have Tina begin labeling them."

"Hold off on that, Nat. I want to see them before they go out."

"Okay, Mrs. Day."

Pearson ended the call and sighed. How was she going to manage running two companies? Her foundation was too close to her heart to abandon. Continuing her father's legacy meant a lot to her as well. Maybe she'd have to tell her mother to find someone suitable to take over the company. Pearson sifted through the files on the desk. She grabbed the one that said Lefton Properties Ltd., and headed to the conference room for the meeting.

Pearson was the first to arrive in the oval boardroom. She sat at the massive mahogany table that mimicked the room's shape. She laid the files on the table and opened up her laptop ready to take notes.

As much as she wanted to be there, her mind kept veering to thoughts about her foundation. There was so much to do in the next few months. This timing was just not the best.

Pearson heard Candice's voice in the hallway. She thought of how she would tell her that she couldn't take the position. After the meeting they could go to lunch and she'd give her the news then. She'd suggest that Walter be considered for the position since he had been with the company from its inception. He was like family and had spent the better part of his life in service to Chamberlin and Associates. Surely he had a stake in seeing it do well.

Finally, Candice entered the room chuckling with the gentlemen Pearson assumed to be the clients. Walter walked in behind the three unknown men and then along came her mother's secretary, a mature woman who wore thick rimless glasses. As sweet as she was, one couldn't tell since her faced appeared to be etched into a permanent scowl. The meeting was successful, Pearson assumed by the way they all smiled and shook hands afterwards, although she hadn't bothered taking a single note. All she could recall was the droning of a collection of voices.

Once the boardroom was clear, Pearson went into her mother's office to wait for her. Candice stepped in with a huge smile, but that smile fell when she gasped and threw her hand to her chest. Pearson had startled her.

"I didn't mean to scare you." Pearson said.

"Oh! I didn't expect to see you." She rounded her desk and sat. "The meeting went well, didn't it?"

"Yes it did." Pearson looked away. "New business is always nice. Let's go to lunch so we can talk...and celebrate."

"Sure. There's a good Asian Fusion restaurant just down the block."

"Okay." Pearson wondered if Candice noticed how lifeless and forced their conversations were. They still hadn't successfully passed being cordial, as if they were both nervous about stepping on any conversational land mines. There were so many. At least Pearson thought so. The other night in Candice's home, was the first time she ever remembered having a conversation with her mother that went as deep as it had. Most importantly, they weren't arguing.

"I'll drive," Pearson offered. "Let me get my purse and I'll be right back."

"Okay," Candice said as she started to paint a layer of soft pink on her lips with one hand while she held a beaded mirror in the other. She pressed her lips together and swiped away the wisp of hair that settled over her right eye. Then she fluffed her flawless salt and pepper bob. Pearson watched for a moment before heading out of the office.

During the ride, Pearson continued trying out words that would help her tell Candice no. She decided to wait until after they ate. When they arrived at the restaurant, it was obvious that Candice had frequented the place. The ultra slim hostess addressed her by name in a heavy accent and asked if she wanted her usual spot.

Once they were seated, Candice sighed, clasped her hands in front of her and rested her head on them. The small chatter that passed between them was more typical of a courteous exchange between professionals rather than a conversation between mother and daughter.

"Looks like a big win for Chamberlin. Congratulations," Pearson said.

"Yes. We've been after their properties for years, but we had to wait until their contract was up with their previous management company. They have a huge portfolio."

Other than placing their orders, not much was said as they sipped on seltzers with lemon. When their food came, Pearson pushed hers around the plate. The questions that she wanted so badly to ask Candice left little room in her nervous stomach.

Pearson knew she'd have to get her questions in before she told Candice that she wasn't going to take the position. Imagining that Candice would not be happy about her decision, she doubted that she'd be open to answering personal questions that could possibly detonate new levels of tension between them.

"I have more questions."

Candice put her fork down and sighed, turning her face away from Pearson.

"I have the right to ask."

"Fine." Candice picked her fork back up and took in a few small bites in the space that Pearson left open as she formulated her questions. Candice then sat back. When Pearson didn't begin right away, Candice threw her napkin on the table. "Come one. Let's get this over with."

"Why did you ship me off to boarding school?"

"It was best."

"For who?"

"You!" Candice said like she was exasperated. "Your future...me…"

"Forgive me if I don't see how beneficial it was to ship me off to some boarding school that was miles away from home right after my father died." Pearson couldn't stop her emotions from raging. Tears spilled from her eyes and Candice looked away. "I just don't get it." She took deep breaths to try to keep calm. Candice still hadn't responded. "Do you know what it felt like to have to deal with the death of my father in the midst of strangers? I had nobody!"

"Neither did I!" Candice yelled. A few people looked in their direction and she retreated. She cleared her throat and sat straight, shifting her chin a little higher as if that alone would restore her dignity. Then she took her napkin and dabbed at a small tear on the side of her eye.

Pearson was shocked. She couldn't recall ever seeing her mother cry, except at her dad's funeral.

"Contrary to what you may believe, I loved your father."

"I didn't question that. Why ship me off at a time when I needed you the most?"

"Pearson!" Candice screamed. "Do we have to do this now?"

"Yes!" Pearson sucked her teeth. "It's never the right time for you, but these are things that I need to know. This isn't easy for me either." Candice shook her head and cast her eyes upwards. Pearson ignored the gesture.

"Fine!" Candice looked around to see if anyone was looking at her again, then lowered her voice and continued, "You won't understand anyway."

"Try me."

"I didn't know what else to do. I didn't know how to deal with it myself, how was I supposed to be able to help you? The counselors at the school assured me that you would be fine."

Pearson felt the heat of anger rise inside of her. Strangely she also felt pity for Candice. The woman had no clue how to be a mother.

Pearson decided she'd had enough for the day. Of course she had other questions that haunted her about her childhood and the wall that had been erected between her and her mother, but for now, she was done. Each question carried so much emotional weight and the response she just received was heavy enough. She was expecting to feel better with answers, but that wasn't happening.

"You know what, Ma? Don't worry about me asking you any more questions about things that I have the right to ask." Dark sarcasm dripped from her words. "Why would I need to…or even want to understand why

my relationship with my own mother seemed to be so…"
Pearson searched for the right word. "Non-existent? Feel
free to take all those answers to your grave."

Candice's head reared back as shock registered on
her face. Pearson savored the response, but still couldn't
stop herself from crying. Her tears flowed so heavily that
she no longer bothered to wipe them from her face. She
noticed that her hands were shaking and decided it was
time to end this exchange. "I'm done." Pearson tossed her
napkin and stood. "And by the way, I won't be taking the
position. I have my own business to run."

Candice's eyes grew wide. Pearson couldn't tell if
it was from astonishment or anger. Needing air, she
ignored her mother's reaction and dug around in her
wallet so she could leave money for her part of the bill.

"Pearson!" Candice called out, but Pearson
refused to answer. "Pearson!" she said louder and again
looked around at the attention she garnered.

Pearson sucked her teeth and continued ignoring
her.

"Pearson," she said again, but more steadily.
"Please!"

Pearson stopped moving. There was a sense of
desperation in Candice's plea that caught Pearson off
guard. She stood still.

"Sit down. I have something very important to tell
you."

Pearson looked away.

"Please," Candice almost whispered and then
reached out and grasped Pearson's arm.

Pearson flopped down in her chair.

"You have to reconsider," Candice said.

Pearson opened her mouth to protest and Candice held her hands up.

"Sweetheart," Candice said gently and Pearson scrunched her brows. When tears streamed down Candice's cheeks and her lips trembled, Pearson really felt baffled. "I have…cancer….breast cancer. There's a good chance that I won't make it through the year."

Pearson felt like a bomb had exploded in her chest. "What!" Her eyes stung from new tears. "No. You can't do this to me. You can't finally come back into my life just in time to tell me that you're going to die!"

Pearson's eyes narrowed into slits. She couldn't speak the rest of the words that bombarded her thoughts. They wouldn't pass her quivering lips.

"You…" Pearson's emotions caught in her throat.

When Pearson felt like she would pass out, she marched out of the restaurant. Once outside, she backed up against the façade, held her hand to her chest and gasped for air. Tears blurred her vision. By the time she made it to her car, her chest felt like it would burst.

Pearson jammed the start button and the car purred to life. She hit the gas and zoomed off a couple of yards until she realized that she still couldn't see. Pulling over, she cried into her hands. Her entire body shook until she calmed down enough to dial Niles' number.

"Babe! What's wrong? Where are you?" Niles yelled into the phone.

She tried to speak through her crying, but her words sounded muffled.

"Where are you?" Niles asked.

"On my way home," she finally managed to say.

"I'm on my way." Niles tone was urgent and Pearson couldn't wait to fold herself inside his arms.

Chapter 28

Ryan

"Hey. How's the movie going?" Ryan tried to sound cheerful, despite the turmoil that she'd been wrangling with since the day she saw Anderson in the restaurant with that other woman.

"Awe, babe! Things are great! We should be wrapping up here in another week or so."

"A friend of mine called me yesterday. She thought she saw you having lunch at Tao the other day. I told her you've been out of town shooting a movie for weeks. She could have sworn it was you, but I told her that was impossible. Funny, huh?"

"Yeah. Funny." The line went mute for a few seconds. "Listen babe, I need to run. You know how it is here on the set—it never stops. I'll call you later tonight when I get back to the hotel."

"Sure." He gave her exactly what she expected—nothing! He'd never admit to his affairs and still believed that she was clueless.

"Later, babe." Anderson hung up without giving Ryan a chance to say goodbye.

Ryan sat at the edge of her bed, still holding the phone. She knew her attempt at trying to get him to say he was in New York was lame. She didn't really expect him to confess. Actually she wasn't sure what she expected. She could only imagine what he would have done if she had approached him in that restaurant—especially when she wasn't supposed to be in the city.

Ryan wrapped her arms around herself, suddenly feeling a chill. Maybe the baby would make her stronger. After her visit with the doctor yesterday, she had a good feeling about the pregnancy, but she would still wait to see how things went before she told Anderson. Most likely, it would be rough and she'd have to spend a good portion of her second and last trimester on bed rest. But she was willing to do whatever she had to do. All she needed was one child—for so many reasons.

Ryan decided that the one person she would tell would be her mother. She dialed her number.

"Hello!" Frannie's greeting sounded rushed as if Ryan caught her in the middle of something.

"Hey, Ma."

"What's up, honey?"

"I'm pregnant." Ryan decided not to waste any time.

"For real this time?" Frannie teased.

"Ma!"

"Hey! We've been here before—several times! I gotta ask these things."

"I was pregnant all the other times. Those times just didn't go well."

"Did you go to the doctor yet? What did she say?"

"So far things look good and that I will probably be on bed rest to make sure it all goes well."

"How far are you?"

"Around two months."

"You didn't waste any time getting back in the sack. What did he say?"

"I haven't told him yet."

"Oh. Well, honey, I gotta go. I'll come by tomorrow and we can do lunch."

"Okay. I'll see you then. Oh! Are you coming with me to Pearson's benefit this year?"

"That fancy smancy benefit she does every spring—hell yeah. I got to meet that cute, famous jazz player last time. Not to mention, I tossed a few of those huge shrimp in my purse and enjoyed them the next day. I ain't neva seen shrimp that big before in my entire life! I'll need a dress, though. Let's start looking this week."

"We'll see. I may be a little bigger by then."

"Just tell me when you're ready. Listen, sweetie, I've gotta go. Got company coming ova. Ya mother's still got it, kiddo!" Frannie hooted and hung up.

Ryan wondered if her visitor was going to be Vonnie's uncle. She cut her eyes at the thought of that. Tossing her cell phone aside, she sat there looking around the large room and sighed. She felt dwarfed in the massive space and a sense of loneliness consumed her.

"You're going to keep mommy company when you get here." Ryan patted her stomach. She stood and made her way to the kitchen.

Certain that the baby would change things in her home, Ryan imagined it would be nice to finally get her husband's attention. She visualized him coming home every night and her traveling with him. If those dreams didn't manifest, at least she'd have her baby.

In the kitchen, Ryan opened the refrigerator. Nothing inside enticed her so she decided to go out for breakfast. Taking a quick shower, she slipped on a pair of jeans, with a black sweater, boots and a mink jacket. She covered her red, swollen eyes with a pair of oversized dark sunglasses. People didn't need to see the anguish that resided in there.

Ryan decided she'd go to her favorite diner, but first she needed to pick up the prescription for her prenatal pills.

Ryan strolled through the drug store and by the time she made it to the pharmacy department, she had a hand full of items that weren't part of her original plan. When her turn came, Ryan gave the clerk her last name and when the woman walked off to retrieve the prescription, she perused the magazines when one caught her attention.

Ryan reached for a tabloid peeking out behind a fashion magazine because she saw Anderson's name. It wasn't just his name that caught her attention, but the woman he was holding hands with on the cover as they appeared to be romping on the beach. It was the woman at the restaurant and the headline read, "Andy Lee Nails New Role and Co-Star!"

Ryan snatched the magazine off the shelf, pushed it behind her back. Her breathing became ragged and she took several deep breaths to maintain control of her rage.

Ryan quickly paid for her items and headed to the car, where she pulled the tabloid open to the spread. Several pictures of Anderson and his young co-star were plastered across the page. Tears rolled down Ryan's face from behind her shades as she scanned the illicit photos of the two in swimwear as well as a few photos of what looked like the inside of a nightclub. The actress looked dreamily into Anderson's eyes and smiled like a smitten teenager.

Ryan started tearing the tabloid apart. "You bastard," she screamed, tossing scraps across the front seat. She banged her hands against the steering wheel, collapsed onto it and cried out.

After she'd gotten out most of her angst, she ran back inside the pharmacy and picked up another copy of the tabloid.

Ryan thought about calling Anderson, but decided she would do this in person. She vowed to muster up the courage to confront him when returned home the next week and wondered what excuse he would offer this time. She finally had proof.

Chapter 29

Vonnie

After a busy week, Vonnie was excited about having a few days off. She and her two partners worked out their schedules so that they would be able to alternately enjoy long weekends and Vonnie wasn't due back in the office until Monday.

Her appearance on the talk show the day before went well and the producer treated her like a true VIP, picking her up and dropping her off in a limo and catering to her every need. She enjoyed everything about the experience like hanging out in the green room with the other guests and getting the chance to meet a co-star of one of her favorite TV dramas. She couldn't wait for it to air the following week so she could see how she actually looked in front of the camera.

The other highlight of the week was getting a call from *Essence* Magazine, and being asked to provide a quote for an upcoming issue. It was hard to contain her excitement; she felt like a child at Christmas.

Vonnie decided that if she was going to be appearing on TV more often, maybe she should pump up her exercise regime and shed a few pounds so she could really look good on camera. Vonnie grabbed her cell phone to reach out to the girls to find a good trainer.

Pearson and Nadalia didn't answer, so she called Ryan. Immediately she knew there was something wrong from the sound of Ryan's voice.

"Hey, Ryan. Everything okay?" she asked. She didn't want to share her good news if the timing wasn't right.

"I'll be fine."

"Well okay. I'm just checking in. I'm off today, so I'll be around if you want to talk."

"Thanks. I'll be fine," she repeated.

"I'll call you later to check up on you."

After Vonnie hung up, she tried both Pearson and Nadalia again. Still neither of them answered. She left messages inquiring about wanting to hire a trainer.

For once, Vonnie had a clear schedule, but with all the excitement reeling inside of her, she couldn't just sit at home. She decided to surprise her husband at his office with lunch and sneak in a few smooches while she was there.

Vonnie changed into a hip-hugging pair of jeans that Mike loved to see her in, a vibrant orange cashmere sweater that wrapped around her waist accentuating her shape, and slipped on a pair of high-heeled boots that were sure to entice him. She busied herself around the house until one of their favorite sushi restaurants opened at eleven.

She placed an order for takeout and picked it up on her way to Mike's office. Balancing the food in one hand, Vonnie walked across the parking lot, through the shrill cold winds as fast as she could.

Pressing the elevator with her elbow, Vonnie headed to her husband's company on the second floor. She walked down the hall to Mike's office and swung the door open. When Vonnie walked up to the receptionist, she noticed something different. This young looking woman with blond hair and long red nails wasn't Pat, the mature black receptionist who had been with her husband's company since its inception.

"Uh, excuse me?" Vonnie caught the woman's attention as she looked around. Mike didn't tell her about any changes to the office or hiring new people.

"Hello. How many I help you?" The woman smiled and her big brown eyes seemed to twinkle.

Vonnie smiled through her confusion. "I'm looking for Cyber Vault."

"They moved months ago. They are now downstairs in suite 110," she said.

"Oh…thank you. I'm sorry to bother you."

"No worries at all. We still get a few people in here looking for them all the time."

"Have a great day." Vonnie smiled, masking her shock. Why hadn't Mike told her about moving the office? They never kept secrets.

Vonnie headed downstairs. Surely Mike would have an explanation. She stepped off the elevator and followed the descending numbers down the hall to suite 110.

This office was a third of the size of Mike's previous location. Vonnie spotted Pat behind a reception desk half the size of the old one.

Pat looked up and stretched her eyes. A suspicious feeling crept over Vonnie. Usually Pat was excited to see her and now she looked nervous.

"Mrs. Howard…Hi!" Pat stammered. "It's been so long. Was Mr. Howard expecting you?"

"Hi Pat. Actually no! I was trying to surprise him with lunch."

"He's not here," Pat said and began shuffling papers around on her desk.

Vonnie watched her for a moment, feeling Pat's unease under her watch. "Will he be back soon?"

"I don't think so. Mr. Madison spends more time out of the office than he does inside these days."

"Oh. Okay." Vonnie thought for a second. "Well, do you like sushi?"

"Uh…yes. I love sushi. Why?"

"Because someone may as well eat this lunch. I don't think it will make it back to my car. Some of the sauce spilled and the bag is falling apart. If you haven't had lunch, you're welcome to it."

"Oh. That's so nice of you," Pat said, taking the bag from Vonnie."

Vonnie gave her a smile that hid just how annoyed she really felt. "Have a great day, Pat."

"You too, Mrs. Howard. And thanks again for lunch."

Vonnie went to walk out and turned back toward Pat. "When did you guys move again?"

"After we downsized," Pat said. "We've been here since November."

"Oh yeah! That's right!" Vonnie pretended to recall. "It's been so long since I've been here and things have been going haywire at the practice." Pat smiled. Vonnie knew that she wasn't buying it. "Well enjoy."

Vonnie hurried to the car, pulled out her cell phone and stabbed the screen to unlock the phone. She swiped her way to Mike's number. Just as she was about to press talk a call came in. She recognized the Connecticut number as being from Noelle's school.

"Hello."

"Mrs. Howard?"

"Speaking."

"Good afternoon, Ma'am. Sorry to bother you."

A chill ran through Vonnie's body. "Is Noelle okay?" She never received calls from Noelle's school.

"Oh yes, ma'am. This is Mrs. Berry. I'm calling from the billing department. I've tried to reach Mr. Howard unsuccessfully, which is why I'm calling you. This is regarding Noelle's tuition balance."

"That's been paid." Vonnie's face scrunched in confusion.

"In fact, ma'am, it hasn't. There's still a balance of ten thousand dollars from the fall semester and this semester has yet to be paid. Would you like to apply that to a credit card today?"

"What? I…I don't understand. Mrs.…." Vonnie paused, trying to remember the woman's name.

"Mrs. Berry," she filled in for her.

"Ah. Thanks, Mrs. Berry. Let me get in touch with my husband and I can call you back regarding that bill and to rectify the situation." Vonnie wanted to tell the woman that she was mistaken, but after finding out that her husband had downsized his business without telling her, she decided that the woman could be right. Vonnie was furious and couldn't wait to speak to Mike.

More than just being mad, Vonnie was hurt. What other secrets had Mike been keeping from her? She ended the call and dialed his number.

"Hey, babe! What's up?"

"Don't babe me!"

"What? What's wrong?"

"You tell me. I just went to your office to surprise you. Guess who was surprised?"

Mike didn't respond.

"Hello! Why didn't you tell me you moved?"

"Babe! I…let's talk about this when I get home tonight."

"Oh, but wait, there's more!" she said sarcastically as if she were delivering great offers in a commercial voice. "I just got a call from our daughter's school about unpaid tuition. What else should I expect today, Mike?"

"Babe, I can explain."

"Damn right you will!" Vonnie's chest rose up and down. "Since when do we keep secrets like this? What the hell is going on?"

"Babe—"

"Where are you?" Vonnie yelled. She felt her cheeks grow hot.

"At work."

"Liar! I'm sitting outside of your office!"

"Babe. I'm still working. I'm about to meet with a client. As a matter of fact, he's ready. I'll have to call you back. I promise I'll explain everything when I get home. Okay?"

Vonnie pressed END and tossed the phone into the back seat. Her hands shook as she wrapped her fingers around the steering wheel. Too riled up to drive, she dropped her hands and rocked back and forth.

When she had her irritation under control, Vonnie started the car and drove home trying not to cry. How could he deceive her like this? They had built their relationship on trust. They shared everything. He had to have a valid explanation for all of this. At least she hoped he did.

She wanted answers and couldn't wait hours for Mike to get home. Once she got in the house, she went into their shared home office and sifted through the mail in search of Noelle's tuition bill. Finding more than she ever expected, she filtered through piles of other unpaid bills, marked with large red 'past due' stamps. Among the delinquent notices included the mortgage payments, car notes, and several credit card bills. The only bill that appeared to be up to date was the membership fee for The Beck, which has just been paid in a few weeks back.

Vonnie couldn't help the tears. The deception made her heart feel like it had severed. She couldn't come up with one valid reason why Mike had hidden this from her. Ignoring important bills while keeping his country club membership payment current baffled her.

Vonnie went to the wine cooler and pulled out a fresh bottle without even bothering to see what kind it was. She uncorked the bottle and drank straight from it. Hours later, she was still sitting in the same spot, waiting for Mike to walk through the door.

Chapter 30

Vonnie

W hen Mike came home that night, Vonnie had already downed at least four glasses of wine. Her lips felt numb, but her anger was still fresh. Normally Vonnie greeted him at the door what a hug and a kiss. Today, she stayed put. Minutes after she heard him come in, he cautiously strolled into the kitchen.

She sneered at him. "And how was your day?" she asked, cutting her eyes at him. She took a long sip from her fifth glass of wine without taking her eyes off him. She slammed the glass down. "Why didn't you answer my damn calls?"

Mike still hadn't stepped all the way into the kitchen. "Babe, I told you I had meetings."

"Until..." Vonnie looked at her watch and squinted. "Ten o'clock at night? Are you lying about that, too?"

"V! I never lied to you."

"Yes, you did!" Vonnie banged her hand against the table and knocked her glass over. Mike walked over to the sink, pulled off a wad of paper towels and cleaned up the spill, while Vonnie continued to lay into him. "Keeping secrets is just as bad as lying. Since when did we start keeping secrets from each other, huh?"

"I can explain."

"Yeah! Well explain these while you're at it!" Vonnie held up the pile of overdue bills and then tossed them at him. "Everything is past due and Noelle's school called me today because they haven't been able to get in touch with you!"

Mike's eyes stretched wide. He opened his mouth to speak, but closed it back, shaking his head. "Just let me explain. Please!"

"I don't even know if I want to hear what you have to say. How many more lies or secrets," she said, curling her fingers into air quotes, "are you going to tell me?" Vonnie went to the cabinet, snatched it open, grabbed another wine glass and walked back to the table.

Mike scooped the glass up before she could pour more wine into it. Vonnie glowered at him.

"It looks like you've had enough."

"I'll tell you what I've had enough of..."

"I know. My lies," he said sarcastically. "I get it. Can I explain now?"

Vonnie snatched the glass out of his hand, but sat down without pouring more wine. "I'm listening," she said, folding her arms.

Mike sat across from her at the table and placed his hand over hers. She pulled her hands back. Mike sighed.

"I ran into some trouble with the business." Vonnie looked away for moment and then refocused on what Mike was saying. "We hit a rough patch, baby. I don't know what happened. The market started changing. Business didn't just slow down. It practically came to a halt. Technology can sometimes change like the wind. Clients were bailing for newer options that cost less money. I went through the company's nest egg to pay salaries until I had to let people go. I've been working with an engineer on a new idea. I need to be able to compete with some of the newer technologies in order to stay afloat. But I needed money to fund these new products." Mike dropped his head.

Vonnie knew he felt ashamed, but refused to give in to the sense of pity that was moving in on her anger.

Vonnie got up and paced. "Our house, Mike. We could lose our home! I can't understand why you would keep this from me." Vonnie swiped at the tears that streamed down her face.

Mike dropped his head into his hands. "Babe." He looked up with pleading eyes. "I'm sorry. I am trying to fix this. I didn't want to worry you. I didn't want to disappoint you and have you think that I failed you!"

"Mike! I could have helped."

Mike slammed his hand against the table. "Dammit!" Vonnie flinched and look at him as if he'd lost his mind. "I said I'll fix it. I told you I'll take care of you...of this and I will. Just give me a chance."

"Well, something needs to be done now."

"I. Will. Fix. This. I don't need your help right now. I have a few things in the works and after that, I will be able to catch up on everything and we will be fine. I can take care of my family."

Vonnie thought for a moment before speaking again. She had a few more pieces of her mind to toss at him, but it was obvious that his sense of masculinity had been bruised. She walked   back to the table and sat down. After a few moments, she put her words together in a way that she hoped wouldn't cause more damage to his ego. She was still furious, but understood where he was coming from. Mike and always prided himself on being able to take care of his family and having a wife who worked only because she wanted to. "Fine! Nevertheless, I'm a part of this too, and I don't appreciate you leaving me out. Now I feel like I can't trust you."

Mike looked into her eyes and shook his head. "Baby. You know you can trust me."

"Keeping secrets from me makes me feel like I can't."

"I just needed time. That's all."

"Okay. I'm telling you now; I'm going to use *my* money from *my* savings to help pay some of those bills. So if you want to get all mad about it, start now. This ship ain't going down without me taking a turn at steering this boat to stiller waters." Vonnie stood. "I'll tally what we owe and see what we have to put toward getting back on track."

"No." Mike held his hands up.

"Don't tell me no!" This time she yelled. "This is my life too."

Mike looked away.

"If we owe more than what's in my savings account, then we'll cash in some investments, take out a loan, or something."

"I really don't want you to do that!"

"Well that's too bad."

"Just leave it alone for now. I have something in the works that will take care of everything."

Vonnie threw her hands up. There was no use in fighting him. Mike was stubborn. However, she was still going to tally her accounts which she now considered their reserve. This made her realize how oblivious she had been with their financial standing and that scared her.

"If you're going to handle this, then fine, but I want to be included in helping to manage the bills from now on. I realize how uninvolved I've been."

"Vonnie!" Mike said her name softly, but looked in the other direction. "Baby," he said. "I said I've got this. Can you please…just trust me?"

Vonnie groaned. She didn't like it but knew that Mike wouldn't put them into a bad situation that he couldn't get them out of. She sighed long and hard and then her mouth said, "Okay," but in her mind, she knew she'd be checking on things when he wasn't around. If his business tanked, there was no way they could afford this lifestyle. The reality hit her hard. If he wasn't able to handle this situation, their entire lives would change.

Chapter 31

Nadalia

N adalia checked her calendar on her cell phone. Tonight was girl's night, which the wives had scheduled the last time they went out to dinner. Nadalia thought the timing couldn't be worse. She didn't feel up to it, but also didn't want to alert the girls to the fact that something was wrong.

"I can get through this day!" she affirmed aloud. She'd been saying the same thing to herself each morning since her conversation with Angela. Moreover, just as Angela predicted, Sage's weekend was filled with 'meetings and appointments.' None of which included her.

The more she thought about it, the timing of the dinner was perfect. She needed an outlet. Hanging with them would be much better than sitting around the house wondering what Sage was doing or who he may have been doing it with.

Nadalia would have to curtail her drinking tonight because she was picking up Angela early the next morning. After her emotionally tumultuous week, she was looking forward to being with Angela. She'd be able to talk about how this situation was affecting her with someone who would understand. There was no one else in her life that she'd dare breathe a word of this to.

Nadalia put on make-up before heading to work. She sighed at her reflection in the mirror. No amount of concealer would hide the puffiness below her eyes. The weary lines in her face reflected exactly what she'd been feeling. Between his long working hours and being too preoccupied to notice, Sage hadn't realized her sullen mood. They'd hardly spoken during the day. He was up and out before she woke in the morning, and returned home after she'd fallen to sleep at night. The one day he did manage to make it home at a decent hour, he was so exhausted that he skipped dinner and went straight to bed. Sage had always been a hard worker and if she found that he wasn't cheating, she would feel like a fool.

As she thought about the limited amount of time they had been spending together, her eyes watered. The excursion she planned was just a week away. Depending on what she and Angela found out, she wondered if their getaway would happen. If he were cheating on her, would she leave him?

Nadalia squeezed her eyes shut. Sage loved her, she told herself. This she knew for sure. If he apologized, asked for forgiveness, promised her it would never happen again and then started paying her more attention, maybe she could give him this one pass. This could just be a bump on their way back to bliss. She wasn't married to the idea of working past his possible infidelity, but she wasn't ready to lose her husband.

The more arrogant side of her was angry and even wondered how he could possibly cheat on a woman like her? She was accomplished and beautiful. Men told her that all of the time.

Nadalia grabbed her concealer and dabbed a few spots under her eyes, covered her face with foundation, added thick smoldering layers of dark shadows on her lids, and coated her lips with a nude gloss. She looked more like she was going to a cocktail party rather than work, but at least her eyes looked 'made up' as opposed to weary.

She got up, grabbed her purse and checked her cell phone as she headed out the door. Angela had called. Nadalia dialed her back through the car's Bluetooth system as she pulled out of the driveway.

"How are you doing?" Angela asked.

"Not good. What about you?"

"Me neither. I can't believe I'm coming to New York to spy on my husband instead of shopping. I don't even feel like shopping. Now that's bad." Angela gave up a weak laugh.

Nadalia laughed slightly, too, but her face quickly turned into a frown and she fought back tears for the umpteenth time that morning. "I don't know if I can do this, Ange."

"I know! This is so hard, but I have to know. I have to know what I'm fighting against and whoever these bimbos are, they need to know what they are up against. I'm not going to just give up my husband and my life...I just can't."

"I'm so scared." Nadalia sniffled and then eased to the side of the road to search her purse for tissue. Her make-up was running and the tears caused the mascara to sting her eyes. The ladies stayed on the line together, but no one spoke until Nadalia started driving again. "So are you all set to leave?"

"Yes, I have a small bag and my mother is coming to get the kids tonight. They are staying with her until Monday. I figured I'd give myself an extra day or so before I go get them, depending on what I find when I get there." Again long moments went by without words. "This is so scary. I've had jitters in my stomach for the past two days."

"Oh my goodness. You too? I haven't slept." Nadalia dabbed her face with the tissue. "My eyes look horrible. I called myself doing the whole smoky eye look so I won't look so ragged at work today and now I just look like a sick raccoon!" This time both girls laughed genuinely.

"I hate that we are going through this and I really hope we find nothing bad. It might sound crazy, but...at least we are not going through this alone. We have each other to lean on."

"I know what you mean." They paused again. "Well, don't forget to call me in the morning before you take off. I've got you set up for one night at the W Hotel. I figured we could have breakfast out here on Long Island before we head to the city for our...stake out." Nadalia chuckled.

"Yeah."

"So...see you tomorrow."

"Yeah. Bye."

Nadalia drove the rest of the way in silence just accompanied by her thoughts. She pulled into her designated spot at work and reapplied her eye make-up before getting out of the car. She put on her game face and marched into work with her head held high.

Locking herself behind her office door, Nadalia ordered her assistant to make sure that she wasn't disturbed unless there was an emergency. Almost two hours into her day, she came knocking.

"What?" Nadalia yelled from her desk.

"I have a delivery." Her assistant's voice sounded muffled through the door.

"Come on in!" Nadalia pushed the sketchbook she was reviewing for the next season's designs aside. As Anna entered, Nadalia folded her arms, making it seem like she was really annoyed by the disruption until she looked up. She was carrying an exotic arrangement of flowers so large that Nadalia couldn't see her face as she brought them to her desk. She gasped, but recovered and made space on her desk for Anna to place the arrangement down. "Who is this from?"

"Your husband, of course." Anna looked at her quite confused.

"Oh, yeah." Nadalia chuckled. "He's been in the dog house."

"Well, I'll assume this will get him back in the big house! These are amazing." Anna smiled and turned to exit Nadalia's office and then turned back. "Let me know if you need anything." She put her hand on the doorknob. "Do you still want your door closed?"

"Yes! Thanks." Nadalia's answer was a lot more cordial.

Once the door was closed, Nadalia spun the vase around and examined the exotic mix of flowers. She smiled at first and then covered her face and cried—again.

Chapter 32

Pearson

Pearson lost count of how many times Niles had called her this morning. Now, he was checking on her again as if she were on suicide watch. Pearson had no intention of killing herself. Interestingly enough, she felt a part of her had come alive when her mother reached out to her and then that same part wanted to die when her mother delivered that dreadful blow about her impending death.

Niles had taken the next day off and Pearson spent it crying in his arms. He went back to work the following day and Pearson spent most of that day drinking herself numb. She couldn't wait for Niles to leave.

Now she worked from home because her eyes were too swollen to face the public and her head felt like it was floating inside of a heavy cloud.

Already, she had drunk half the bottle of vodka she opened in lieu of breakfast. It was her balm. She didn't feel pain in the same way when she was drunk. Vodka made her feel lighter and whenever the heaviness returned, threatening to weigh her down, she'd take another drink.

Niles wouldn't let her drink the day he stayed with her and every time she broke down, he'd pull her into a warm embrace. Though she appreciated his effort, the refuge his arms provided didn't soothe her the same way. In his arms, she cried, but when she drank, she forgot.

Pearson's cell phone rang and she sent the call to voice mail and it rang again. Pearson didn't feel like speaking to anyone and directed her assistant to respond to most of her calls through email, which had become her preferred method of contact for the day. Despite being intoxicated, she was handling business just fine. Her employees got the message, stopped calling, and started emailing and texting her all of their questions and updates.

Pearson's phone rang again and she rolled her eyes. Whoever this was wouldn't relent. She at least looked at who was calling and saw Candice's number. She felt a tightening in her chest.

Holding her hand over the phone, she deliberated with herself. Tears had become her natural response. She'd been ignoring her mother's calls because not only did she not know what to say, she didn't know what to feel.

When the phone vibrated again, Pearson turned the phone over and continued working.

After a while, she got an email from Niles asking her to call him because she wasn't answering her phone. She made that call.

"Hey, babe," she puffed up her voice so it wouldn't sound so heavy.

"I've been trying to call you. You had me worried."

"Sorry. I was wrapped up in work. I'm trying to tie up all the loose ends for this benefit. I only have a few weeks left."

"I know. How are you doing?"

"Okay."

"We are playing at the restaurant in the Hamptons tonight. Why don't you come with me? We'll have some special guests and Mom and Dad would love to see you."

Pearson fished for a reason to say no. She felt better being alone with her bottle. Suddenly, she remembered. "Wait!"

"What?" Niles responded.

"Aw shoot! I think tonight is our girls night out."

"With who?"

"Nadalia, Ryan and Vonita."

"Perfect! You should go. It will be good for you to get out."

Pearson didn't completely agree, but would consider it. Then she thought about it. "Yeah." She didn't quite offer a definitive answer.

"Oh, and your mother called me. She said she was trying to call you too, and didn't get an answer. I told her that when you're working, you sometimes get in a zone and you don't take calls."

"Okay. I'll call her back," Pearson lied.

Pearson reached for her glass and took another gulp of her vodka.

She heard Niles sigh. "Don't forget. She's worried about you." Pearson rolled her eyes. "I am too. I've got to go, but you better answer my call the next time or I'm coming home," Niles threatened and she believed him. "I'll be home a little early anyway so I can get ready for our set later tonight."

"Okay."

"Love you, baby."

"Love you back," Pearson said and heard Niles toss her a kiss through the phone.

"We'll get through this. We can get through anything."

Pearson appreciated his support, but wasn't sure how true his statement was. She had no idea how to get through this. Turning her phone back over, she worked for a little while longer before deciding that she would go ahead and get together with the girls. However, in order to do that, she'd need to see if she could be squeezed in for a facial. Her face and eyes were far too swollen to go out with that bunch and not be subject to a host of questions and she wasn't ready to talk about her mother with anyone.

Pearson sent one last email to her assistant letting her know she was headed off to appointments and wouldn't be available for the rest of the day. Then, she headed to her bedroom, washed her face and applied a light coat of liner and mascara to mask some of the puffiness. She called up the spa to see if her regular girl was available for a massage and facial. She was able to be squeezed in, but would have to get to the spa in the next half hour.

Pearson retrieved a travel mug from the cabinet and filled it to the brim with ice and vodka and headed out the door. She nearly dropped it along with her purse when she opened the door and found Candice standing on her steps.

"What...what are you doing here?" Pearson felt like a little girl caught doing something naughty. "I'm about to leave."

"We need to talk, honey."

Pearson cringed when Candice said 'honey.' "How did you know I was home?" she wondered aloud.

"Niles told me. I called him when you were ignoring my calls."

"I wasn't ignoring..." Candice gave Pearson the side eye. "I was working."

"I know, sweetheart. I work a lot, too."

"I'm sorry, but now is not a good time. I have an appointment." Candice looked at her watch. "And if I don't get going, I'll miss it."

Candice released a long sigh. "Okay. Call me when you get back. If you don't, I'm going to show back up."

Pearson's shoulders slumped. "Fine. I'll call you. But I won't have much time then either because I have plans tonight."

"No problem. It won't take all night."

"Fine." Pearson stepped outside and turned her back to her mother to lock the door. "See you later, Ma," she said as she hastened to her car.

Pearson pulled out as Candice stood in her yard watching. She wondered how she could avoid running into her later that day as well. She just needed a little more time. Pearson opened her travel mug and downed half of the vodka, winced at the large gulp and drove off.

Chapter 33

Ryan

R yan was all cried out and had spent the last few days avoiding contact with everyone, including Anderson until he left an angry message on her cell phone, telling her she'd better call him ASAP or else. Ryan chuckled at this audacity and purposely took at least another hour to call him back.

"Hello!" Anderson was obviously still angry.

"What's up?" Ryan's response was nonchalant.

"Where are you? I've been calling you. Why aren't you answering your phone?"

"I was taking a nap."

Anderson released something that sounded like a grunt. "I don't like it when you don't answer when I call."

In her head, Ryan repeated his words and then said, "You never answer my calls," under her breath.

"What did you say?" Anderson snapped at her.

"Nothing."

"Listen. We are all wrapped up here. I'll be home tomorrow."

Ryan was barely listening as he made awkward small talk. She realized how much their communication had diminished. She figured she might as well try her hand at being a little more firm.

"Andy!" she said, interrupting him.

"What!"

"I saw those pictures of you in that paper." Ryan's lip trembled as she spoke. She couldn't even recall the name of the tabloid.

"What the hell are you talking about, Ryan?"

"I saw the pictures, you're on the cover with that woman from the movie and inside you're at the beach together. I saw them. It was embarrassing."

"I don't know what you're talking about."

"Yes, you do. I'm not going to put up with this anymore Anderson." Ryan felt strength coming from somewhere inside. "I'm tired of this."

"Are you threatening me?"

Ryan stayed quiet for a moment and started pacing. "I'm just saying." She heard Anderson suck his teeth. "What about the lady in the restaurant?"

"What? Are we back to that again?"

"I was there, Anderson."

At first he didn't respond. "You were where, Ryan?"

"At Tao, last week. I saw you myself."

Again, Anderson didn't respond right away and she heard him breathing hard into the phone. "How could you have seen me in Tao, Ryan?"

She knew she was taking a risk admitting that she was in Manhattan. Right now she was less concerned about getting scolded and more concerned about the truth.

"What were you doing in Manhattan?"

"What were you doing in New York, in a restaurant with another woman?"

"Ryan!" she heard a big bang as if he'd punched a wall or tossed the phone. "Don't play with me, answer my question."

"Why can't you answer mine?" She enjoyed her new boldness.

"I was working. Now answer me."

"You came that close to home and didn't even call your own wife?" Ryan was doing well and proud of it.

"I'm not doing this with you. I'll see you tomorrow and I want to see how much mouth you have when we are standing face-to-face."

He called her on her boldness and she felt her confidence deflate. She realized that he'd hung up on her and she swallowed hard. If she wasn't pregnant, she'd have a drink. In all that audacious talking, she hadn't thought about what she would have done if he were in front of her. She almost didn't want him to come home.

Ryan put her phone on the charger and started getting ready for her night out with the girls. Their dinner couldn't come soon enough. Her nerves were frazzled and hanging out with them would be sure to help calm her down. Too bad she couldn't ask them to come back home with her so they could be there when Anderson arrived.

Ryan dressed for the night and left the house. They weren't scheduled to meet for quite some time, but Ryan felt like she was suffocating and needed to get out. She could already feel Anderson's rage.

She arrived an hour before the other girls and sat at the bar drinking seltzer water with olives until the other ladies arrived one by one. Pearson was the last to show up and they were seated. Ryan had prepped the waitress before Nadalia, Vonnie and Pearson arrived, telling her to bring her seltzer water in a martini glass with olives whenever they ordered drinks. She wasn't ready to explain why she wasn't drinking.

"So we made it to round two. Are your husbands happy? I know mine is," Nadalia said.

Ryan couldn't help but stare at her. She'd never seen Nadalia wear so much make-up. She looked away when Nadalia turned in her direction. Not sure if she had caught her looking, Ryan complimented her to avoid being embarrassed. "Nadalia, you have on make-up tonight."

"Yeah. Been trying some new things lately. I'm trying to master the smoky eye thing. I love the way it looks on people."

"Yeah. You're so pretty. I don't think I ever remember you wearing make-up before."

"I try to keep it looking natural," Nadalia said and called the waiter over to order a bottle of wine. "Pearson. What's the name of the wine we had last time?"

"I don't even remember. Order anything. I'll have a glass, but I'm feeling more like having a dirty vodka martini tonight. Actually, I'll probably have quite a few. You ladies can enjoy the rest of the wine," Pearson said.

Ryan expected her to laugh, but she didn't.

"That sounds good," Vonnie said. "I'll have one of those too. Make mine extra dirty. I love the olives."

The waitress gave them a friendly nod and turned toward Ryan with a discreet wink.

"So what's up in the lives of the rich and famous?" Nadalia asked and chuckled.

At first no one answered. Vonnie broke the silence. "Hey Nadalia, how was the getaway with Sage?"

"Oh. It's next week. I'm looking forward to it," Nadalia said with a slight smile before taking a sip of wine. "And I tried some of that spontaneous action," she said and winked.

"Woo!" Vonnie said, lifting her glass to Nadalia.

"How's Noelle doing in school?" Pearson asked.

"She seems to be fine, but I'm still having separation anxiety," Vonnie said. "I find all kinds of silly reasons to call her. She knows what's up, so she indulges me."

"I hated that place," Pearson said without looking up.

"What? You are the one who recommended that school to us."

"It's a great school even though I still hated it. I was never good at making friends," Pearson admitted. Nadalia made a sound, chuckled and sipped. Pearson cut her eyes at her. "Surprised?" She directed her comment to Nadalia. "Anyway." Pearson turned her attention back to Vonnie. "I'm sure Noelle is more sociable than I ever was. Most kids love it and the education is unmatched. It's one of the best in the country."

Vonnie put her hand to her chest. "Oh. You scared me for a moment. I was about to ride up there and pull my baby out." All the women laughed. "But really, sometimes I do want to take her out just to have her closer to home. She seems to be adjusting well, but I worry about her a lot. Don't be surprised if you hear that she's back home attending private school."

"Oh leave her be. She'll be just fine," Nadalia said. "I went away to prep school. It looks good for college."

Apparently no one was in the mood for a large meal, so they ordered several appetizers. Ryan being the only sober one noticed that they drank a lot more than they ate.

"How's the benefit coming along?" Ryan asked Pearson and picked around the salad she ordered.

"Oh great." Pearson brightened up a little. "You are all coming, right?"

"Of course," Vonnie responded first.

"Sage has been working extra hard lately, but he wouldn't miss an opportunity to hang out with his buddies." Nadalia put her hand to her mouth and looked at Pearson. "Oh. It's not that the foundation doesn't matter. It's a great cause. It's just that I'm sure he's missing his friends. It's been a while since they've gotten together. Don't worry. We will be making a hefty donation like we do every year."

"It seems like everyone has been so busy," Ryan added.

"What have you been up to Ryan? Everything groovy on the home front?" Nadalia asked.

Ryan resented the question yet almost wished she could tell the truth. However, she couldn't reveal anything, no matter how trapped she felt inside of her disappointing reality. "Anderson finally comes home tomorrow. He's been gone so long. I can't wait to finally see him." Immediately she stuffed her mouth with a forkful of salad.

Ryan noticed that Pearson had changed from martinis to scotch. She was way ahead of the rest in terms of drinks. As much as she looked forward to this dinner tonight, it wasn't turning out like she had expected. Pearson was unusually quiet and her conversation was void of her sarcastic quick wit. In addition, her and Nadalia's insulting, but entertaining dance was missing and the atmosphere felt weighted.

The chatter at the table subsided a bit against the backdrop of the noisy restaurant.

"I don't know about you ladies, but I needed this outing," Nadalia said.

"Me too," Vonnie chimed in.

"Yeah," Ryan said.

Pearson remained quiet.

Ryan noticed Nadalia looking her way and cast her eyes down, avoiding contact. She wished she would stop looking at her. It made Ryan feel like she was under a microscope.

"Ryan," Nadalia called her.

She looked up and thought she read pity in Nadalia's eyes. "What's up?" she said, hoping to mask her concern. She felt her composure unraveling. *Could Nadalia tell that something was wrong? Did she hear something?*

"Oh, hell! I'm just going to come out with it."

Everyone looked up.

"Come out with what?" Pearson slurred.

"All right. I was in the supermarket and saw this magazine that had Anderson on the front with another woman and a bunch of pictures on the inside of them holding hands at the beach," Nadalia said.

"Nadalia!" Vonnie scolded.

"Here we go," Pearson slurred again.

"It's in a public magazine. If she hadn't seen it by now, she's bound to see it. They're everywhere."

At first Ryan didn't know what to say, but quickly recovered. "Oh that. I know about it. In fact, Anderson and I were talking today about how they turn things around for a story. That's actually Andy's co-star and those photos were taken on the set of their movie." The lie slid right off of Ryan's lips with ease.

Nadalia looked at her crossways for several moments. "If you say so."

"I can't stand those tabloids. They don't give a damn about what they print. That stuff can ruin people's lives," Vonnie said.

Vonnie had come to her aid and Ryan smiled at her. Her lie seemed to work.

Pearson ordered another drink.

"Wow, girl. You're really putting them back tonight," Nadalia said.

"What? You're jealous?" Pearson teased.

Ryan snickered.

"Hardly! Keep drinking and you're going to need a designated driver. Don't look at me." Nadalia laughed.

"I won't need anyone to take me…" Pearson stopped talking and her eyes stretched wide.

The other women sat up wondering what was wrong. Pearson held up her hand, indicating that she was okay, but then gagged and quickly covered her mouth. Without an ounce of grace, she tried to get up from her seat and stammered. Pearson's body lurched, her eyes stretched wider, and before she could get away from the table, she vomited. The girls scattered.

Vonnie grabbed an empty bowl from one of the appetizers, held it under Pearson's mouth and rushed her to the bathroom. Nadalia turned away completely. Other patrons watched like it was for their entertainment.

Ryan felt her stomach stir and churn. Shooting up from the table, she ran toward the bathroom herself, almost slipping in Pearson's vomit on the floor.

When Ryan got to the bathroom, Vonnie was holding Pearson's necklace and patting her back as she released the rest of the contents in her stomach into the sink. Between the smell and the sound of Pearson's gurgling and heaves, Ryan's weak stomach couldn't take anymore. She rushed to the closest sink, lowered her head and threw up right beside them.

"Oh, Lord. Help me!" Vonnie said and moved between both women.

Ryan was the first to recover, running water and washing out her mouth.

"Are you okay now?" Vonnie asked rubbing Ryan's back.

"Yeah. I guess I just have a weak stomach."

"Okay." Vonnie turned her attention back to Pearson, whose head was still in the sink. "Come on, honey. Let's get you cleaned up."

Pearson grabbed the sides of the sink. Ryan stood on one side and Vonnie on the other with a handful of paper towels, helping her stand. Pearson's face was filled with blotches and she looked like as though the heaving had worn her out.

"Are you okay, Pearson?" Ryan asked.

Instead of responding, tears spilled down Pearson's face. Ryan was shocked, but Vonnie reacted right away.

"Oh, honey." Vonnie pulled Pearson into her arms and rocked her.

Ryan stood by not knowing what to do. Eventually, she patted Pearson's back as she cried into Vonnie's shoulder. Ryan assumed the toxic mixture of wine, vodka and scotch was the root of her strange behavior. She was used to seeing Pearson tipsy, but never to the point where she was right now, and definitely not emotional.

"Get Niles on the phone and let him know we are bringing her home," Vonnie instructed.

Ryan ran to the table to get Pearson's phone and Nadalia was standing, waiting as the bus boys cleaned up the mess.

"What's going on in there?" Nadalia asked.

"Pearson's sick."

"She's not sick. She's drunk. There's a difference." Nadalia flipped her hand.

Ryan waved Nadalia off. "Vonnie is going to make sure she gets home. I need to call Niles to let him know she's on her way."

"I guess that means dinner is over." Nadalia pulled out her credit card. "This one is on me. Go ahead and get Ms. Tipsy Pants situated. I'll call Niles."

Ryan was almost afraid of what Nadalia would say, but headed to the bathroom anyway to bring Pearson's stuff.

Vonnie was on her way out with Pearson crying and mumbling in her arms. Together, they helped Pearson into her coat and carried her to Vonnie's car. Nadalia met them outside. She leaned beside the passenger seat to get a good look at Pearson slumped over.

"Stick to the wine next time, girlfriend." Then she did something that surprised all of them. It would have surprised Pearson had she been more coherent. Nadalia kissed her on the cheek. "Get our girl home safe, Vonnie. Until next time!" she said over her back as she trotted to her car.

Vonnie waved at Ryan as she pulled off. They were all in a rush to get home while Ryan stood there wishing she had somewhere else to go. She didn't know exactly what time Anderson would be getting in, but she did know that she didn't want to be there when he did.

Despite the biting cold, Ryan took her time getting into her car. She started it and sat for a long while contemplating whether or not to go home. She didn't have many options and she would have to deal with Anderson one way or the other. She wondered how upset would Anderson be if he came home and she wasn't there.

Knowing that would really irk him, she put the car into drive and headed to her mother's house. Using her key and being careful not to disturb her mother's sleep, she tipped to the guest room, slipped under the covers and fell asleep.

Chapter 34

Nadalia

Nadalia pretended to be in a deep sleep when Sage slipped in late the night before and pretended again when he left early in the morning. The routine morning kiss that he placed on her cheek every day, even while she slept, made her at least feel hopeful, yet it didn't stop her stomach from churning as she thought about what she would possibly find out by the end of the day. Once she heard his car pull out, she pulled back the covers and jumped out of bed.

Nadalia had a little more than an hour to get dressed and meet Angela at the airport. Anxiety tormented her gut, bubbling along with her stomach acids and left no room for food. A cup of tea would have to hold her until she and Angela stopped for breakfast.

Nadalia dressed quickly and was mindful enough to make sure she looked fabulous. If she did run into Sage with another woman, she'd needed to be able to send her a message with just her presence, while reminding Sage of what he had.

Nadalia picked the jeans that accentuated her hourglass shape the best. She added a cashmere sweater that wrapped perfectly around her cinched waist and threw on her most expensive pair of stiletto boots. While she dressed, she soaked her five-karat princess cut diamond and matching antique band in cleaner so that it would gleam in the light. Despite the cold, Nadalia grabbed one of her personally designed mink ponchos instead of a coat and her newest designer handbag.

Nadalia applied a light coat of makeup. When she looked in the mirror, she was pleased, but as pulled-together as she was on the outside, she was equally disheveled on the inside. Her stomach groaned and rolled. The air whirling in her chest made her feel like her lungs would explode and her heart felt like it would fail if she found her suspicions to be true.

Quietly, she prayed that she and Angela wouldn't find anything incriminating. She hoped to find two hard working men making deals that would make their wives proud. Yet the feeling deep in her gut prevented her from believing they were innocent.

Coffey was the one doing all the traveling. Maybe Sage was just covering up for him, she hoped. At this point in their careers, Coffey was the popular one. He played in the league much longer than Sage and went on to live his life in front of the camera. Sage, as handsome as he was, spent his recent life behind the scenes and out of the spotlight.

Nadalia looked around before walking out of the house, feeling like she needed to see it as it was one last time. Depending on what happened after her and Angela's 'sting' operation, there was no telling how her home would change.

Taking a deep breath, Nadalia pulled the door open and exhaled. "Here we go," she said aloud.

Riding in silence with the looming presence of her apprehension, Nadalia made it to the airport in record time. She pulled up to the passenger pick up area for Angela's airline at JFK and hoped security wouldn't nag her about sitting there until Angela came out. With her nerves so frazzled this morning, she couldn't take any additional friction. Lying back on the head rest, Nadalia closed her eyes and tried to calm down. She jumped at the light tapping on the passenger side window, huffed and prepared herself to deal with the pushy airport security. When she looked over, she saw Angela motioning to her.

"You made it." Nadalia tried to muster as much excitement as possible, but her words still came out lacking enthusiasm.

"Yes, I made it." Angela's tone matched Nadalia's. A brief nod between them expressed their understanding.

"Should I open the trunk?" Nadalia asked as she unlocked the doors.

"That won't be necessary. All I have is this overnight bag." Angela held it up for Nadalia to see before putting it in the back seat.

Angela climbed into the car and gave Nadalia a hug. The embrace bonded them in their despair. When they pulled away, there were tears in both of their eyes.

"Hungry?" Nadalia asked, wiping her tears away as she drove the winding road to exit the airport.

"Yes and no."

"I know what you mean. We'll head straight to the city and find a Starbucks for some tea before we embark on our," Nadalia raised her brows when she said, "adventure."

"It took so much for me to get on that plane this morning." Angela shook her head and looked out the window.

"If I didn't have to pick you up, I wouldn't have left my house."

"I can't believe I'm in New York to spy on my husband."

"I know."

After an unplanned moment of silence, Nadalia reached over and took Angela's hand in hers, which was just as clammy. A huff unified their sentiments. They continued to drive in silence until they reached Angela's hotel in midtown. Once Angela was checked in, they went to her room to review their plans.

"I have a copy of his schedule," Angela said. She placed her bag down on the chair near the desk and paced the floor rubbing her hands together.

"Yeah?" Nadalia didn't know what else to say other than expressing her strong desire to abort this mission. However, she was here now. She took a seat at the end of the bed. Standing seemed strange, pacing made her crazy, and sitting helped to keep her still.

"You still want to go through with this?"

Nadalia closed her eyes and sighed. Either Angela had penetrated her mind or she was also having second thoughts. "We're here now."

"You're right." Angela paced to the window and looked out over the Manhattan skyline.

"Let's get this over with," Nadalia said, rising from the bed. "I can't stretch this out any longer. Where are they…or where should they be now?"

Angela rummaged through her purse and pulled out her cell phone. Thumbing through the screen, she looked up at Nadalia. "They should be at the hotel. I'm still checking."

"What are you checking?"

"I put a little something in his cell phone so that I can track him."

"Angela! How do you even know how to do these things?"

Angela giggled and then winked at Nadalia. "I'm a gadget girl."

Nadalia looked at her like she wasn't buying her excuse.   "Really. There's this website where you can buy all kinds of spy equipment. It's amateur stuff, but works. I have a tracker on his car and his phone. I just haven't been able to get the tap working properly so I can't hear his calls."

"Are you kidding me? You got this stuff from a website?"

"Yep." Angela stood proudly.

"Girl! I'm scared of you and Coffey should be, too." They laughed.

"Okay, Doc Brown!" Nadalia said, referring to the inventor of the time machine from the movie *Back to the Future*. "Get your gadgets together and let's do this already." Nadalia picked up her purse from the bed and headed to the door.

Laughing, Angela said, "Funny, but I bet you'll appreciate my inner Doc-ness."

Outside, they hailed a cab a few blocks to the hotel where Coffey had registered. Angela walked in with Nadalia right behind her.

"Hi!" Angela said cheerfully. "I'm here to pick up the key to my room." She started rummaging through her bag. "Oh goodness! I can't seem to remember the room number." She played with her cell phone as if she was looking for the information in her messages. "Jeez! My husband came in yesterday. His name is Coffey Davis and I'm Angela Davis." The young looking black hotel attendant looked at her knowingly and smiled. "Yeah. I know. Angela Davis." She held a fist in the air, acknowledging the coincidence of sharing a name with a famed activist, whom she looked nothing like. Angela was tall, a darker shade of brown with a weave that reached her lower back.

The attendant laughed. "Let me check on your room for you."

"He probably has both keys and forgot to leave one down here for me. We have such a busy schedule today. He had a couple of meetings this morning, so I told him to leave a key for me at the front desk. He's here

Renee Daniel Flagler

on business. I'm here to shop!" Angela threw her head back and laughed heartily. "We're gonna have dinner and catch a show on Broadway tonight. I'm so excited. I don't get to New York much, but you can probably tell, right?"

Nadalia was impressed by Angela's acting skills and figured the woman would give her a key just to shut her up.

"Oh! Silly me!" Angela tapped herself on the forehead. "You must need my ID, right?"

Nadalia was nervous and started checking messages on her cell phone to busy herself.

"Thanks!" The attendant took the ID, glanced at it and smiled politely. "Okay, ma'am. I have your reservation right here, just give me one moment."

Angela smiled and Nadalia turned around letting her eyes wash over the people moving about in the lobby.

"All right! Would you like two keys or one?"

"Go ahead and give me two and thank you so much. I'm a mess when I get to New York. I get so excited. I know I'll need a backup."

"You're welcome. Please enjoy your stay!"

Angela hurried to the elevator with Nadalia on her tail. When they entered, both of them exhaled.

"You are a mess! I was so nervous. I swear I really feel like I'm on some kind of covert operation," Nadalia said.

Angela laughed. "That was fun."

Nadalia turned to Angela. "You've done this before, haven't you?"

Angela smirked. "For other wives." Her smirk faded. "But never for me."

The air in the elevator dissipated suddenly. Nadalia couldn't wait to get off. A fragile silence dominated for a few moments until Nadalia broke it.

"Do you think they're in the room?"

"I doubt it because I think he's scheduled to meet someone for breakfast. I couldn't get a read on his phone. I was hoping to find some undeniable proof before approaching him. You know, like some bimbo he left waiting for him, or the panties she may have left in his bed. I just want to check things out."

"I'm following your lead." Nadalia couldn't think clearly enough to be strategic and she was sticking to her suspicion of Sage being Coffey's cover up.

"We are going to be in and out, quick. Then maybe we can get something to eat before our next move. We can hang out in the lounge, then we'll be able to see them when they come in."

"Okay."

The elevator doors opened and they looked at each other before stepping out. Looking for the direction of the room numbers, they headed right.

At the door, Angela tapped and said, "Room service," in a bad Spanish accent. There was no answer, so she tapped once more time before sliding her key in the door. A small green light flashed and Angela turned the knob. Together they tipped inside the huge suite and paused when they heard a sound coming from the bedroom.

"Did you hear that?" Angela whispered.

"What was it?"

"I don't know. Let's go see."

Nadalia's heart dropped into her stomach and she wanted to bolt out of the door. She turned back and Angela grabbed her by her arm. "What are you doing?"

Nadalia sighed, but continued to follow Angela toward the sounds. The two of them stood still and tried to listen more keenly. Neither could make out what they heard, so they continued moving forward. Half empty bottles of liquor and clothes were tossed about in the living room. Music filtered through the suite. When they got to the door of one of the bedrooms, which was wide open they paused.

Nadalia peeked in and noticed the bed sheets were ruffled. The shower could be heard running from the other side of the room.

A deep groan bellowed out of the cracked bathroom door. The women froze and looked at each other again. Red undertones flushed underneath Angela's brown skin. Nadalia could tell she was upset as her lips twisted into a tight circle. Another groan flowed through the space. Nadalia's hand flew to her heart. She felt for Angela. It was obvious that Coffey wasn't in that shower alone.

Another deep moan resonated from the bathroom. Angela's chest heaved and she charged into the bathroom screaming Coffey's name. Nadalia was stuck in her spot, unable to move. She didn't follow Angela because she didn't want to witness his infidelity and cause Angela any more embarrassment.

Nadalia watched Angela disappear into the bathroom and then for a quick moment everything was silent. Nadalia wondered what happened until she heard Angela's deafening scream.

Nadalia wanted to cover her ears. It sounded like Angela had seen a dead person. Curiosity made her want to see what Angela had seen. Fear kept her feet glued to the floor.

"You bastard!" Angela screamed again and then yelled her name, "Nadalia!"

Nadalia ran into the bathroom. Coffey was wet and naked, pleading with Angela as he tried to pick her up off the floor. She was fighting him off.

Nadalia stepped in, but looked up and found herself unable to breathe or move at the sight of another wet masculine body stepping out of the shower.

Chapter 35

Nadalia

"Nadalia!" Sage's voice sounded like it was coming through a tunnel.

But Sage was not alone. Yet another naked man emerged from the shower.

Natalia did the only thing she could do. She turned and ran.

"Nadalia wait!" he screamed as he ran after her.

Nadalia ran through the suite and tried to make it out the door, but Sage caught up with her. He pried her hands from the doorknob.

"Nadalia, wait!"

Finally, his voice started coming through clearly. She looked at him as if he was a stranger, refusing to process what he was saying. Nadalia started punching him on his bare chest.

"Get off of me! Don't ever touch me again!"

"Dali, calm down. Let me explain." Sage pleaded.

"Don't call me Dali! Men, Sage? You disgust me!" Nadalia continued pounding her fists into his chest and landed a few lucky ones on his face. He tried to contain her wild arms.

She couldn't believe she had just witnessed her husband with not one, but two men.

From the bedroom, Nadalia heard Angela cursing and crying while Coffey pleaded. Looking down at Sage's exposed body, she felt repulsed, fighting the urge to vomit. The same body that had turned her on for years was being shared with men. Growing weary, Nadalia stopped punching him and tried for the door again.

But he blocked her way. "Please, Dali. I can't let you go like this."

She glared at him sideways. "Move out of my way."

"We need to talk first."

"I have nothing to say to you!"

"Baby!"

Nadalia slapped him. "I'm not your baby!" Emotions she couldn't explain whirled inside. She didn't know how to feel. Maybe if it had been women…she stopped and shook her head. It didn't matter if it were men or women, this betrayal was more than she could handle. She pushed him hard. He tripped and his back slammed against the door.

And then she saw the other man, someone she didn't know tiptoeing into the second bedroom. And Nadalia crumpled to the floor.

Sage lowered himself and tried to comfort her. She slapped his hand away. All the episodes of his recent inability to respond to her sexually and finally, she understood why.

Sage left her alone long enough to put on some pants and a shirt, and then came back to her.

Nadalia had wanted to, but, she hadn't moved. She couldn't.

He knelt beside her. "Nadalia," he called her name. The pain in his voice made his words sound like whispers.

"Stop it!" she snapped and stood to her feet. She wanted to leave, but she needed to check on Angela.

Nadalia carried herself to the bedroom. Each step felt like her body weighed a ton. Not caring whether or not she was intruding on their private business, Nadalia went straight into the room without warning. Angela was seated on the side of the bed and Coffey was standing in front of her, pleading. Seeing his exposed body embarrassed Nadalia; she turned away when they looked up at her.

"I need to go, Angela."

Angela stood up. "I'm going with you." Coffey tried to block Angela's path and she pushed him. His brawn body didn't budge. "Get out of my way, Coffey."

"Please, Angela. We have to finish this."

"You've already done that. To think I told Nadalia I intended to fight for you when I suspected that you may have been cheating on me. But it's obvious that I can't compete with men."

Coffey dropped his head and his hands. "Baby. It was just...I love you."

Angela pushed at him again. "Stop saying that!" she screamed.

"Let's go, Angela!"

Angela stepped around Coffey and took the hand Nadalia held out for her. Holding one another tight, they limped through the suite as if they were physically wounded. When they entered the living room, she looked up at Sage. His eyes were red and strained. Though she hadn't seen any tears, Nadalia assumed he was crying. She sucked her teeth. He started to walk over to her, but she held her hand up. Angela squeezed the hand she was holding for support.

Coffey finally entered the room. Nadalia could tell when Sage shifted his eyes to focus behind them, and then shifted his hopeless expression back to Nadalia. Refusing to witness the desperation and pleading in his eyes, she turned away, lifting her chin she reached for the door.

Coffey ran over to them. "You can't tell anyone about this!"

Nadalia's jaw dropped and Angela glared at him with a look as if she smelled something putrid. Sage turned to face another direction.

"After what we just witnessed, all you care about is other people finding out? You're pathetic. Just wait until I tell your son."

Coffey lunged forward. Nadalia pushed Angela out of the way. Sage ran over to block them. But instead of hitting Angela, Coffey melted to his knees and cried out.

"You can't do that!"

Disgusted, Nadalia grabbed Angela, who had been staring at Coffey in awe, and dragged her out of the room, slamming the door behind them.

Chapter 36

Ryan

R yan was up having coffee with her mother when the call came in. She braced herself to answer, knowing Anderson would be upset. She got one last smile in before her stomach began to flutter in anticipation of the impending scolding.

"Where are you?"

"I stopped by my mother's house. Why?" Even the little lie felt good to her. It was her way of getting vengeance—gaining some ground. "You made it home," she said as if all was well.

"Get your ass here now!" Anderson hung up the phone.

"I'll be there shortly," Ryan said into the dead line as her mother watched her over the rim of her coffee cup. "Did you eat?" She paused a moment. "Okay. See you soon," she added for good measure.

"The old bugger found his way back home, huh?" Frannie said, placing her cup down and getting up from the table. "I guess I'll see you later. It was a nice surprise seeing you this morning."

Frannie reached across the table to take Ryan's cup, but Ryan stopped her. "I'm not done."

"You're not leaving?"

"I… I just want to finish my cup of coffee. Sit down and finish it with me."

"Oh!" Frannie slowly sat down. "Okay. I figured you'd want to hurry home and see your man. It's been weeks since you've laid eyes on him. I know if it was my man, I'd want to jump his bones!" Frannie hooted.

"Ma!"

"Ah, girl. I'm just kidding you. Go ahead and finish your fake coffee."

"Why do you keep calling it fake?"

"I mean really. Why even bother drinking decaf. What's the point?"

"I like the taste and I'm trying to pull back on the caffeine because of the baby."

"Whateva!" Frannie waved away Ryan's explanation. "Anyways, you thought of any names yet?"

"No. I have plenty of time for that. Right now I'm just trying to focus on taking care of myself. I want this pregnancy to go well."

"Well, I think you should name her after her grandma. Ha!"

"I bet you would, Ma." Ryan finished off the last bit of coffee and stood. "Thanks. I'll call you later."

Ryan wasn't ready to go home, but with all the nervous energy spinning around inside of her, she found it hard to continue to sit still. She got in the car and pulled away from her mother's house, but a few blocks down, she pulled over to get her nerves together. She was in no rush to face Anderson, but knew that if she took too long, it would only make things worse.

Flutters took flight in her stomach as she pulled into their driveway. Anderson's Maserati was sitting in front of the garage, which meant he had been out since he came home—probably looking for her.

Slowly, Ryan got out of the car and took her time getting to the door. It swung open just as she reached it and Anderson stood there with fire in his eyes. He snatched her inside with one strong pull.

"What took you so long?"

"I...I was just finishing up with Mom."

"I told you I'd be home today. You should have been here when I arrived."

"You say a lot of things, but don't always do them."

Anderson scowled at her. Ryan didn't back down, but inside those flutters sloshed around in her stomach and chest.

Anderson stormed off to the back of the house. Ryan followed him because she knew she was expected to. He snatched the remote from the side table, plopped down and turned on the TV.

Without looking her way, he continued talking, "What were you doing in the city?"

"I..." Ryan was at a loss for words at first. She almost forgot about telling him she was the one who saw him with her own eyes. She could have kicked herself.

She would have never said that to him if they were face to face. "I wanted to see a show."

"I told you how I feel about you going out there without me."

"I was bored," Ryan whined. She was still standing. "You leave me here for weeks at a time. You won't let me work. You won't let me go anywhere. Besides my mother, I have nobody to talk to."

"You don't need to work. You're my wife. And you have Nadalia, Pearson and Vonnie to talk to."

"They all have jobs. They're business owners who lead busy lives. They're not available all of the time. Besides," Ryan dropped her head, "I'm not even sure if they like me that much. So, I get lonely."

Anderson looked over at her for the first time, but just for a moment. She thought she saw him soften a little.

"And what's this crap about some tabloid?"

Ryan went into the kitchen and pulled out the magazine. She took it back to the room, dropped it on the couch next to where Anderson sat and stepped back. "That's the same woman I saw you with at the restaurant."

Anderson picked up the paper, scanned it and tossed it aside, laughing.

"What's so funny?" Ryan was getting frustrated.

"I told you not to believe that silly tabloid stuff."

"I saw you with her." Ryan raised her voice. Anderson's neck snapped in her direction. She adjusted her tone. "Tabloid or not, what am I supposed to think?" Anderson's eyes were still locked on her, but she pressed forward, determined to stand her ground. "I'm tired of this, Anderson." She waited for his response.

Anderson drew in a deep breath. She was expecting the thunder of his harsh words, but instead he began explaining.

"I'm not messing around with her. Those pictures are from the set. Somebody on the crew must have taken them and sold them for a nice price. You'll see when the movie comes out. The only reason we were in New York that day was to do a photo shoot for the promo materials. We had just enough time to do the shoot, have lunch and get back on the plane to head to the next location. That's why I didn't bother telling you because I wouldn't have had the time to see you anyway."

Anderson got up, went to the kitchen, got a beer and sat back down.

Ryan wanted to believe him and since this was the first time he ever offered any kind of explanation, she decided that it would be sufficient. She thought it was ironic that she had given the same story to the girls when Nadalia told her about seeing the tabloid at dinner.

"Well you could have at least let me know."

"Next time I will."

Anderson took sips of his beer in silence as he watched the screen, flipping channels.

She loved Anderson and despite the fact that he wasn't perfect, she still felt lucky to be with him. This baby would help change things. She just knew it. Ryan was also relying on showing a little more firmness. He hadn't flipped out on her as she expected him to. Maybe if she did it a little more often, things would get a little better and she'd have more say.

"Andy."

Instead of responding he looked over at her.

"I want you to be around more. No more coming and going as you please without at least letting me know where you are. That's not fair to me."

"Anything else, Ryan?" he said sarcastically.

"Yes." Anderson turned to face her. "I just want you to know that I'm fed up with the way things have been. If things don't change. I'll…I'm going to have to…"

"What, Ryan?"

"Leave…" Ryan was proud of her audaciousness—scared, but proud.

Anderson studied her. She became uncomfortable under his gaze. Then he reached for her, pulled her close and kissed her. That same spark that ignited between them on the steps months back had returned.

Ryan kissed him back. Anderson crawled on top of her and squeezed her small breasts in his hands, pulled up her shirt, and took her nipples in his mouth.

Ryan felt like she had gained some power. She tugged at his belt, unzipped his pants, released his erection and massaged it. Then, wiggling free from under him, she knelt down in front of him on the couch and took his rigidness into her mouth, stroking him until he called out her name. She rose just before he reached his peak and sat facing him. He guided himself inside and with the power she felt, she matched him thrust for thrust until his face twisted in sweet agony and he released himself, grunting in staccato. He kept pumping until Ryan's muscles twitched and she cried out in ecstasy.

Even in her pleasurable exhaustion, she felt like she had gained some ground again and wondered if her firmness was a turn on for him. She also knew that if she said she would leave, she'd have to actually be willing to do it in order for Anderson to become a true believer.

Chapter 37

Vonnie

Vonnie didn't know whether to be scared or angry. She hadn't seen nor heard from Mike since she left to go to dinner with the girls the evening before. Dialing his number once again and praying that he would answer, Vonnie walked circles around herself. Now the calls were going straight to voicemail.

"Mike!" she yelled. "At least call me!" she screamed as if he could possibly hear her.

One the verge of tears, Vonnie went to her room and threw herself on the bed. This wasn't like Mike at all. He'd never just disappear this way. Vonnie's mind was a frenzy of wild thoughts. She prayed to keep herself sane.

"Lord, please don't let my husband be dead. I don't know what I would do without him. And if he isn't dead, forgive me for trying to kill him when he finally walks through that door!"

Vonnie's cell phone rang and she dived over the bed to retrieve it from the nightstand. "Hello!" she said, hoping it was Mike and then realized she hadn't even bothered to look to see who was calling. It was a wrong number and Vonnie felt like tossing the phone across the room.

Vonnie imagined Mike stranded along the side of the road, hurt, unable to get to his cell phone to call for help. For a moment she thought about getting into her car and riding around to see if she could find him. Maybe he had been car jacked and the thugs took everything, his wallet, cell phone, car, and all of his money. Then she thought that he would have walked somewhere and called for help and would be home by now.

Then she imagined him lying asleep next to another woman, intoxicated by a night of wild sex, which made him forget his wife, the time and his wits. Then Vonnie thought, what if he was with another woman? Would that mean the end of them? Did he love her? He couldn't love her if he was reckless enough to spend the entire night with her without even trying to cover up his philandering ways. Would she be willing to leave? They had so much history and he had never been unfaithful before. Should she give him a second chance? She couldn't turn off her love for him like a light switch.

Vonnie grumbled, filling the room with the sounds of her frustrations. She was running out of possibilities. Each thought made her heart pump a little faster.

"Okay, girl," she said to herself. "Get it together. Something had to happen." Vonnie looked around the bed and picked up her phone. She couldn't recall him telling her where he was going so she wasn't sure who or where to call first. She decided to start with his friends and make her way to his family. She dialed Pearson's number so she could speak to Niles. There was no answer. Vonnie knew he couldn't have been with Anderson because he was out of town. Sage was her only option. She dialed Nadalia. No answer again.

Vonnie ran back to her room to get her iPad. She looked up the numbers to all of the hospitals in the area and called each of them. None of them had Michael Howard in their care. She even tried calling 911 to see if they received any reports for fatal accidents in Nassau and had to bite her tongue to keep from cursing the operator, for not having answers to her ambiguous questions. Vonnie knew she was reaching, but her desperation drove her to the edge of insanity.

Mike's family would be her last resort. Since she didn't have any of their telephone numbers, Vonnie grabbed her purse and ran to the kitchen to get her car keys. She knew where his aunt and cousins lived. They weren't exactly close, but Vonnie didn't care. Nor did she care about the gossiping that would be sure to follow her visit because she needed to find her husband. She prayed that she'd find him alive.

Vonnie made it to the Grand Central Parkway when her phone rang. It was one her sister, Nadine's friends.

"Hey, Trisha! What's up?" Vonnie answered wondering why she was calling. *Please don't let something be wrong with Nadine.* "Is everything okay?"

"That's what I called to ask you."

"Huh! What do you mean?"

"Mike and Andrew are here."

"Here, where? Your job!" Vonnie almost slammed on the brakes right in the middle of the parkway. Trisha worked at Queens Courts as a Correction Officer.

"Mike came to bail Andrew out!"

Vonnie felt her insides grow warm with the slow heat of anger. Mike was alive, which was great, but what was he doing bailing his career-criminal brother out of jail when they had huge financial problems at home?

"No! Both of them are in the cell!"

Vonnie felt a tight squeeze in her chest. "Jail." She was barely audible. Her breathing made it difficult to speak for several moments.

"Vonnie! Are you still there?"

Vonnie was still trying to catch her breath and now tears fell as she imagined Mike in a dank cell alongside real criminals.

"Vonnie!" Trisha called her again.

"What…what happened?" What could Mike have possibly done to be sent to jail?"

"I'm about to get the full story. I just got on duty. I called you as soon as I saw them."

"Did you call Nadine?"

"Don't you worry, baby girl. You're the first call I made. No one will hear this from me."

"Thank you, Trish. I'm on my way." Vonnie picked up her speed.

"If you come now there's not much you can do besides sit and wait for him to be arraigned."

"I can't see him?"

"No! Go home and try to relax. I'll keep you posted and when it's close to the time for him to be arraigned, I'll call you to come."

Vonnie groaned. "There's absolutely no way I can see him?"

"Sorry, hon. No can do."

"Okay. I'll go somewhere and grab a bite to eat. Any idea how long it could take?"

"Anytime from now to practically midnight and that's if he even gets arraigned today. It can be anytime from now to Monday morning, depending on how crowded it is."

"Are you serious?"

"I'm afraid so. If he has a decent lawyer, there's a chance he'll push to get him arraigned sooner but there are no guarantees."

Vonnie remained silent, not knowing what to say.

"Listen, Vonnie. Try to chill out for a while. Let me go in and find out as much as I can and I will call you back. That way, you'll have a better idea of what to do."

"Okay," Vonnie said. Her entire spirit had deflated. She felt like she had been run over by a truck and hadn't slept for days.

"I'll call you back as soon as possible. Okay?"

"Yeah."

Vonnie got off the parkway at the next exit and headed to the diner with all the blue decorations on the corner of Francis Lewis and Horace Harding Expressway.

She didn't have an appetite, so she sat and nursed a few cups of tea waiting for Trisha's call. When her phone rang, she grabbed it with trembling hands. It slipped from her grasp, bobbing in the air a few times before she caught a hold of it and answered.

"Trish!" Vonnie sounded as if she were out of breath.

"Okay, hon. This is what happened. Mike and Andrew were pulled over last night, but were arrested because they found a gun and more than three hundred and fifty thousand dollars cash inside of the car."

Vonnie's heart felt like it stopped, and then plummeted into the pit of her stomach. Her bottom lip trembled. Tears pooled in her eyes.

"What?" Vonnie thought about all of their financial problems and dropped her head back against the head rest. She recalled Mike telling her that he would take care of everything. It must have been much worse than he admitted. Mike was taking desperate measures. Trisha was talking, but Vonnie only heard bits and pieces of what she was saying.

"This sounds crazy and so unlike Mike. But Andrew, that's another story." When Trisha mentioned Andrew, Vonnie paid attention. "Apparently the police have been watching him, but he's always managed to elude them because he doesn't come out much. Both of their lawyers are here and are pushing to get them in front of the judge ASAP so chances are, they will both be arraigned sometime this evening or possibly tonight."

"Thanks, Trisha." Vonnie's voice was small. She wiped her tears. "I'm heading over there now."

"Okay, but you may have to wait a while."

"I don't care. See you soon." She tossed a twenty dollar bill on the table, covering her few cups a tea and a hefty tip.

Vonnie was happy that her husband was alive, but her heart pounded rapidly at the thought of him sitting in a dank cell. He probably felt a little more comfortable with Andrew being with him. She wondered why they had been stopped, but then thought about the fact that in Jamaica, Queens, there wasn't much a black man had to do to be arrested.

Suddenly she was angry at Mike all over again. What stupid thing had he done to end up in jail? How dare Mike place them in such a predicament? What if he was convicted and sent to prison for a long time? What would happen to them? Their life? Their home? Noelle? What would the wives think?

Chapter 38

Pearson

W hen Niles walked out of the room, Pearson rolled over and watched him leave. She was thankful, but felt horrible for him having to babysit her the way he did. Although she had barely been able to lift her head from the pillow the entire day and was probably dehydrated because of all of the throwing up she'd done, yet she craved another drink. She didn't want to think about her mother dying. She didn't want to anticipate how that loss would make her feel.

Pearson wrestled all Niles' efforts to make her better, refusing the water he tried to force her to drink and pushing away the soup he'd made for her from scratch. She even rejected the BLT he tried to feed her piece by piece, which was her favorite.

Pearson reached under her bed and felt for the flask she had hidden there. When she couldn't reach it with her hands, she leaned farther until her head was nearly touching the floor.

"Looking for this?"

Pearson jumped up, whipping her head in Niles' direction. Her breath caught as he stood near the end of the bed dangling her flask. She hadn't even heard him enter the room. Niles shook his head. Ashamed, Pearson looked away and gnawed on her bottom lip.

Niles took a deep breath and sat on the edge of the bed. Neither of them spoke and Pearson could feel the heaviness of what both of them wanted to say.

After a while, Niles got up and repositioned himself next to her. Pearson turned her back to him so he wouldn't see her tears if she started crying. She knew when she caused him pain and hated being the source because she never knew how to soothe him.

Niles slid behind her and spooned her, wrapping his arms around her tight. Pearson's tears came despite her efforts to keep them at bay. She sniffled quietly as if she could succeed in not alerting Niles to the fact that she was crying. Niles held her tighter.

"Pearse," he whispered softly. She cleared her throat, but didn't respond. "I can't say I know exactly what you are going through. I can only imagine how much it hurts." He paused, apparently waiting for some acknowledgement. Pearson remained quiet. "It hurts me to see you in pain, but I cannot—I will not stand by and watch you drink yourself to death."

Pearson's body shook as the tears rushed her. The lump in her throat made it hard to swallow. Niles turned her over and let her cry into his brawny shoulder. Pearson sobbed until her eyes dried out. The release took some of the weight off her, but she still desired the numbing that affects that liquor afforded her.

"I need you to promise me something," Niles said.

"What?" Pearson looked into his eyes.

"Promise me you will keep letting me in." Pearson shook her head. "Don't shut me out. And for your sake, chill out on all the drinking before you get to a point when you can't turn back."

"Niles, I—"

"Don't!" Niles gently placed his finger to her mouth. Pearson looked away. "Okay." She turned back to him.

He wiped away her tears with his thumb and then kissed her eyes. Pearson folded her arms around him and squeezed him tight. She'd do anything for him, including slowing down on her drinking even if it meant having to face her pains head on. With him she could do it or at least she felt like it could be possible.

"Okay!" Niles said, his tone sounding lighter. "I have plans for us tonight. I figured both of us needed to do something to get our minds off all the stuff that's been going on."

"What's that?" Pearson smiled. It was small, but she was making an effort to pull herself out of her slump. She glanced at the clock and then glanced up quickly. "Aren't you supposed to be gone by now? You have a gig in Chicago tonight."

"I cancelled."

"Why?"

Niles looked at her as if the answer should have been obvious. "Did you really think I was going to leave you here the way you were?"

Pearson turned away at first. "Well, where are we going?" She didn't bother trying to convince Niles that she would be fine without him. Once his mind was made up that was it.

"We are going to a comedy show." Niles got up from the bed and stood proud and reached for Pearson. "Remember how we used to always go to comedy shows when we first got together?"

Pearson took his hand and stood with him. "Yes. I remember following our favorite comedians around to all of their performances. That was fun."

"Tonight should be fun." Niles pulled her into his arms.

"Yes. That would be nice."

"Wait right here." Niles disappeared and came back with a large box. "I picked this up after I got the tickets to the show."

Pearson scrunched her brows. "What's this?"

"Open it," Niles coaxed.

"That's why I disappeared earlier." Pearson dropped the box on the bed and ripped it open. Inside there was a black dress and a brand new pair of boots. "Thanks, baby." She kissed Niles and felt like the passion that had taken a back seat in her recent turmoil could possibly return.

Niles held his hand out to Pearson once again. She rolled her eyes playfully and took it. Leading her to the kitchen, he pointed at one of the stools behind the kitchen island where she sat while he prepared a bowl of soup and watched her eat. After that, they got ready for their night out on the town.

Hanging with Niles helped tremendously. Pearson loved how he entertained her with his silly antics. She threw her head back and laughed at his re-enactments of scenes from the comedy show.

"Niles!" she said with a naughty smile. "You are a fool!"

Niles laughed with her as he mimicked a funny gesture from one of their favorite comedians.

Pearson was bent over. "Stop!" I can't take anymore." She put her hand on her chest and tried to stop laughing, then suddenly clenched her knees together. "Ahhh. I have to pee!" Pearson ran in the direction of the powder room, giggling all the way.

She stumbled a bit along the way and thought about the fact that she'd only drank wine during the show, except the few shots of cognac she slipped in when she went off to the bathroom and when Niles left to bring the car around.

She enjoyed the burn of the potent amber spirit created as it slid down her throat. She popped dinner mints after each shot to mask the scent.

Niles' attention had been trained on her the entire night. Pearson melted each time she looked up and noticed him stealing adoring glances. He ran his fingers along her cheek and took her by the hand, giving her loving squeezes.

When they got home, Niles spun her around taking her in.

"Um! You know you can give any twenty-something woman a run for her money." He looked her up and down and smiled, admiring her figure.

"Thank you," Pearson said, trying to get her footing. The spinning made her dizzy.

Niles loosened the cufflinks on his shirt and placed them on the dresser. Stepping out of his shoes, he slid them against the wall. The entire time, his eyes were on Pearson as she undressed, trying to keep steady.

Pearson didn't want to disappoint Niles, but she was getting sleepy. She felt the stirring in her stomach from the mix of wine and cognac and prayed she wouldn't have to vomit. The liquor made the night funnier, more enjoyable, but now it was hitting her. Pearson was slipping into that familiar place that she usually yearned for, but tonight she didn't want to be taken under. She didn't want her memory to fail her.

For the first time ever, she regretted sneaking in extra sips. Pearson wanted to give Niles what he desired. He wanted her affection, but she wasn't sure how much she could coherently offer to him.

"Woo." Pearson had made it out of her clothes and stumbled again.

Niles smile faded when Pearson fell into his arms causing him to lose his balance himself.

"Let's go to bed," she said. Pearson brushed her hand across his groin and giggled. His erection responded immediately. Stretching her eyes wide, she raised a brow and concentrated on the bulge in his slacks. "Is that a sax in your pants or are you happy to see me?"

Their kiss was passionate, but she knew it was sloppy. Entangled in his embrace, Niles pulled her body closer. Pearson hoped she wouldn't pass out.

Chapter 39

Pearson

Before dawn broke, Pearson stirred, reached for Niles, and found his side of the bed empty. She sat up looked at the clock. It was after five in the morning. She felt a familiar thump pounding at her temples and rubbed circles around them. She pulled back the covers, whipped her legs over the side of the bed and took her time standing.

"Niles," she called out, sliding her feet across the rug toward the bathroom. A glow of moonlight sifting through the window illuminated the way for her. Peeking in, she flicked on the light. Niles wasn't there.

Pearson grabbed her robe from the back side of the bedroom door. "Niles?" she continued to call out as she tipped around the house looking for him. She peeked out of the front window. All of his cars were still there. Pearson searched for him in the family room and was struck with the harsh stench of liquor. Broken bottles were strewn across the floor. Dried splash marks created ragged circles in the carpet and spotted the walls with lines. Pearson looked around in awe. Nearly three thousand dollars' worth of liquor had been wasted.

"Niles!" she yelled. There was still no answer. Racing around the first floor of the house, Pearson called his name repeatedly.

Finally Pearson noticed the door to the basement was slightly ajar. She pulled it wider and called his name some more. Pearson ran down the steps and through the basement, peeking in the media and work out rooms before she found Niles sprawled across the floor of his studio, on his back, with his sax still in his hand.

For several moments she watched his chest rise as he slumbered, thinking of the possibilities that drove him to break every bottle of liquor in the house.

Despite the scene before her, she thought about how much a drink could help her deal with Niles' disappointment when he finally woke up.

Pearson backed out of the room, turned and sprinted the two flights to the bedroom. She rummaged through the drawers of her walk-in closet and found a hidden pint of cognac. She twisted it open and took a long sip. Wincing, she wiped her mouth with the back of her hand, looked at the bottle to see how much was left, took another sip and then twisted the cap back on and put it away. She slid to the floor and sat there waiting for her impending confrontation, accompanied by tears that wouldn't stop flowing. If she managed to become numb enough, she could handle the impending fight.

It wasn't long before she heard Niles' footsteps approaching. She hugged her legs, wishing she could simply disappear. Her heart thumped louder as he drew near.

Moving as fast as she could, Pearson reached for the bottle again as she tried to gauge Niles' steps. He was getting closer, but she believed she had enough time to take a quick gulp before he entered the bedroom. The burn soothed her as it went down. She closed her eyes to savor it for a short moment, but when she opened her eyes, Niles stood before her. His eyes were tight slits. Disdain dripped from his expression and he shook his head. Pearson looked from him to the bottle in her hand. Her body shrunk under the mass of shame.

In a swift motion Niles snatched the bottle from her grasp.

"I'm tired of trying to compete. No matter what I do, this," Niles shoved the bottle in her face, "always seems to win." He tossed it across the closet.

"No!" Pearson screamed flinching at the sound of it crashing.

Glass splattered everywhere and the odor filled the space. Niles turned his back and walked off, eating up the length of their large bedroom in just a few steps. Pearson ran over and grabbed him by the arm.

"Niles. Wait!"

He turned, snatching his arm from her grasp. The cutting look he gave her made her release him. "I can't wait anymore, Pearson." His intent wasn't lost on her. He continued toward his closet on the opposite side of the room.

Pearson stayed on Niles' heels. When he reached for his overnight bag, fear catapulted her into action. "You can't leave."

Pearson tried to grab the bag from his hands, pulling with all her might.

"Stop. Stop!" Niles yelled.

Regardless how unsuccessful she was in getting the bag from his grip, she persisted.

"Pearson!" Niles yelled. "I can't do this anymore. Do you know that you fell asleep with my face between your legs last night? Because of your drinking, we can't even make love anymore." Niles walked up to her, pointing his finger. The hurt in his eyes was piercing. "You think I don't see you taking shots behind my back?" Pearson covered her gaping mouth. "I'm tired of fighting a battle that I can't win. All this time, I thought that if I loved you hard enough you would eventually choose me over the bottle." He turned away.

Pearson was compelled by a desperate force. She ran after Niles and stood between him and his clothes, holding her hands out to the side. "Don't you leave me, Niles! I'll stop..." she panted, "but I can't do this one my own."

"I've heard that before," he said and pushed past her.

There was no way she could let him go. With tears streaming down her face, Pearson ran through the room pulling bottles from the backs of drawers and behind furniture.

Niles watched in confused awe.

Pearson took the bottles and tossed them in the tub. With trembling hands, she poured the remnants from each down the drain. After emptying the last one, she melted beside the tub, taking deep breaths. "It's over, Niles. I promise." She looked up at him. "Just don't...." Her words caught when she noticed the tears flowing down his face.

He shook his head, turned and walked out. Pearson wanted to go after him but couldn't find the strength to move. She covered her face with her hands. Her cries rocked her entire body.

Chapter 40

Nadalia

Nadalia had spent the better part of the past hour in the great room with the lights out. The sun had tucked itself in for the night, but Nadalia found that she preferred the dark. It mimicked her mood. This way, she wouldn't risk catching a glimpse of her red, swollen eyes in any of the decorative mirrors.

By late evening, Nadalia couldn't seem to produce any more tears. Her phone still buzzed, chirped and rang, but she refused to look at it, afraid to see Sage's number. The only person she called was Angela to make sure that she made it back home safely after she'd dropped her off at the airport.

Nadalia wondered what she would even say to Sage when he came home—if he came back home. The betrayal was enough to deal with. She may have been able to fight for her man had she found that he was unfaithful, figuring they could get past it. Couples overcame infidelity all of the time. She loved Sage enough to give him a second chance. Not that she intended to make it easy on him. He definitely would have had to work to regain her trust.

Nadalia shook her head and her eyes stung, but no tears fell. How could they ever overcome the fact that he cheated on her with men?

There was no conceivable way to get past that. She couldn't successfully compute the whole ordeal in her mind. She wished she could just flick a switch and turn off the love she had for him. Then she wouldn't feel so tormented. Maybe then, her heart wouldn't feel like it had been snatched out of her chest and trampled on, causing her chest to ache.

How could she face the next day knowing that her life had been changed forever? What would it be like without Sage? What would she tell her mother? What about their friends? She wondered if Niles, Mike and Anderson knew about Sage's penchant for the male kind. Nadalia doubted that they were aware. But what about the wives? She had finally gotten to know them and was actually starting to like each of them. She could never tell the other couples the truth. Separating herself from the pact seemed like her only option.

Nadalia's phone rang again and she continued to ignore it. But, she decided to at least see who tried to reach her. There were calls from her mother, Vonnie, and another from Angela.

There were no messages or texts from Sage. In spite of how upset she was with him, the fact that he hadn't tried to reach out was disheartening. He should be trying harder, but would it have mattered? Nadalia dropped the phone onto the sofa and rested her head against the back.

The locks clicked on the door and Nadalia jumped up. Her heart raced, pounding against her chest at the sound of Sage's footsteps as he entered and walked through the house. She stood, waiting to be discovered, refusing to be the first to call out. Listening, she heard him place his keys on the hook in the kitchen and walk around some more. When he arrived at the entrance of the great room, her breath caught and she stood stark still.

Sage paused at the entrance and stayed there. Apparently he was unsure as to whether or not he should venture inside the room. Nadalia didn't invite him either. She remained steady. The outline of Sage's body shifted and she saw him stuff his hands into his pants pocket. He did this a few times before finally speaking.

"Hey."

Nadalia sighed. That's all he had, she thought and didn't bother to respond.

"Can I come in?" Sage asked.

Nadalia sat back down. That was her answer. Her breathing was returning to normal. Sage cautiously walked into the room. Nadalia wished he had stayed away for a few days rather than just one. Maybe with more time, she would have figured out how to handle seeing him.

Right now, her heart felt like it would just stop beating at any moment. The love she had for him wrestled with the turmoil from his betrayal and deep sense of inadequacy, leaving her feeling emotionally tangled.

"I just want you to know that I never stopped loving you."

Nadalia covered her ears and screamed through the darkness. "Don't you dare say that to me!"

Sage shifted his weight back and forth, from one foot to the other. "I didn't expect this to happen."

"You didn't expect to get caught." Nadalia turned away from him. "How long have you two been slapping penises with other men?" Nadalia stood and held her hands up. "You know what? I don't even want to know." She blazed past him and went back into the kitchen.

Sage followed, keeping a safe distance and turned on the light. "Dali." She shot him with a penetrating glare. "Nadalia," he corrected himself.

Her breath came in gasps and a fresh stream of tears began to fall. "I loved you…trusted you and this is what you do to me! Men, Sage! Freaking men!" Nadalia picked up a plate resting in the dish drainer and tossed it at him. She followed that up with two wine glasses and a bowl, missing him by mere inches.

Sage jerked and flinched avoiding the flying objects, which crashed and shattered across the marble tile. "Get out!" Nadalia tossed the entire dish drainer in his direction and fell to the floor in a wailing heap. "Get out of my sight!"

Sage tried to help Nadalia up and she clawed at him, scratching his face and neck. "Don't touch me!" she cried, arms flailing, she landed several blows on his chest. Sage released her and stepped back.

Nadalia cried into the floor and screamed for him to go, wondering why he wouldn't move. Finally, she lifted herself from the floor, slowly making it to her feet, and then hobbled back into the darkened great room.

Sage followed her again, shaking his head. "Please, Nadalia."

"Please what?" Nadalia glared at him.

"We can find a way to work this out." He pleaded with his whole being.

"This can never ever be worked out."

"I made a mistake. I'm not sure how I even got caught up in this mess. It just happened. I didn't expect it to…" The fire in her eyes seemed to have made him rethink his words. "I love you." Sage changed his direction. "You can't tell me that you don't love me anymore. Can you say that?" Sage's tone was desperate.

Nadalia walked over to him with an eerie calmness about her. "Love has nothing to do with it. Don't worry about leaving. I'll go." Quietly, she walked to their bedroom to pack.

Chapter 41

Vonnie

Mike was released the following day. His attorney worked to get him before the judge before noon. Mike's clean past earned him a release on his own merit without bail. Andrew had to pay $25,000 bail, which a very attractive woman in tight designer digs, long flowing wavy hair, and sunglasses—despite the fact that it was night time—paid for in cash.

Mike locked eyes with Vonnie in the back of the courtroom and she blinked away tears. Mike wasn't cut out for the criminal system. He looked like he had aged since she saw him the day before.

Mike turned away and wouldn't look directly at her again. Once his paperwork was properly stamped and his court date given, he was all set to go.

Vonnie stood as he approached where she was seated on the bench. Mike walked up to her, but still wouldn't make direct eye contact.

"Let's go," he said and walked past her.

Vonnie expected at least a hug. She imagined he would be happy that she was there to support him after this ordeal. She was on his heels as they exited.

Andrew was outside chatting with his lawyer holding the hand of the woman who had bailed him out. Mike walked up, shook the lawyer's hand and whispered something to Andrew. Andrew looked over at Vonnie right behind him and nodded.

Andrew walked over to Vonnie and said hello. She sneered at him. His girlfriend frowned and went to say something and Andrew raised his hand for her to be quiet.

"I'm sorry about all of this, sis." Vonnie crossed her arms and looked away. "I understand," Andrew said and leaned over to plant a kiss on her cheek anyway. Vonnie let that happen.

Andrew put his arm around his woman and waltzed away like he didn't have a care in the world. Vonnie heard the woman say, "Why she mad at you? It wasn't like you dragged him into this."

Andrew told her to mind her business without breaking his stride.

Mike appeared by Vonnie's side. She glared at him, shook her head and headed for the car. Mike followed silently.

Inside the car, Vonnie started the engine and was about to put the car in gear, then sat back. Moments passed in slow motion until Vonnie broke the silence. "Why, Mike?"

"Everything will be fine."

"I don't want to hear that. Do you have any idea what it's like to sit up half the night and day wondering whether or not the person you love is dead or alive? I called friends, hospitals, precincts. People thought I was crazy. What happened to your one phone call? I had to find out about you being in jail from Trisha. Do you know how embarrassing this is? What were you doing in the car with a gun anyway? What were you thinking?"

Mike looked away and then finally focused on Vonnie seething in her seat. "Andrew was helping me out. He was going to invest in the business. We were pulled over. I didn't know he had a gun in the car."

"Are you kidding me? He's a known felon! You know what he does for a living. And don't expect me to believe this crap about him investing in your business." Vonnie curled her fingers into air quotes. "Don't insult my intelligence like that. We come from the same neighborhood." Vonnie paused, waiting for him to come clean.

Mike avoided eye contact at first. Several moments passed before he finally said, "Okay. He was going to flip some money for me."

"Mike! You gave him money to buy drugs?" Vonnie threw her hands up in the air. "Don't you realize you have put our entire family and livelihood in jeopardy? What if you go to jail?"

"I'm not going to jail," Mike said as if he were very sure.

"How can you be sure? You were picked up on a gun charge."

"Drew told them that the gun was his and that I had no clue he had it on him. He took the fall."

"What about us?"

"I did this for us!" Mike shouted.

"No! You did this for you! Do you think Noelle and I care if we live in a mansion or a shack? It's not necessary that Noelle goes to the most prestigious prep school on the east coast. What matters is that we can be a family together all in one place. What matters is that we don't have to strip down and be searched just to spend time with you."

"I care!" Mike yelled, and turned to look out of the window.

"Well I don't. We've been broke before and if we're broke again, we will survive! It's not like we would have to move into the projects."

"It's my responsibility to take care of my family."

"And dammit, it's my responsibility to make sure you don't go to jail trying to do it. Close the damn business if you have to and start a new one."

Mike looked out of the passenger window and wouldn't say anything more. Vonnie jerked the car into gear and sped home.

Words didn't pass between them until they made it inside the house. Vonnie displayed her frustration by taking her shoes off and tossing them into the corner. She stomped over to the console in the foyer and slammed her keys into the draw before marching off toward the bedroom.

Mike lagged behind. Vonnie mumbled to herself when he walked into the room and he stood in the doorway watching her. She rolled her eyes and stripped down to get into the shower. Snatching her robe from the hook inside the door of her walk-in closet, Vonnie continued mumbling as she marched past him on her way to the bathroom.

Mike grabbed her arm. She tossed him a scathing glare.

"I'm sorry."

Vonnie didn't want Mike to witness her softening from his apology, so she tried to pull away, but Mike held on to her.

"You're right. I was desperate and didn't think of how this would affect my family. All I could think of was how to maintain the lifestyle that I had gotten you and Noelle accustomed to living. With or without money, I need you and her in my life." Vonnie sighed. "I'm going to fix this." Vonnie raised her brows. "The right way," Mike added and pulled her into his strong arms.

"You went too far this time."

"I know. However, in order to fix this, we are going to have to make some serious changes. Noelle may have to come out of that school. We may have to find a new place to live. A lot will change."

"We could put this house on the market tomorrow for all I care. I miss Noelle anyway. The schools here are great. We'll start by getting you a good lawyer and getting past this legal mess. Don't do anything stupid like this again."

Mike smiled sheepishly. "Never again."

Vonnie drew in a long breath. "I'm exhausted and I need a shower. You coming?"

Mike took Vonnie by the hand and led her to the bathroom. They showered, washing away the stress and anxiety of the day as much as possible. Together they crawled into the bed and lay in each other's arms.

"Let's talk about our game plan in the morning," Vonnie said.

"Alright."

Mike was alive and safe, but sleep still didn't come easy. She was serious when she said that the money and lifestyle they'd become accustomed to didn't matter, but she knew she would miss it. What would they tell their friends about all of the changes they would have to make? What would she tell the wives?

Chapter 42

Ryan

Ryan wanted to leap off the chaise and shout when Anderson told her that she needed to buy a dress to attend a benefit where he had been asked to speak. If she wasn't pregnant, she would have jumped up and down. Instead, she squeezed her knees together and squealed, clapping her hands like a seal.

"So find something beautiful and elegant. Cameras will be following us all night," Anderson told her.

"I can definitely do that."

"Maybe you can ask one of the wives to help you pick something out. Nadalia has great taste."

Ryan's smile faded, remembering how Anderson had been caught eyeing Nadalia at their Christmas party. She didn't need Nadalia. She had taste, too. "I can pick out something on my own." Her tone was flat.

"I didn't mean anything by it. Anyway. Just go get something."

"Okay. When is the benefit?" Ryan's toothy grin returned.

"Tonight," Anderson said, swiping at the New York Times on his iPad Air.

"Tonight?" Ryan yelled. "And you're just telling me now?"

Anderson looked up at Ryan as if he wondered what the big deal was.

"Yes. Why? What's the problem?"

Ryan threw her head back and grunted. "Anderson!" Ryan looked at the watch hanging from her thin wrist. "I need to go and get something right now. What about my hair? My nails look like crap. You couldn't have told me before now?"

"No."

Ryan waited for more of an explanation and when he went back to reading the news, she and walked out of the room. For a moment she thought about wearing something she already had, then thought that wouldn't work. The few times she did accompany him to awards dinners and benefits, paparazzi was all over them and some of those pictures ended up on the internet and in the rags. Not that they cared about her, but she had been standing right by his side. Surely some big-eyed fashion critic would slam her for repeating an outfit when her husband was a celebrity. That wouldn't look good for Anderson.

Ryan jumped in the shower and headed out in search of a perfect dress for the evening. Then she asked her mom to call in a favor and get her squeezed in for a last minute appointment with her good friend who owned a hair salon over in Rockville Center.

Ryan wasn't much to make a big fuss over getting dressed, so within hours she had her act together, surprising Anderson when she strolled down the stairs with the grace of Elizabeth Taylor in her heyday.

With his cell phone plastered to his ear, Anderson paused, training his eyes on Ryan with his mouth slightly ajar. Her green gown brought out the matching hue of her eyes. Her straight hair was swept into a chic bun with wisps of sweet tendrils gracing her neck and temples. She turned slightly as she descended so that he could see how the back dipped dangerously into her lower back, while still maintaining its elegance. The long strip of dangling diamonds cascaded down the sides of her jawline like crystal waters—a perfect complement to the diamond bracelet she wore. Silver stilettos completed her ensemble.

"Let me call you back," Anderson managed to say when he finally found words.

Anderson's gesture made Ryan feel beautiful. Even with a million dollar wardrobe, Ryan couldn't remember the last time her husband actually made her feel pretty. A coy smile spread across her face and her cheeks grew warm.

Anderson met her at the bottom of the staircase and held his hand out to her. Ryan took it, allowing him to guide her for the last few steps in old Hollywood style. A giggle escaped and she covered her mouth, trying to maintain her elegant stride.

Anderson looked quite dapper himself. His long, lean body poured into that tuxedo like it was molded just for him. His eyes twinkled.

"Let's get your coat. The driver should be here momentarily," he said still holding her hand.

What he did next surprised her completely. Anderson leaned over and planted a sweet peck on her lips for no reason at all.   Ryan swallowed hard before she could breathe again. Closing her eyes, relishing in the moment for as long as she could, secretly wishing this would last forever. He hadn't been that randomly affectionate with her in years.

"Um," Ryan finally managed to croak out. She cleared her throat. "We're not driving?"

"No! They agreed to have a car pick me—I mean us—up and bring us home when they asked me to speak at the event."

"Oh. Very nice."

Ryan headed to the guest room that she had turned into a ballet studio to retrieve her fur coat. Normally she wouldn't have worn it, but tonight was special.

Anderson held her hand as they engaged in small talk while waiting for their driver. The perfect gentleman, Anderson draped her coat over her bare back, held the door and guided her into the car once it arrived.

Already giddy from the attention Anderson showered on her, Ryan tried her best to remain graceful once they arrived at the event, which was held at another one of those ritzy venues in The Hamptons.

Ryan took a deep breath and smiled before Anderson guided her out of the car. The moment they stepped out, blinding flashes of lights flooded her vision. She held Anderson's hand tight. Even after being married to Anderson for more than five years, absorbing all of the attention that was being showered upon him was a bit much for her to adjust to.

A woman on the sidelines, called out to Anderson, declaring her affection for him, despite Ryan being right by his side. Ryan kept her smile pinned to her face as they walked the red carpet waving to screaming fans. She twisted her small frame just right for the media's volley of photos.

Once inside, she sighed with relief. A young woman with a head full of curly red hair and hopeful eyes approached her and Anderson with an extended hand.

"Thank you so much for coming on such late notice." She nodded at Anderson and then Ryan, and then swept her arm in the direction of a scrawny young man to her right with thick black curls set atop a thin face. "This is Paul. Let him know if you need anything. He will take care of you tonight."

Paul nodded. Taking Anderson by the hand, he gushed. "I'm a huge fan, sir. It's an honor." He turned to Ryan and flashed a toothy grin and nodded politely. "My pleasure, ma'am. Just follow me."

The young man led them off to a draped area just outside the hall. Behind the curtain sat a few mod sofas, a couple of high top tables, and a private bar.

"Can I get you something, sir?" He turned to Ryan. "Ma'am?"

"Sure," Anderson responded loosening the button on his tuxedo. "I'll take your best scotch."

"We've got a fine selection. You will be pleased. And you, ma'am?"

"Cranberry with a twist of lime will be fine for me."

"You got it. Just get comfortable and I'll bring you to your table once it's time to get started."

Anderson stepped away to greet a few of the other male celebrities in the room. Ryan looked around taking in the scenery, recognizing several entertainers, a few of Long Island's richest and a handful of local politicians. This was obviously the VIP area.

Her gaze swept across the room taking in the vibrant atmosphere and that's when she noticed her—— the same woman from the restaurant and the tabloids. Anderson's co-star. Their eyes locked and it was evident that she had been watching Ryan from the second she entered the room.

Never one to invite conflict, Ryan wanted to look away, but didn't want to appear intimidated. The woman didn't smile, she just kept Ryan fastened in her gaze. Ryan could have sworn she saw the woman's upper lip curl up into a slight sneer.

A touch on Ryan's shoulder pulled her from her trance. The young man handed her the drink.

"Thank you." Ryan smiled politely and took her glass.

"The pleasure is all mine," he said and scurried away.

When Ryan looked back in the woman's direction, she was gone. She looked around and couldn't find her anywhere. Then she scanned the room for Anderson and spotted him engaged in a conversation with a few other polished looking gents in tuxedos. Throwing his head back, he let out a hearty laugh, holding his belly.

Shortly after, everyone was escorted to their respective tables. Unlike when they first came in, the room was now filled, buzzing with chatter and aglow with the elegant sparkle of sequence encrusted gowns and gleaming jewels. They were seated at a table near the stage so that Anderson could have easy access when it was time for him to speak. A few of the fellows that he was chatting with were also seated there with their wives or significant others. Everyone at their table greeted each other politely. All seats were filled except one on the other side of Anderson.

Ryan discreetly searched the room again looking for the woman and snapped her head toward Anderson when he and the other men at the table stood. Being the perfect set of gentlemen, they all waited for her to sit before taking their seats again. Ryan craned her neck around Anderson to see her up close. One of the wives at the table scowled and turned away.

"Hey! You made it," Anderson said to the woman who had locked her eyes on Ryan in the other room. He wrapped his arms around her.

She nodded to the men at the table and offered up a weak, but cordial smile to the woman. The women who scowled before rolled her eyes and looked away.

"You never met my wife Ryan before, have you?" The woman looked around Anderson, uninterested and sat back. Anderson seemed to be oblivious to her sneer. "Ryan, this is Carmen Childs. My recent co-star and an unbelievable up and coming actress," he said proudly. "Carmen, this is my lovely wife, Ryan!"

Carmen flashed a fake smile that ended flat, but offered no words. The woman across the table sniffed and peered at Ryan and then shook her head. She put her glass down and tossed Ryan a quick warning glance before getting up from the table.

Ryan leaned into Anderson and pushed her hand into his. He held her in his grip.

The lights dimmed, the music stopped, and the redhead took to the podium to welcome all of the guests. After she thanked everyone for coming she called Anderson to the podium to deliver his speech. Ryan knew her husband well, but hadn't seen his charismatic side in years. He seduced the crowd. They gave him a standing ovation, partly because of his speech and partly because he pledged a half million dollars to the organization for their diligent help with displaced families recovering from the devastating aftermath of Hurricane Sandy.

Ryan's eyes glassed over as she stood with the rest of the guests clapping as he descended from the stage. Her admiration for him had been restored. The consummate actor, and perfect gentleman when he chose to be, Anderson pulled Ryan into his arms and kissed her forehead before taking his seat. From her peripheral, she caught the way Carmen's mouth twisted at Anderson's display of affection. Ryan wondered what her problem was.

The redhead ordered everyone to continue eating, drinking and being merry before taking her leave from the podium. The band played a familiar, lively song that brought many couples to the floor. Others took to the open bars and silent auctions taking place in the back of the room. Anderson had a line of people waiting to chat with him, and shake his hands, until he was whisked away for more red carpet photos with some of the other VIPs in the room.

Ryan gave him his space and headed to the bar for a Shirley Temple. Enjoying the vibe, she swayed to the music until a voice close to the back of her head arrested her attention. Turning slowly, Ryan already knew who it was.

Ryan no longer felt pretty when she was finally face to face with Carmen. She assessed how Carmen's flawless almond skin glowed. Her pink sweetheart shaped lips parted slightly, her tall, lean frame held small curves. However, the envy that flickered in Carmen's hazel eyes dulled the perfection of her beauty.

"So you're the wife. Didn't know he was into white girls. He keeps you well hidden," Carmen said, leaning up against the bar.

Ryan tilted her head to the side to finish taking her in. She was used to bold women when it came to her husband and usually didn't pay them much attention. "And?"

"My suggestion would be that you hold on tight. There are a lot of predators out there," Carmen said slyly, pushing her full lips into a pouty smirk.

"Yes, Andy loves this white girl. Don't you worry about the predators because I sure don't. Like you said, *I'm* the wife!" Ryan took her drink, gave the bartender a polite smile and a hefty tip before turning back to Carmen. "Enjoy your evening," she added and sauntered off with one hand on her belly.

Walking straight up to Anderson, Ryan smiled at him and lifted up on her toes with her lips puckered. Anderson leaned in to meet her, planting a series of pecks on her lips. Ryan glanced back at Carmen who was taking the whole scene in and winked. Carmen returned a hard scowl.

"This was great, honey. I'm coming to all of your events from now on," Ryan said and smiled, watching Carmen from the corner of her eye.

For Carmen's sake, Ryan stayed glued to Anderson's side until she had to go to the bathroom. Inside the restroom, she relieved herself and took to the mirror to freshen up her lipstick. Carmen appeared in the mirror beside her.

Ryan swallowed hard, cleared her throat, and then snapped her purse closed. She didn't want Carmen to know how much her presence affected her.

Before she could walk away, Carmen closed the space between them. Her eyes bore into Ryan. She braced herself for whatever was to come. This wouldn't be the first time some bold groupie or green actress tried her. Things were finally better between her and Anderson so

Ryan was ready to let her know that she didn't stand a chance.

With her hand on her hips, Ryan turned to Carmen. "What do you want?"

"For you to leave already."

"Excuse me." Ryan's race wrinkled in confusion.

"I'm tired of waiting on the sidelines so if he doesn't have the nerve to tell you then it would be my pleasure."

Ryan felt her hands tremble, but she couldn't let it show. "Tell me what?" Ryan's hands were on her hips. She dared Carmen with her stance.

"That he wants a divorce. He loves me now. When the baby comes," Carmen leered and delicately placed one hand on her flat stomach and in her other, she held up a sonogram picture before she continued, "he's going to put you out, but why should I have to wait?" She smirked and lifted her shoulders in a confident shrug.

This time, Ryan couldn't hide the trembling in her hands. She held her back rigid to keep from doubling over. Carmen's verbal blow felt like a punch in the gut and rendered her immobile. Seconds later, Ryan's hand connected with Carmen's face. She hadn't even realized that she'd slapped her until the she heard her scream and saw Carmen holding her cheek.

Before Carmen could respond in any other way, Ryan hastened out of the bathroom in search of Anderson.

"You bitch!" Carmen's words hit Ryan's back.

Ryan dismissed Carmen's cursing. Her only focus was getting to Anderson. Her skin grew warm as she scanned the crowd. She finally spotted him near the center of the room. Ryan sailed toward him.

"Anderson!" She blew out his name in a rush of air. Her chest heaved. Tears stung her eyes. "You bastard." Once again, she'd struck before she realized it.

Anderson stood looking dazed. He held his cheek in the same fashion that Carmen had moments before. "What the—"

"Anderson!" Carmen came yelling behind them.

Ryan turned and shot Carmen a look so scathing, she halted mid run. Then she glared at Anderson. "Congratulations on the new baby, jackass!"

Anderson's mouth hung ajar. With that Ryan turned and walked out.

Chapter 43

Pearson

P earson looked up, ready to scold the person who just burst through her office door and found Candice standing in the entrance. Her assistant peered around Candice as if she had just lost a battle. As annoyed as she was, she hoped to look up and see Niles standing there. She hadn't seen or heard from him since he walked out on her the other day and he wouldn't answer any of her calls. She tried her best not to drink herself into an incoherent stupor, but loneliness wrapped its painful hands around her neck. A drink here and there was the only thing that helped her breathe. She had at least made a conscious effort to monitor her intake.

"I'm sorry, Mrs. Day. I tried to tell her that I would notify you, but she just kept walking," her assistant said.

Pearson's brows cinched.

"No worries, dear. I understand that you are just doing your job, but I don't need an appointment to see my own daughter," Candice said, removing her gloves as she invited herself all the way into Pearson's office.

Nat shrank and started to back out of the door.

"It's, okay. I'll deal with my…" Pearson looked at Candice and noticed that she looked thinner than the last time she'd seen her. The realization gave her pause. After another beat, she finished her sentence, "…mother."

Once the door closed, Candice eased on to the couch and paused to take in a labored breath. Making a noticeable point of glancing at her watch, Candice said, "It's lunch time. Shall we go out or have something delivered?"

Pearson folded her arms across her chest. "Who said you were staying?"

Candice's gaze swept around the office and then she yawned, apparently unaffected by Pearson's attitude. The creases in her worn eyes deepened.

"Tell me. What do you feel like having today? Sushi? I know how you love sushi. Try to decide quickly. I haven't eaten a thing all day."

"I feel like asking you to leave. I have a lot of work to do. Getting ready for this benefit has taken up a lot of my time." Pearson walked to the door and opened it for Candice to leave.

Candice looked at Pearson and chuckled. Pearson slammed the door shut, crossed her arms and cut her eyes toward the ceiling. Candice's appearance unnerved Pearson. Her tired eyes and thinning face were the visual indications of her debilitating condition thus far. The sickness was beginning to claim her normally polished and well-cared for skin. As familiar as Pearson was with loss, the last thing she wanted to witness was her mother's lingering demise. She was better equipped to manage anger as opposed to pain.

"Alright, Ma. What do you want? Let's make it quick."

"I want to talk to my daughter." Candice hid her smile behind her pout.

"We can talk another time. I have so much work to do now." Pearson walked back to her desk and began shuffling files across the top.

"We can talk another time," Candice mimicked and chuckled again. "You remind me so much of myself it's unbelievable." Candice got up and moved toward the window taking in the mountains of snow still sitting in the parking lot. "We could talk if you would answer the phone when I called you or open the door when I tried to visit. If you would just stop avoiding me."

"I'm not avoiding you." Candice pursed her lips at Pearson. Her low cast eyes belied her words. "I mean."

"Sweetheart, I know what you mean, but that's not what you are saying."

Pearson looked baffled.

Candice sighed, walked over and sat on the edge of Pearson's desk. She lifted Pearson's chin and searched her eyes, watching them become glossy. Pearson jerked her face away. Candice touched her chin again. More gently than before. "Look at me, Pearson." Sighing, Pearson turned back to face her mother. "I'm dying." Candice's words sunk in. Pearson averted her eyes again so that Candice wouldn't witness the strain of her holding back tears. "I can't change that," Candice finally added.

Tears belied Pearson's will. She wanted to pull away, but her mother continued to hold her firmly allowing the tears to tumble onto her hand.

"I hate it, but I have to face it." Candice choked on her admission. "But it's a reality that we all have to face." Candice let go of Pearson, went to her purse, pulled out a tissue and dabbed her eyes.

After a deep breath, she continued. "I haven't been the best mother. Woo. There I said it." Candice blinked rapidly and sighed. "I didn't have the best example myself so I didn't know how to be a good mother." Candice took a moment, crossed her arms and walked back to the window, looking out as she continued. "Facing the end of my life has made me reevaluate some things. There is so much that I would change if I could. There are some things that I wish I could still do, but probably won't get the chance. Of all of those things, there is one that I can't leave this earth without doing. And that's giving you the explanation that you deserve."

"Mom." Pearson wanted her to stop. Already unstable, Pearson teetered on an emotional edge. "You don't have to do this." Pearson walked to the opposite side of her office putting distance between her and Candice's words.

"If I could have given you away, I would have, but I was too selfish to let you go, but too messed up to do you any good."

Pearson's head snapped in Candice's direction as a lump lodged in her throat. Her lips parted, but only succeeded in trembling. She gasped and felt incapable of producing words. The weight of the pain in Candice's eyes, matched the pressure pressing down on her own chest.

"I didn't have a pretty childhood." Candice shrugged her shoulders. "I didn't think I had anything to offer a child, but I loved you." Swiping at a steady stream of tears, Candice shook her head. "Mama was…a mean woman…just mean." Blinking rapidly, Candice pursed her lips and shook her head again. "Mm," she added as she reminisced. "In fact, as a child, I thought she hated me. She's been gone for so many years now and it was just recently that I realized she loved me the best way she knew how no matter how it looked or felt. Her mama was mean, too." Candice chuckled and punctuated her statement with a nod. "I remember being so scared of that woman." Candice drew in a deep, sharp breath and let it out as she walked over to Pearson.

Taking Pearson by the hand, Candice looked into her eyes as if she were trying to reach her soul. The pressure of Candice's gaze made Pearson blink. She tore her eyes away.

"Your father knew this. He tried his best to love me enough to fill all of my voids. I loved that man more than my own life and didn't know how to show it… but he understood—he understood," she said again, choking on her emotions. Candice didn't bother wiping the tears that flowed more heavily now. "He wanted a house full of children." She tittered, her sad eyes glazed with memories of her lost love. "That crazy fool believed that having kids would help me learn how to love better.

Instead, having you scared the Bejesus out of me."
Throwing her head back, Candice chuckled. "And when
he died, I sent you away because I didn't want to ruin
you." She turned back to Pearson to search her eyes once
again. "Not because I didn't love you. But then, once the
distance settled in between us, I didn't know how to fix it
so I let it remain there. The next thing I knew, you
became a woman and that was that. I know now that it
was entirely my fault, but I refuse to let my mistakes ruin
what we could have in the time I have left." Candice
inclined her head toward Pearson and held out her hand.
"If you're willing."

Pearson got up and walked over to the window
that her mother had just come from. Slow breaths helped
to keep her calm. Her mother had just said things she'd
wanted to hear all of her life and now she wished she
could take them back.

"I know how you feel, Pearson." Candice touched
her back and she flinched. "It doesn't seem fair. Finally I
come around, but now our time is limited. I will
understand if you don't want me in your life now. I just
had to get this out. You deserved to hear it." Candice
moved toward the couch and retrieved her purse. "I won't
ask you for much. If you can find it in your heart to
forgive me for being such a poor example of a mother, I'd
like to spend whatever time I have left with you making
up for what has been lost. If you don't want to...then...I
understand." Candice headed for the door.

Pearson heard her walking away. Letting her
endless tears fall, she continued looking out over the

parking lot. Her blurred vision prevented her from seeing anything clearly.

The doorknob turned. Pearson wanted to call out to her mother. Tell her not to go or even tell her that she was forgiven, but she couldn't get the words past her quivering lips. Pearson knew pain well and had learned to cope in it. Forgiveness and all of the other messy emotions that came along with it were foreign to her. She wasn't sure if she could handle that kind of freedom.

"I truly love you, honey. Always did," Candice said. Pearson could tell by the slight tremor in her voice that she was still crying, too.

Shaking, Pearson held herself tighter while Candice walked through the door. Minutes passed with Pearson's gaze fixed on the stillness of the parking lot. She expected to see her mother make her way toward the car.

Closing her eyes, Pearson inhaled slowly, and then let her breath out in a rush. She had to get herself together. There was work to be done.

Her office door suddenly crashed open, banged against the wall, and seized her attention.

"Mrs. Day! Your mother passed out in the elevator!" Nat yelled, breaking into her thoughts. "Hurry."

Pearson's heart clamored against her chest as she ran behind Nat, her pencil skirt limiting her stride. Guilt shrouded her at the thought of how she'd just treated her mother. How could she have been so selfish? Silently, she prayed that the Lord wouldn't let Candice die before she had a chance to turn things around.

Chapter 44

Nadalia

Once again Nadalia was in the dark. Daylight had fallen into the night as she sat in the family room of her mother's Long Island home. The only illumination came from the flickering embers of the fireplace, casting moving shadows along the walls. Nadalia had come to like the darkness, where she could wallow in her agony or avoid the lines that creased her tired face from all of the crying she had done.

Since she left home, she only journeyed to the office and back to her mother's house, moving through her days like a zombie. Cutting herself off from the world, outside of work, she wouldn't answer any calls. Eventually, she'd have to come out of the darkness, but right now, it embraced her and she liked it.

At first, she thought she was hearing things when the doorbell rang, followed by a knock on the door. She blamed it on her imagination. No one, including her mother, knew that she was there. Mina only ventured to her home on the Island in the summer so it couldn't be her. Besides, she wouldn't knock at her own door.

The knock came again and she knew it was happening outside of her head. Still, she didn't move to answer. Nadalia nudged herself deeper into the couch, stared into the dark and tried to think of something other than Sage's betrayal. She'd thought about that every way she could, turning the scenario over in her mind like a Rubik's cube. Every angle brought the same amount of pain.

The series of non-stop ringing and barrage of knocks slamming into the door got her attention. It sounded like the police were pounding their way through with a battle ram. Nadalia stood and took cautious steps through the dark toward the banging. Peering out the window, she saw Pearson.

"Open the door, sister. I know you're in there. I see your car in the driveway."

Nadalia closed her eyes for just a moment and then walked to the door and peeled it open slowly. She put her hands on her hips. "How did you know I was here?"

"Your lovely husband. Well, from the looks of things, your stupid husband told me." Pearson welcomed herself inside, pushing passed Nadalia laughing. "They are stupid when they make you mad."

"What!" Nadalia tensed, wondering how much Pearson knew. "What did he tell you?"

"What's with the darkness? Mama didn't pay the light bill?"

Nadalia walked into the nearest sitting room and flicked on a lamp, casting a low light around the room.

Pearson followed her. "Aww, that's better." She looked around before sitting on an antique Queen Anne chair. "This is fabulous."

"Thanks," Nadalia said watching Pearson scan the European decor with admiration.

"Is that your mom?" Pearson asked, getting up and walking over to a huge portrait of Mina wearing a Victorian-styled gown.

"Yes. My mom always liked those old world paintings so she had one done of herself. Now. Why are you here?" Nadalia asked, snapping at Pearson.

"After I called a hundred times and didn't get an answer, I decided to stop by your house. I was trying to see if you guys were going to make your usual donation to the auction at the benefit. Sage told me that you weren't there and that he couldn't tell me when you'd be coming back. He looked like a lost puppy, so I knew he'd done something to piss you off. I just went ahead and asked the dummy what he did and of course he wouldn't tell me."

Nadalia released the breath she'd been holding.

"Men never fully admit anything but anyway, he said he messed up bad. He assumed you were here and asked if I would just check up on you."

"Oh. Well, I'm fine and I will be donating a coat from the new season for the benefit as well as making our usual donation. So if that's all..." Nadalia got up to let Pearson out.

"Whoa!" Pearson put her hands up. "Look, Nadalia. I'm not trying to get in your business, but it's obvious that there's something very wrong. You're sitting in this big scary ass Victorian, looking like a haunted house from lifestyles of the dead and famous—in the dark, mind you—with eyes redder than Ruby Woo. The bags under your eyes are big enough to fit a few pairs of Jimmy Choos. You don't have to tell me exactly what's wrong. Truthfully, I don't even want to go down that path, because I have more issues than you can imagine and it would take the next five years for us to swap problems. But, I'm not about to just leave you here. You need some...support." Pearson ended with a gentleness that Nadalia wouldn't have expected. "You don't have to talk. I'll just sit here so you know you've got somebody."

Nadalia burst into tears. Pearson got up and wrapped her arms around her. "I know, honey. I know."

Nadalia pulled her head back, wiped her tears and chuckled. "Goodness. I know you didn't see that coming."

Both ladies laughed.

"We all have issues, honey." Pearson led Nadalia to the floral love seat, sat and cupped Nadalia's hands between hers.

"Some of ours are bigger than others," Nadalia said.

"Girl, please! Why do you think I drink so much?"

Nadalia twisted her lips and looked at Pearson sideways.

"Yeah! I know I drink way too much." Pearson snorted. "But it helps me," she said in a near whisper.

"Sometimes things hurt so much that I just want to stop myself from feeling." Pearson looked away. "I'm trying to control it now, but it taunts me sometimes, promising that it will make me feel better. There are times when I feel like it's more of a friend to me than my real friends are. It never judges me." A lone tear fell down Pearson's cheek.

Nadalia remained quiet, but squeezed her hand.

Pearson swatted the tear. "Hey. The girls said you kissed me the night we went out. Of course I don't remember anything."

"Yeah!"

"There's a heart in there after all."

"You're talking?"

They shared several moments of easy laughter.

Pearson rubbed the back of Nadalia's hand and smiled. "This life! I tell ya."

"I know!"

They welcomed the next few moments of silence. Nadalia was actually glad Pearson was there. She gave her the first genuine laugh, and a flicker of hope that she might be able to come out of the dark well that she had crawled into.

"I never thought I'd say this, but I'm actually glad you are here," Nadalia said and shoved her playfully.

Pearson smiled and stared off in the distance. After a few beats she opened up again. "I never made friends well. I never really trusted people. Somehow you women have snaked your way into my gate and I like having you there. Even you…and Ryan." Nadalia gasped and swatted at her again. Pearson dodged the hit. "I'm being honest."

Nadalia shook her head and laughed.

"Hey!" Pearson said, snatching Nadalia's attention. "Since you don't want to talk about your problems, I'll tell you about some of mine. Then you'll probably feel like your life isn't so bad. I'm tired of keeping all this stuff to myself. It gets heavy and frankly, I no longer give a shit what people think because we all got issues. Ha!"

Nadalia flinched. Pearson's outburst startled her and for a moment, Nadalia couldn't stop herself from laughing.

"Woo. Okay! You ready?" Pearson straightened her back.

Nadalia stretched her eyes and took a deep breath.

"Niles is at the end of his rope with my drinking. I've promised him I'd stop numerous times. I lied then, but now I've tried and don't even know if I'm capable of stopping. It lures me with the promise of making life lighter for me, like a mischievous friend." Pearson put her head down for a moment. "I don't want to lose my husband." She paused long enough to fill the space between them with awkward discomfort. "He's my safe haven, my best friend and he's about to be all I've got since my mother's dying."

Nadalia's hang flew to her mouth, covering her gasp." Oh my goodness, Pearson. I'm so sorry."

Pearson looked at her with glistening eyes and pursed her lips. "I've never had a great relationship with my mom. Always wanted to." Her bottom lip quivered.

"In fact for years I thought she just didn't like me. Recently she tried to reconcile with me...even apologized for being a bad mom, but I rejected her and then she passed out. I thought I was going to lose her then." Pearson hunched her shoulders, donned a sheepish grin, and choked on her emotion when she tried to speak again. "She'll…she'll be gone soon." She paused, pressing her lips into a tight line. Wiping the tears from her chin, Pearson cleared her throat and continued. "I think it's so unfair. I almost don't want to get close because I know it's going to hurt so much more when she goes." Nadalia squeezed her hand tighter. "And how have I been dealing with all of this...drinking." Pearson held her hands up and let them fall into her lap hard. "It's driven a wedge between my husband and me. He was so upset with me last weekend that when I woke up Sunday morning, every bottle in the house had been smashed…and then he left me."

Nadalia sucked in a heap of air and blinked at Pearson.

"Pearson," she called her name gently.

"He came back when my mom got sick. I'm trying to do everything right to make sure he stays. See, Nadalia. You're not alone." Pearson sniffled. "We've all got issues and some of ours can really trump others." Pearson laughed a little. "I bet if the other women were here, they could tell of so much more. Ryan with that controlling, womanizing Anderson. Vonnie and Mike with..." Pearson thought for a minute. "I swear Vonnie and Mike seem like they have never had any problems." Both women laughed.

Nadalia put her head down. She really felt for Pearson, but still wasn't ready to reveal her own truth. She couldn't imagine telling her that facing life without Sage seemed impossible, but he had left her with no choice. She could never admit that she felt like less of a woman because Sage cheated on her with a man. If she could help it, no one would ever hear any of this from her lips.

Chapter 45

Vonnie

Mike and Vonnie sifted through scores of envelopes, dividing the house bills from his company's bills and then organizing them by due date. The pile of those that were past due towered high over bills that were current. Mike rested his head in his hands and let out a frustrated breath.

"What do we have in savings again?"

Vonnie got up from the table, yawned and stretched her back. They had been maneuvering funds from their savings and investments trying to work out strategies to fix their financial problems for hours.

"From my savings, I can bring the car notes, utilities and some of the credit cards up to date. We'll have to cash in some investments to get Noelle's tuition back on track. We can loan the business a little money to pay one of the bank loans, but the bottom line is we are going to have to pull Noelle out of that school. We just can't afford forty-five thousand a year for tuition anymore, especially if we plan on sending her to college someday." Vonnie sat back. "It would be great to have her back home. She can go to the public school right here in this district."

Mike shook his head. "Where do we stand with the business accounts?"

"It doesn't look good. Based on what's going out on a monthly basis to cover rent, the bank loans, and your regular creditors, you may be just making payroll."

Mike dropped his head back. "I may have to let a few more people go. This new project will get things moving again."

"But Mike, without the money you need to invest in developing the software, there's nothing we can do. You're maxed out with the creditors and the banks are refusing to loan you any more money. And you better not even think of going to Andrew." Vonnie let him know just how serious she was with her tight expression and pointed finger.

This time Mike stood and started pacing. "Think!" he chanted to himself. "How many people would I have to cut to maintain again?"

"At least six."

"I'm just going to have to do it." He shook his head.

"You may not want to hear this, but the reality is we just can't afford this house anymore. We have three options; we can take some money and pay a few months of the mortgage to buy us some time. That way we can put the house on the market and hope it sells before the bank takes it. We could do a short sale, or we just let it go and let the bank foreclose on it. If we can sell it, we may be able to walk away with a few dollars to put on a more affordable home. If the bank does a short sell, we walk away clean, but we won't have any money for a down payment on the new house and all of our accounts are cleaned out, lastly if we let the bank foreclose on us, we lose it all."

Vonnie read the frustration in the lines of Mike's stressed eyes. She didn't mention the fee his lawyer was charging to represent him in the case for the gun charge, which could wipe them out if it went to trial.

Vonnie sat back in her seat and sighed. Mike was still pacing, his bloodshot eyes narrowed in deep thought. His cell phone rang, pulling him from inside of his mind.

"What's up, my man?" Mike said cheerfully, masking his irritation from the person on the other end of the phone. Vonnie looked up at him, and shook her head at the fake smile in his voice. "Yeah that sounds cool...when...I know this weather has been crazy, but I hear the weekend is supposed to be nice...Yeah... you think the course will be clean enough? Cool...sure...count me in. Look man, I gotta run and handle some business. I'll call you back."

Mike ended the call and tossed his phone onto the teak wood table a little too hard. "Dammit." The smile had left his voice. Mike leaned against the counter and folded his arms. His eyes narrowed and his mouth twisted as he gnawed on the inside of his bottom lip. A gesture that gave Vonnie a clear indication that his anger was getting the best of him. Mike wasn't much of a liar and Vonnie knew that the little game he just played on the phone would affect him. The man in him wouldn't allow others to see him sweat.

Vonnie wanted to mention that they couldn't afford for him to go golfing right now until she remembered that one of the only bills he did pay was his country club membership. The little reminder made her scream on the inside, yet she understood. The Beck was their haven. Had he not paid his dues, the others would have known right away that they were having financial problems. Mike was too proud to expose himself like that.

But, how long would it take for them to realize that they had been ejected from their economic status? Would they remain friends with Mike?

"Dammit!" he yelled again, startling Vonnie.

"Mike! Relax. We will get through this."

"I messed up. I messed up bad," he repeated with his teeth clenched tight. "I fu—"

"Mike!" Vonnie yelled again before he released the expletive on the tip of his tongue.

"I did this to us. I ruined us." Mike's hands flopped against his thighs.

"Everyone has ups and downs."

"This wasn't supposed to happen to us!" With a single swipe Mike sent the invoices, cups and calculators that were scattered across the table crashing to the floor.

Vonnie grabbed the laptop and jumped out of her chair. "Mike!" she yelled, but he wasn't listening.

With a growl, Mike swung his arm again and sent the rest of the paperwork fluttering to the floor, then lifted the table. Vonnie screamed his name one more time before he turned it completely over. She placed the laptop on the granite counter and pulled on his arms until he let the table go. She called him repeatedly, trying to bring him from the dark rage that had come over him. She hadn't seen him that mad in years.

"Stop it!" she yelled and melted into the chair beside her, burying her muffled tears in her hands.

Mike finally came around. Spent, he crumpled to the floor and held onto her legs.

"I'm sorry." Mike was out of breath, panting as if he'd just completed a marathon. "I sorry for messing up our lives, baby. I promise I'll make it up to you. Just don't leave me."

"I'm not going anywhere," she said in a tone that let him know how absurd he sounded. She continued wiping her tears. "We will get through this." She rubbed Mike's head. "We'll be fine."

Getting over the issue of their finances seemed like the easy part to her. She always felt like she'd been living a dream—almost like she was living someone else's life. The wealth seemed surreal.

Now it was time to float back down to reality. She would always cherish the memories they made while they were filthy rich. The hard part would be facing everyone else once their lifestyle had been downgraded.

Vonnie patted Mike on the shoulder letting him know she wanted to get up. He lifted himself and together they cleaned up the mess he'd created. Picking up the mail, Vonnie came across the elegantly designed invitation for Pearson's annual gala. At five hundred dollars a ticket, she and Mike certainly couldn't afford to attend, but what excuse would she give Pearson for not showing up? Surely she couldn't tell her the truth.

Chapter 46

Pearson

Today would be Pearson's day of full reconciliation. Candice's health scare and Niles' absence were too much to bear. After Candice passed out, Pearson had an opportunity to speak with her doctors when they arrived at the hospital. She realized just how fragile life was for her mother. Dehydration had claimed her strength, leaving her listless on that elevator floor. *What if she died?* Pearson couldn't imagine losing her mother without making the most of what little time they had left. She planned to prove to herself and everyone else how strong she could really be.

Her visit with Nadalia helped her come to this decision. Pearson's world was small and she was at risk of losing the two most important people in it.

Pearson had gotten up early and taken a long walk down her beautiful tree-lined street. The pre-dawn stroll gave her much uninterrupted time to tangle with her thoughts.

As she expected, Niles was still in bed when she got back. Pearson peeked in on him, feeling grateful for his return. He was rolled snugly inside the covers and she quietly pulled the bedroom doors together, leaving a small crack and then headed to the kitchen to start breakfast. Quickly whipping up fried eggs, turkey sausage and a toasted English muffin, Pearson poured a tall glass of ice cold orange juice and carried it to the room on a wooden tray.

"Niles," she called softly, pushing the door open with her foot. She nudged him awake. "Babe. Wake up. I made breakfast."

Niles woke with a start, staring past Pearson with wide eyes.

"Niles," she said again gently.

Niles pushed himself up until he was sitting, squeezed his eyes and stretched.

"Morning," he finally said, his voice gruff from sleep.

"I made you breakfast," she said again, hoping he would see this as the effort she intended it to be. "Come on, eat."

Niles stared at her for a moment before taking the tray. Pearson walked around to the other side of the bed and climbed in. For a while, she let him eat without interruption.

"I'm sorry."

Niles stopped chewing, but did nothing more to acknowledge her apology.

I just need you to tell me that you won't leave me again. Even if I...mess up...while I'm trying to get it together."

Niles released a long sigh and put his tray to the side. Tears had found their way down Pearson's cheeks. Niles turned to her and wiped them with his thumb. "If I were going to leave again, I wouldn't be here now."

Pearson leaned into him, wrapping her arms around his firm body. For a while they just held each other until Pearson pulled back.

"How do you want to do this, again?"

"I'm going cold turkey. If that doesn't work, I'll seek out a group, attend meetings, I'll do whatever I have to do. These next few months are so important and I need to be able to absorb every minute of every hour of every day." Her tears streamed faster as she thought about spending more time with her mom and her desire to be fully in those moments. "I won't be able to do this without you."

"I've got your back, baby."

"I'm glad that you're not mad at me anymore. Those days without you were unbearable."

"I was never mad at you, just frustrated. It felt like I was fighting a battle that I wasn't equipped to win. If I were losing you to another man, I would know how to handle that. But how do I win against a force as strong as..."

"Alcoholism." Pearson saved Niles the agony of actually putting the label on her issue. The sad look Niles gave her confirmed that he was hesitating to say the same thing.

"Yeah. It had you, baby. You've been slipping away for a while."

"I know. Eat your breakfast, I need to jump in the shower and head over to my mother's house. If she's up to it, I'm going to take her out for brunch."

The way Niles paused midway as he reached for his breakfast told Pearson that he was surprised. "You want me to come."

"No." Pearson kissed his cheek. "But, thanks. I need to do this alone."

"I'll be here if you need me."

Pearson kissed him again. Niles pulled her in, looked into eyes and kissed her a few more times before letting her go.

"I'm proud of you."

She paused a moment to absorb Niles' admission before heading toward her walk-in closet, smiling.

The crisp cold air whirled around her when she stepped out her front door, pulling her coat tighter. The chill seemed harsh when she was sober and she realized her drinking had numbed more than her feelings.

Pearson climbed behind the wheel of her two-seater Jaguar and took a long breath before starting the car and pulling out. The glare of the eastern sun poured through her windshield, forcing her to dig in her purse for a pair of sunglasses. Fortunately, the ride to her mother's wouldn't take more than twenty minutes.

Finally ready to move past her fears, Pearson looked forward to the surprise visit to her mother's lavish home. She pulled into the circular drive, got out and rang the bell, listening for the chime to resonate through the spacious corridors. She waited a while giving her mother a moment to respond since the hour was still early.

Glancing at her watch, she rang repeatedly until Candice showed up at the door clad in a silk robe and slippers.

"Pearson?" Candice smiled and moved aside inviting her in.

"Good morning, Ma," she said, stepping past her mother. "You look better. How do you feel?"

"Fine. And to what do I owe this," Candice looked around and took Pearson's arm to look at her watch, "early visit?"

"If you're up to it, get dressed. We are going to spend the day together. We'll come back if you get too tired."

Candice's face illuminated like a child on Christmas Day. "Really!"

"Yes." Pearson started walking up the steps toward Candice's bedroom and Candice followed eagerly. "While we are out, we've got a lot to discuss, like your plans for...well, you know." Both women knew she was referring to her final arrangements. Pearson couldn't bring herself to say it. "Also, you'll have to bring me up to speed about the company."

"Oh, Pearson. You're going to take over?" Candice all but squealed.

"I didn't say that just yet. But we'll need to at least get me on the board."

"Done."

"And I could use some advice. I never really had another woman who I could run certain things by, you know." Pearson continued down the second floor corridor toward Candice's room. "No offense, but it's the truth." Stepping into Candice's room, Pearson stopped when she noticed a figure lying under the sheets in Candice's bed. "You didn't say you had company," she whispered.

Candice walked past her straight into the room. "Oh, it's no problem at all! Walter, dear! Pearson is here." Candice sat down on the edge of the bed and nudged his pecan colored back. "Wake up, honey."

Pearson's hand flew to cover her gaping mouth. "Mr. Walter," she said as he began to stir. Pearson turned so she wouldn't mistakenly gaze upon any of his private parts. The sound of Walter's stretch reached her ears, the groans along with a few snaps and cracks from his joints.

"Hey, sweetheart! How are you doing?"

"I'm fine," Pearson said with her back still turned.

"Walter, she came to spend the day with me. Isn't that wonderful?"

"That's good to hear. Have you had enough rest, honey?"

"I feel fine." Candice's excitement rang through her words. "In that case, you ladies have a great time."

"Thanks," Pearson said. "And don't worry. I'll make sure she doesn't overdo it. Mom, I'll wait for you downstairs."

Pearson was shocked. It was interesting to actually see the man in her mother's life. Since childhood, she couldn't recall meeting a single male friend. As she thought about it, the only man who had been around the family was Walter, who had been a great friend of her dad's for many years. Pearson thought of him as an uncle. Now it was obvious that he was a little more than that.

The whole idea of her mom dating tickled Pearson and she covered her mouth so they wouldn't hear her sudden outburst as she laughed. Her stiff mother was getting it. Seeing this made Pearson feel like Candice did have a softer side. She found herself wondering how long they had been dating, screwing, or whatever it was that they called themselves doing. Then she thought about her mother's limited time.

The laughter in her heart and the smile on her face faded. Pearson swallowed hard as she tried to keep tears from falling. Candice was going to die. Pearson would never get used to that reality. Soon she would be in this world by herself, with no other family besides Niles.

Candice's foot hit the landing, bringing Pearson back to the present moment. As stylish as ever, Candice had on a pair of jeans, a gray flowing top and matching gray suede booties. No one could ever guess that she was well into her sixties.

"You look cute," Pearson said, taking her mother in. "And I love the boots."

"It will all be yours eventually. These," Candice twisted her foot giving Pearson a better view of her ankle boots, "this house, the cars, the business—all of it."

Pearson cringed at the cavalier way her mother referred to her own death. "Ma!" She rolled her eyes.

Candice waved away her concern and then paused, studying Pearson's weary expression. "Come; let's chat a little before we go." Candice led the way to the gallery, sat on the sofa and patted the seat beside her for Pearson to sit.

Pearson hesitated, dropped her shoulders, and then took slow steps toward the couch. She felt like a child about to be reprimanded. Instead of looking at Candice, she looked around the artsy space, focusing on some of her father's favorite paintings, sculptures and artifacts from his travels. Her mother made sure that everything was preserved well.

"Pearson."

Finally, she looked her mother's way, trying to keep the tears from falling. Candice cupped Pearson's hand between hers.

"I'm dying." Candice's admission hung in the air for a few moments. "And I have accepted that fact. The most important thing to me was making sure I made amends with you before I went. Now that it seems that I have, I couldn't care less if I had one month or one year left. As long as I know I have my daughter in my good graces, The Lord could take me today."

"She didn't mean that!" Pearson said looking up.

"Ha!" Candice slapped her thigh and shook her head. "Really Pearson, I didn't want to leave here without reconnecting with you the right way. I'm content now."

"So...how long do you have?" Pearson didn't want to ask the question and wasn't sure if she was ready for the answer, but she had to know.

"Does it really matter?"

Pearson thought for a moment.

"No," Candice answered for her. "We matter."

"You don't look that sick."

"I'm wealthy and vain!"

Pearson chuckled. She completely understood. "You're not going to tell me, are you?"

"Nope. All I want to focus on when I'm with you is enjoying your company. I don't want you or anyone else trying to count down my days. I plan to live them out as fully as I can so I don't need pity or reminders. I've lived a robust life. I have no regrets. Well, I had one." Candice looked at Pearson and pouted. "But now that we are on better terms, my life really feels complete."

Pearson sighed again, feeling like that's all she'd been doing in her life lately, living from one sigh to the other. "Did you tell Walter?"

"He knows I'm sick, but he doesn't know how much time I have left either. Now I have some paperwork in the safe in the back of my closet." Candice transitioned to the next subject as if they were simply talking about the weather. She pulled a small key from her jean pocket and pressed it into Pearson's hand. "It contains everything you need to know and all of the important paperwork. Besides a few donations I'd like for you to make on my behalf, everything else is yours to do with as you wish."

"Ma—"

Candice put her finger to Pearson's mouth and shook her head. "If you don't want to take over the company, that's fine too. I realize you have a life of your own. All I ask is that you remain as the chairman of the board."

"Remain."

"Yes. In the case of my death, that position goes to you. Just keep an eye on it for your dad and me."

"Okay," Pearson said, voicing her surprise.

"Walter could run the company just fine until you decide if you want to take it over—or not." Candice shrugged. "Okay?" Pearson nodded. "Now." Candice clapped punctuating her orders and then stood. "That's all the talking about death we are going to do. Let's get on with our lives."

When Pearson stood, Candice pulled her into a long embrace. Pearson wrapped her arms around her mother's slim waist and held her back just as tight. When Candice pulled back, her eyes glistened. "Thank you, Pearson. You have given me the greatest going away present ever."

Pearson snorted and shook her head at the way Candice so easily shifted from one matter to another in such a no-nonsense manner. At that moment, she realized just how much her personality mirrored her mother's.

Chapter 47

Ryan

Ryan woke with a start, looked around the room and then remembered she was at her mother's house. She looked at the piles of clothing around her and sighed. When she left Anderson and his pregnant mistress at the benefit, she ordered the driver to take her back home immediately. She tossed a few twenties as an incentive and he followed her instructions.

Frannie met her there and they stuffed everything they could into her mother's SUV. Ryan knew starting over with a baby and no income would be hard, but she looked forward to the peace her new life had to offer. She had already begun to develop a blueprint for the next phase.

"Ryan." Frannie whispered from the opposite side of the door.

"I'm up, Ma."

Frannie pushed her way into the room, traveling through a trail of Ryan's belongings while balancing a tray.

"I brought you some toast, eggs, bacon, and a cup of tea, honey," Frannie said and sat the tray on the night stand. Flopping on the bed, Frannie yawned and then patted Ryan's leg. "How ya doing, kiddo?"

Ryan felt proud for taking a stand, regardless of how costly.

"Good! I can't believe that bastard went out and had a baby on you. I swear, when see him, I ought to pop him one good time."

Ryan chuckled and shook her head. "That won't be necessary."

"I know, but it would feel awfully good!" They shared a laugh. After a few beats, Frannie asked, "Did you tell him yet."

"No." Ryan instinctively placed her hand on her stomach and thought for a few moments. "I'll let him know soon enough."

"You do that. He's obligated to take care of that baby and the money will certainly help until you get on your feet." Frannie stood. "I'll leave you to your breakfast. I'm going to get ready to run a few errands. Let me know if you're up to going with me. I'll even let you ride shotgun. Ha!" Frannie laughed at her own joke.

Ryan offered up a chuckle for support. "I will."

When Frannie left the room, Ryan got out of bed. She wanted to continue making her list of all the things she would need, but the phone interrupted her plan.

Ryan saw Anderson's number, rolled her eyes toward the ceiling and then answered, "Hello."

"Ryan?"

"Who else would it be?" she smarted.

"I need you to come home so we can straighten this out. We need to talk."

"Is the baby yours?"

The phone went silent.

"Is. It. Yours," Ryan repeated.

After a few more beats of stillness, Anderson finally responded, "Yes."

"Then there's nothing for us to talk about. When you're ready to marry your mistress, contact me about the divorce. Until then, have a great life." Although she couldn't see him, she could tell by his breathing that Anderson was angry. "Oh and when our baby gets here, I'll let you know so you can send child support payments. Goodbye, Anderson."

"What?" Ryan heard him yell just before ending the call.

She snickered imagining how that bit of news must have hit him. Her phone rang right after she hung up. For a moment she contemplated sending the call to voicemail.

"You're pregnant?" Anderson asked as soon as she picked up. He sounded out of breath.

"Yes," Ryan confirmed and waited for him to respond.

After a long pause, Anderson said, "Come home, Ryan."

"I can't."

"Then I'm coming there."

The line went dead.

Immediately, she got up and went to freshen up. It wouldn't take long for Anderson to get to her mother's house, but she was ready for him.

Anderson arrived just moments after Frannie left. The timing was perfect.

Ryan opened the door as Anderson approached the small porch. She was surprised by his disheveled appearance and wondered if he had actually been crying. Anderson was always a hard man so she dismissed the possibility.

Anderson followed Ryan into the cozy living room. She gestured for him to sit and parked herself on the opposite sofa, folding her feet under her.

"Oh. I'm sorry. Did you want anything to drink? I don't mean to be rude."

For a while, Anderson just looked at her. "No. I'm fine," he finally said. "Why didn't you tell me," he asked, nodding toward her belly.

Ryan looked away at first. In the short time they'd been apart, she felt free. She was no longer afraid to handle intense matters with Anderson. "I was going to tell you after the benefit, but your girlfriend's news changed that."

"We can work this out, Ryan."

Ryan pursed her lips and sighed. "No we can't."

"I love you!" he said as if he were ordering her to believe him.

Ryan rose from where she was perched, sat on the couch next to Anderson, and took him by his hand.

Gently, she lifted his chin until they were facing each other eye-to-eye.

"It's too late. I tried everything I could to keep this marriage together and took everything you threw at me. For so long I was afraid of what life would be like without you, without the lifestyle you provided for me, but for the first time ever, I realize that my own peace, sanity and dignity are so much more important. I can't stay with you, Andy."

"What will you do without me, you don't have anything?"

"I know." Ryan shrugged. "I'll still be fine."

"Ryan-"

She interrupted him, pressing her finger against his lips.

"I'm not changing my mind. You can keep your money, the house, cars—everything. I don't want any of it."

Anderson cocked his head to the side and looked at her as if she were out of her mind. He shifted his gaze around the room as if trying to think of what to say next.

"Don't be upset because I'm not."

His face scrunched in confusion.

"What are you saying?"

I'm saying that I deserve so much more. I'm praying that this time everything goes well with the pregnancy and when the baby gets here, we can make arrangements. I won't stand in the way of you having a relationship with your child."

"This time." Anderson tilted his head at her. "You were pregnant before."

Ryan sat back and chuckled. "Yes, but I miscarried each time."

Anderson looked down at his hands. Ryan could have sworn she saw them quiver.

"It's okay, Anderson. That's in the past." She found herself rubbing his back.

"Things were changing with us," Anderson said.

Ryan was surprised at the pleading in his eyes. This softer side of Anderson had been missing during most of their marriage. "I thought so too…until the benefit."

Anderson dropped his head. Together they sat silently absorbing her words. After a while Ryan stood.

"Thank you for coming by. You were right. We needed to talk. I'll let you out." Ryan began walking to the door.

It took some time before Anderson followed her. Ryan waited by the door. When he finally reached her, she saw the glistening in his eyes. Anderson lowered his lips to hers. She turned away. Turning her head back toward him, he kissed her hard, showing more passion than Ryan had experienced in years.

Anderson released her and rested his head against hers. They stayed that way for a while. Ryan stepped back first, pulled the door open and said, "Goodbye, Anderson."

Without responding, Anderson solemnly walked out. As soon as he made it past the threshold, Ryan closed the door and leaned against it. She knew this would be difficult, but from the moment she decided to let go, she felt lighter. She had made the right choice.

Starting over wouldn't be easy, but it would be her way.

Chapter 48

Nadalia

Nadalia closed the lawyer's office door behind her, but continued holding the doorknob to keep her balance. She had given her attorney the game face as he handed her copies of the documents that she'd paid him extra money to draw up quickly. Now she was on her way to deliver them to Sage personally. First, she had to catch her breath.

Nadalia got herself together and headed for her car. The drive home seemed surreal since it had been almost two weeks since she set foot in her own house. But she had no intention of going back there. There was no way her house would ever really feel like home again. Too many reminders lived there.

When Nadalia pulled up in front of the house, she sat in the car for a long time thinking about what she was about to do. Sage wouldn't be home for a few more hours, which gave her enough time to pack a few more of her things to carry back to her mother's house. She'd wait until he came so she could serve him the papers before she left.

Finally, Nadalia got out of the car, stuffed her keys in her coat pocket, and lugged up the walkway. She pushed her key in the door and it opened. Frightened for a quick moment, Nadalia looked up and stared directly into Sage's red eyes. She drew in a sharp breath and for a second, thought about turning back. Sage stepped aside to let her in and then leaned over to plant a routine kiss on her cheek. She turned away.

Nadalia wondered why he was home, but refused to ask, not wanting to show concern. His disheveled look had already clued her in on the fact that he wasn't handling the separation well. Either that or he was afraid that she may have let out his secret. She was glad to find that she wasn't the only one suffering, but she was even happier to find that it also showed that at least he cared.

"Um. I came to bring you these and get a few more of my things." Nadalia handed him the papers and headed up the steps to their room as swiftly as possible.

"Divorce papers!" he yelled as she retreated.

Nadalia's gut tightened when she heard his footsteps trailing hers.

"Nadalia! Don't you think this is a little rash? We haven't even had a chance to really talk about this whole thing."

"I've heard all I needed to hear," Nadalia said, tugging an overnight back from the depths of her closet. "And, I can't get what I saw out of my head."

"Can we at least give this a little more time?"

"That's not necessary. My decision is made." Nadalia pulled a few blouses off the hangers and stuffed them into the bag. She wanted to get out of there.

Sage stood with his back against the wall and the papers dangling from his hands, watching her throw clothes in the bags. "I need time."

Nadalia stopped, placed one hand on her hip. "For what? I'm not going to change my mind."

"Babe!" Nadalia cringed and then tossed a few pairs of shoes in the bag. "It's too soon. Maybe you'll feel different after a little while. We could go to therapy. People get over infidelity all of the time."

"Sage! You slept with men! There's no getting over that!" She slammed the shoe that she had in her hand into the bag and punched at the clothes inside so she could close the zipper.

"I'm not gay!"

"Well, what do you call it?"

"It's just something…different."

Nadalia threw him a sharp glare. Had it been a blade, it would have cleanly sliced his head off his body. She threw her hands up in frustration. "Look. I can't do this," she said and flopped down on the bench in the center of the closet. After a while she asked, "How long has this been going on?"

Sage dropped his head.

"That long, huh?" Nadalia sucked her teeth.

Sage looked the other way.

"You and Coffey thought no one would ever find out, didn't you? Does Niles, Anderson and Mike know about this?"

The frightened look in his eyes told her they didn't. Another concrete answer without words.

"Have you been tested?"

"Come on. I don't have HIV or AIDS."

"Answer my question!" she yelled.

"Yes," he said quietly.

Fear struck her. What if she was infected? "What were the results, Sage?" Nadalia stood to her feet, closing in the space between them.

"Negative," he answered in the same small tone.

"I can't hear you!" Nadalia shouted, needing to hear him again for confirmation.

"I'm clean!" he shouted back.

Nadalia's exhaled. She felt like she was watching her life play out in a drama. It didn't feel real. Nothing did. She thought about the possibility of having contracted HIV and became even angrier.

"You put me at risk." Nadalia ran to him and pushed him hard. His brawn body absorbed her assault without moving. She realized her attempts at inflicting any physical harm would prove futile. She sat back down.

Nadalia grew nauseous and charged past Sage, with her hand folded over her stomach. Pushing the toilet seat in the master bath back, she heaved, but nothing came out. Her emotions pooled into the center of her stomach forming a huge knot.

Sage was behind her, patting her back. She shrugged him off, cutting her eyes at him. She didn't come here for this. She thought she was done with all of the crying and stomach churning. Now in his presence, the hurt and anger twisted inside of her with the force of a tornado. She needed air.

Nadalia ran down the stairs and out to the expansive back yard to take in fresh air. She looked up and again, Sage was at her side. Nadalia turned and went back inside.

"Forget it. I'll get my stuff another time." She headed for the front door.

"Dali, wait!"

Nadalia ignored him, walking as fast as her legs could take her in three inch heels.

"Dali!"

Stopping short, she turned and scowled at him.

Seeing the look on her face, he dropped his shoulders and shook his head. He looked pitiful. Nadalia shifted her gaze so she wouldn't be affected.

"Just give me some time."

"Sign the papers!" Nadalia snapped back. She turned on her heels and ran to her car.

Halfway down the block, she reached for her purse to pull out her cell phone. She needed to speak to Angela. The only person she wasn't ashamed to talk to about this situation. Realizing her bag wasn't in the car, she slammed on her brakes. She had left her bag in the house.

Nadalia screamed, banging her fists against the steering wheel. The last thing she wanted to do was go back to that house, but she had no choice.

Nadalia whipped her car around in a hapless U-turn. Pulling into the driveway, she slammed the car to a screeching halt, and charged out, leaving the keys in the car and the doors wide open. She tried the knob to the front door. It was locked. Nadalia punched the door with the sides of her fist until Sage opened it. Seeing his face again made her want to scream. She clamped her mouth, ran up the steps and grabbed her bags from the padded bench in the center of her walk-in closet. Nadalia raced downstairs, refusing to acknowledge Sage, and then jumped back into her car and sped off.

Pulling over down the block, she dug into her purse for her phone and stabbed in Angela's number.

"Angela!" Nadalia didn't wait for Angela's greeting. After a few beats of silence passed by. "Angela."

"I'm here." There was silence again. "I'm not handling this well. What about you?"

"Well." Nadalia heard Angela release a heavy breath into the phone. "I guess you can say what we have now is more like a business arrangement."

"Angela?" Nadalia was appalled by her response.

"I know what you're going to say, but first let me explain."

A part of Nadalia didn't want to hear what Angela had to say. She sucked her teeth. "Go on."

"You see, I get everything—and I mean everything—I've ever wanted and need in exchange for my silence. I keep my house and my lifestyle as well as the opportunity to live my life as I please, and he gets to keep his image intact. It's a win-win."

"Is it really, Angela?"

At first she didn't respond. Nadalia let her hang in the silence. "Nadalia, I still love him. I can't just turn it off. Plus, he begged me not to leave. I have my family to think about. He said they were merely experimenting. He'll never do it again." Angela tried to sound convincing, but only came across as pitiful to Nadalia. "So...yes." Angela paused. "I'm staying with him."

Disgusted Nadalia looked at the phone as if it had just given that ridiculous excuse. "Goodbye, Angela," she said and tossed the phone into the backseat.

Angela's actions surprised her. She couldn't imagine why Angela would consider staying with Coffey. It didn't make sense. She couldn't believe that they were more worried about his image than the things he'd done to betray her.

Nadalia swore that the moon would first turn to blood and drip from the sky, while Jesus rode on a cloud before she would take Sage back. Forgive him, she could, but return to him...that would never happen.

Chapter 49

Vonnie

A somber quiet had filled the house as Vonnie sat alone in the kitchen watching the display on her telephone light up with Pearson's name and number. Like she had for the past several weeks, she let the call go to voicemail and still hadn't listened to any of the messages she or the other wives had left. Bowing out silently was what she preferred, despite the fact that she wasn't sure if that would work. Maybe they would stop calling and not even notice that she and Mike had dropped out of the scene.

At the sound of the bell, Vonnie braced herself on the edge of the kitchen table and lifted up. Mike was off somewhere in the garage trying to navigate the city of storage boxes that they had erected and Noelle was most likely in her room group texting her circle of friends. Making her way around a bunch of boxes in the spacious foyer, Vonnie trailed her way to the door, touching the empty spaces on the wall where paintings used to hang.

The area, turned gallery, now held an eerie emptiness, mirroring how she felt about having to leave her cherished home.

Vonnie paused, took a breath and pasted a smile across her face before opening the door. The buyers were back again, bringing more family to see their new home. She and Mike had been lucky enough to find an enthusiastic young couple with deep pockets only two weeks after discreetly putting the house on the market, receiving an offer they couldn't refuse. They went into - contract immediately, looking forward to making enough on the house to get them out of foreclosure status while also affording them a hefty down payment on a much smaller, but still beautiful five-bedroom Tudor home that was full of character a few towns away.

Politely, Vonnie greeted the fresh young executive, his pregnant doe-eyed wife and their three young children, along with the additional member of the family. Less than two seconds in, the overwhelmed mom was calling after her toddler who had taken off toward the family room.

"Please excuse him." She nodded apologetically, wobbling after the quick-moving tot. "Kaitlin, go and get your brother," she said to her older child who looked to be about five years old.

Vonnie gave her an understanding smile. It seemed that every time another family member came into town, they called to see if they could come by and show the house off. Each excited visit drove a stake further into Vonnie's heart. Their new neighborhood was still considered affluent, but paled sorely in comparison to their grand twelve room mansion, complete with a three-car garage, circular drive, exotic gardens, water features, and a pool house the size of a modest single-family home.

"We'll only be a minute, Mrs. Madison. My uncle was in town and we wanted him to see the house. Thanks for making time for us."

"No problem at all," Vonnie said, forcing that cordial smile again, hoping they wouldn't see the pain she hid behind her eyes. "Feel free, to show him around." Vonnie stayed in the background as the couple showcased the home and spoke of all the things they wanted to do to make it their own. Vonnie trailed behind the happy bunch as they went from room to room and then out to the massive, bi-level backyard.

Saying her goodbyes from there, Vonnie reminisced about how excited she was when she and Mike had found this house. Prior to their search, she had never seen homes so grand in person. The thought of actually living in one tickled her to the point where she pinched herself every time their realtor showed them a house. She hadn't labeled the process as mere 'house hunting.' Walking through elaborate mansions that were large enough to fit the house she grew up in at least five times couldn't be something as regular as house hunting. It was a fantastical adventure. When she walked into her current home, she felt like she had entered into her personal Shangri-La. The place spoke to her, inviting her in with its exquisite grand foyer, spacious layout, yet cozy feel. She decided then that she would fill her foyer with beautiful things so that they would be the first thing she saw when she entered her new home.

Once they moved in, the feeling of living a real life fantasy took years to wear off. She loved pulling up into their cobble-stoned circular driveway, curling her car around the serene fountain, and the beautiful shrubs and flowers planted around it. Vonnie couldn't even sleep during her first few nights there. A part of her couldn't believe the home actually belonged to them. Now they were leaving—too soon.

Vonnie rushed back inside, ran up to her bedroom and buried her tears in her pillow. Less than two months ago, life was still perfect. In that short time, the ugly truth unveiled itself. Mike's business had been downsized even more, they were saying goodbye to their dream home, and Noelle was attending the local public school. Fortunately, her daughter adjusted well to the transition since she had missed her friends when she went off to boarding school anyway.

Mike was no longer his usual jovial self. He spent most of his time at home in intense research to find ways to recapture the success that had slipped through his fingers. Other times he apologized to Vonnie for putting them in this situation. Now that she had a much more active role in handling their finances, she often tiptoed around topics of past due accounts in an attempt to keep from further bruising Mike's already fragile ego. She knew they'd get past all of the angst once they were settled in their new home. It wasn't as if they had to go back to Jamaica, Queens.

Vonnie lifted her head and listened keenly. She thought she had heard the doorbell ring once again and then, the happy chime flowed through the house. Vonnie pushed herself up off the bed. Mike wouldn't hear it from the garage and Noelle's ears were probably plugged with some pop song.

On her way to the door, she peeked into Noelle's room. As she suspected, her daughter lay across the bed with her head hanging off and her feet against the wall, snapping to the music filling the room from the wireless Bluetooth speaker as she video-chatted with friends. Noticing her mother's presence, Noelle smiled and waved. Vonnie smiled back and shook her head before closing the door.

The doorbell rang again. Vonnie sniffed back a slight attitude. "I'm coming already. How many times are you going to ring the damn bell?" She assumed it was the family once again. They probably left the two year old in the backyard and had driven a few miles before they realized he wasn't with amongst the boisterous brood.

Vonnie trudged to the door, stopping just before to pull down her shirt, take a deep breath and paint on a fresh smile. Without peeking through the glass, Vonnie opened the door, flashing her killer Hollywood smile, adding a warm tilt to her head before she froze.

"Hey, Sweetie!" Pearson said and stepped passed her, inviting herself into their home. "What's up with you? It's been weeks since we've talked. I was in the neighborhood, collecting last minute donations for the silent auction at the gala tonight so I decided to stop by. Girl, I thought you and Mike dropped off the face of the earth. No one has heard from you. I called you earlier. Did you get my message?"

Pearson's rambling gave Vonnie time to think. She had hoped that Pearson didn't taken notice of the storage boxes and the bare walls, but a blind person wouldn't have missed that.

"Hey, Pearson." Vonnie tried to force some elation into her greeting so it would seem like she was happy to see her. Her hand never left the knob of the door after she opened it and prayed that Pearson's visit would be short.

Pearson continued talking, seemingly oblivious to the sparse surroundings. She removed her shades and moved closer to Vonnie. "I'm running my mouth and I haven't even greeted you properly." Pearson squeezed Vonnie in a genuine embrace and air-kissed the side of her cheek.

Vonnie's mind was searching for a way to get Pearson out before she started asking too many questions. Pearson hadn't seemed to notice Vonnie's lack of conversation as she continued to fill every available space with her own voice.

"You guys are coming tonight, right? I never got your RSVP back in the mail."

"Oh my goodness! The benefit is tonight!" Genuinely surprised, Vonnie's hand shot to cover her gasp. "I completely forgot. We've been so busy," she offered a valid explanation. She wasn't going to mention that she hadn't planned on attending. "Noelle's home and I don't have a babysitter."

"So. Bring her. She's so well behaved. If I ever had kids, I'd need your help raising them to make sure they didn't come out as screwed up as me." Pearson hooted.

Vonnie jerked, startled by the unexpected outburst. "But we haven't bought tickets."

"So you're good for it." Pearson waved Vonnie's concern away. "As a matter of fact, just come. Don't even worry about the tickets. I had a few last minute cancellations and I still have to pay for those plates anyway. It's so important for the girls to see successful people and couples like you and Mike. I love telling them that you're a doctor. They're always so impressed."

"Goodness, Pearson. I've nothing to wear."

"Girl, please! Find something in the huge closet of yours. I'm sure you can put something stunning together in no time." Pearson looked down at her watch. "Listen, honey," she leaned in and gave Vonnie another air kiss, "I'll see you guys later, okay? I've got so much running to do before this thing kicks off, it's unbelievable." Then Pearson finally looked around. "Where's Mike?"

Vonnie held her breath. From the change of expression on Pearson face, Vonnie knew that she noticed the empty foyer.

"You're doing some remodeling?"

"Um." Vonnie toyed with the idea of lying. "Not exactly."

Pearson raised her brows at the ambiguous answer.

"We're moving," Vonnie said flatly.

Pearson's surprise showed in her furrowed brow line. "Moving? Why? When?"

Vonnie drew in a long breath, pushed the door closed and gestured for Pearson to follow her to sun room. As they sat, she gave Pearson the short version of the recent changes in her lifestyle.

"Vonnie!" Pearson held her hand to her chest. "Why didn't you guys come to us? We could have—"

Vonnie held her hand up, stopping Pearson. "Mike wouldn't have it."

"How are you handling all of this?"

"Better than before," she admitted. "We'll be fine," she added dismissively.

Pearson shook her head. "You just never know what's going on behind closed doors."

At first Vonnie didn't know if she should take offense to Pearson's remark until she continued.

"Life hasn't exactly been a bowl of cherries over at the Day's residence either." Pearson proceeded to share the problems with her tough journey to sobriety and efforts to rebuild her relationship with Niles and her mother while facing the harsh realities of Candice's impending demise. "It's been so hard. I'm proud of myself. I haven't had a drink in three weeks and two days. At first, I would sneak a few drinks in here and there, but Niles found my stash." Pearson paused, holding back possible tears. "I'm doing better. I can't afford to lose Niles. Soon he'll be all I have in this life."

Vonnie wiped the tear that trickled down the side of her nose and took Pearson's hand in hers as they wept together.

After a while, Vonnie broke the silent cries. "Things aren't always what they seem, huh?"

"Tell me about it, girl!" Pearson wiped her tears with the back of her hand, sniffed and stood. "Believe it or not, this is like therapy for me. I never really had people to talk to. Now I can't seem to shut myself up. But it helps," she tittered. "I need to get going." They hugged again, smiling as they pulled away.

Vonnie hadn't expected it, but sharing her story with Pearson made her feel lighter. She smiled inwardly as she walked her to the door.

"Hey," Pearson said. "Have you heard from Nadalia?"

Vonnie thought about it. She had ignored calls from Pearson and Ryan but didn't recall any missed calls from Nadalia. "No." She thought a moment longer. "Not since we went to dinner that last time," she said.

"I guess we've all been hibernating, handling our business." On the way out, Pearson turned back toward Vonnie. "Promise me you won't stop being my friend when you move."

Vonnie pursed her lips together and smiled before she said, "I promise." She held three fingers up like a girl scout. Both women laughed.

"Love you, girl!"

Vonnie blinked. "Love you too," she said slowly, surprised at Pearson's expression.

"I know. I've been trying those words out on certain people lately. Everyone seems to give me a similar response. But it's true."

The girls hugged one last time before Pearson left.

Vonnie headed to the garage to check in on Mike, realizing he'd been in there for a while. She found him sitting on one of the boxes with his head in his hands.

"Hey."

Mike looked up. "Hey."

Vonnie came over and tapped the box he sat on, gauging its stability, before climbing onto his lap. She put one arm around his neck. "You okay?"

Mike smiled and Vonnie's heart quickened for a second. That was the first genuine smile she had seen from him in a while.

"Believe it or not, I'm good. I was just thinking about some of the memories we made in this house. I hate to leave, but we'll just make more in the new house." He raised his brows and grinned.

"You got that right!" Vonnie winked. She let a moment pass before saying, "Pearson was here."

Mike raised his brows. "Yeah?"

"Yeah. She knows we're moving."

"Niles knows, too. He kept questioning me, talking about something hadn't seemed right with me for a while. Finally I had to break down and tell him a few things. He just wouldn't let up on me."

"What did he say?"

"He wanted to help."

"And you said, no!" Vonnie interjected before Mike could say anything else.

"I've been praying."

Vonnie's eyes stretched wide. She and Mike had always been consistent church members, but other than grace, she hadn't seen him do much praying. "Wow."

"I think He heard me."

"Of course He did."

"No really because things have been happening and I feel different." Vonnie looked at him curiously. Not that she didn't believe him, but she had never heard him speak this way before. "Seriously, babe," Mike said responding to the look she was giving him. "I even got a message from the lawyer saying that the case was going to be dropped because of something the police didn't do properly."

Vonnie closed her eyes and thanked God herself for answering her prayers. She wrapped her arms tightly around Mike's neck. She couldn't imagine having to live apart from him or explain to her daughter why her father was in jail.

"Plus all the stress that I've been feeling is starting to go away. All of a sudden, I'm not so upset about leaving here. I'm actually looking forward to starting a new chapter and having Noelle home. I mean, we can't get it on as spontaneously as we used to, but I can deal with that. Instead of focusing on what we're losing, I've been counting my blessings. I realize I've got quite a few."

Vonnie's joy started on the inside and spread to her lips and eyes.

"I've always said that life was good as long as I had you. We started from the bottom, now we're here." Vonnie swatted Mike playfully for his sad rendition of the popular line from the rapper Drake's song. "And we're going to be just fine." Mike nuzzled his nose into her neck.

Vonnie threw her head back and laughed. Mike was becoming himself again. She too was sure that they would be alright. Mike laughed, and then wrapped his arms around Vonnie, who leaned in for a kiss. One that started as a series of sweet pecks, but quickly turned into a passionate lock, ending abruptly when the box they were sitting on collapsed underneath them and sent them crashing on to the cold garage floor. They looked at each other, laughed, and locked lips once again.

Chapter 50

Nadalia

N adalia wondered how she would deal with being in the same room with Sage after weeks of avoiding contact with him. Tonight, not only would he be unavoidable, but also she wondered how she would manage being in his presence with everyone else around. Everyone knew they were separated since she had permanently moved back into her mother's Long Island home.

Nadalia applied a saturated coat of red lipstick, pressed her lips together and turned from side to side checking her reflection. Although the pain of Sage's betrayal was still fresh, it had been a while since she cried herself to sleep, giving her eyes much needed relief. A facial and massage gave her an added lift in both her spirit and appearance.

Satisfied with her make up application, Nadalia slipped into a black, beaded gown that hugged the curves of her hourglass figure. A fresh trim gave her jet black shoulder length hair a polished finish. She could set any red-carpet ablaze.

The closer she got to leaving the house, the slower she moved. She couldn't stand Pearson up after promising to donate a fur coat for the auction. The designers worked overtime to create an exquisite mink cape.

Nadalia and Sage had always been such an integral part of the auction. She was sure that Sage was donating his usual pair of prime tickets for club seats at the Met Life Stadium.

She just hadn't figured out how she would handle being around him with everyone else there.

Nadalia exhaled and shook her head. Delaying the inevitable was senseless. She grabbed her silver evening bag and crystal covered pumps and headed out the door. The ride to the Hamptons seemed longer without Sage, yet she managed it without breaking down. However the closer she got to the venue, the more nervous she felt.

Nadalia wheeled her sports car up to the valet, pushed her red lips into a friendly smile as she handed the young man her keys and walked into the posh venue with her head held high. Slipping passed the red carpet, she headed straight to the hall where the cocktail reception was being held, glanced around and then she went into the ladies' room to check her reflection. Nadalia fluffed her hair, and ran her finger along the lines of her mouth, cleaning up any of the lipstick that may have run outside the lines of her full sweetheart lips.

Stepping out cautiously, Nadalia moved into the cocktail reception with her chin forward, winding through throngs of elegantly dressed woman, and polished men sharply decked out in tuxedos. As she passed, she offered cordial nods and delicate waves to familiar faces. A festive air hung in the atmosphere, but Nadalia's nerves were too frazzled to be swept up in it.

I can handle this. She pepped herself up and released the breath that she'd been holding as she leaned on the edge of the bar.

"One Louis XIII and one Cabernet Sauvignon please," she told the bartender. Her intention was not to get drunk, but she needed the cognac to take the edge off quickly. Throwing the liquid back, downing it in one gulp, Nadalia winced at the slow burn passing through her chest and closed her eyes. She put the snifter down on the marble bar top, picked up her purse and turned to leave.

"Hello, Nadalia."

She froze right in the middle of her turn. The depth of Sage's voice flowed through her with the same sting as the cognac she had just downed. Nadalia closed her eyes and swallowed long and hard, before turning in his direction.

"Sage." She was proud of how steadily her voice held up in that single word.

He stuffed his hands in his pants pockets. "How have you been?"

"Fine." After a few ticks, she added, "And you?" She wanted so badly to appear unaffected, but remembering how much she loved the richness of his voice made it difficult. She had yet to look him in his face, fearful that she would break.

Sage touched her hand and her breath caught. She swallowed hard again and pulled her hand away from the familiar touch of his strong fingers.

"Please don't do that."

"I miss you."

Nadalia shifted her feet.

"I just want to know if we can at least be friends."

Nadalia exhaled, relived that he understood that what they once had would never be again.

"I still love you. Always have and always will. I understand that you can't...don't want to be with me anymore, but I can't see you not being a part of my life in some way."

Nadalia nodded. Not in a way that responded to his friend request, but in more of a non-committal way that let him know that she'd at least acknowledged him.

He went to touch her hand again and immediately she pulled back. Squeezing her eyes shut, she fought to keep it together. Encouraging herself, she repeated in her head, *you can do this.*

"I'll try to stay out of your way tonight; you don't have to avoid me. I'd just like to be able to talk to you soon."

Nadalia shook her head. "I know. I just need a little more time." She looked away.

She could feel him staring at her. She could smell the cologne mixed with the natural scent of his body emanating off him. She could see his rigid manly stature through her peripheral vision, but still refused to look at him. She couldn't trust herself just yet. Proud of the fact that she was keeping it together and hadn't run out of the event, she decided it would be best not to look at him. Even stealing a glance could have thunderous affects. She didn't want to be reminded of how handsome he was. Of how much she still loved him. It was too soon to handle looking into the depths of his brown eyes, or taking in the strong jut of his chin. She kept her eyes on the people. The beautiful dresses. The smiling faces. The other men.

"There you are!" Pearson's voice cut in, piercing her concentration. She was focusing hard on everything and everyone else that she could.

"Hey," she said. She received Pearson's hug and gave her an air kiss.

"Pearson!" Sage greeted. "You look great."

"Why thanks!" Pearson said, spinning to offer them a better view. "We'll be moving into the other room momentarily. You'll be sitting at the front table with me."

"Okay," Nadalia said.

Pearson's look let her know that she sensed that something wasn't right.

"I need to run to the ladies room. I'll see you two inside." Nadalia hurried off, thankful for Pearson's interruption and the opportunity to make a clean escape. She had gotten through the initial part of their encounter and was confident she'd make it through the rest of the night. It would take time for the love she had for Sage to wear off, if ever. However, she knew now that she could make it. Not that it would be easy, but it was doable.

Then, she could work on being his friend. She could at least give him that.

Chapter 51

Pearson

nderson was Pearson's emcee for the benefit and he had yet to arrive. She dialed his number.

"I'm five minutes away," he answered, jumping right to the reason for the call.

Pearson barely heard him over the music playing in the background. "Well, come on already. You're making me nervous."

"I'll be right there, Pearson."

She tapped the phone, ending the call and went in search of her mother before checking back in with her staff. Candice was seated in the same place where Pearson had left her twenty minutes before, which was just outside the room where the cocktail reception was being held.

Candice's decline had become much more evident in recent weeks, taking her to a point where her money and vanity were no longer able to hide the fact that she was seriously ill. Pearson could see that Candice was thinner and her movements were slower. Seeing that her mother was fine with Walter by her side, Pearson kept moving.

The young firecracker of a PR agent pulled on her to take a few pictures with some of her prime investors.

Pearson saw the event manager scanning the crowd in search of her. The look on her face gave Pearson no doubt that she was coming to deliver some bad news.

Niles appeared by her side to let her know that there were still a few issues with the sound equipment and that would affect the music from the live band that was setting up. Telling her not to worry, he promised to handle it.

Pearson realized that she no longer had the two manila files that she'd been holding in her hand. She stopped, closed her eyes and tried to recall where she left them. Trying not to panic, she turned to retrace her steps. Those folders contained the emcee's speech, the program outline, and several checks for vendors she had to pay at the end of the night.

With so much going on around her, she craved a drink. If she could just have one, it would help mellow her out just a little. Pearson had kept her smile all through the ensuing chaos, but the more that came her way, the more she wanted to crawl into a corner with a bottle of scotch. Right now, a single glass of wine would help settle her nerves.

"Babe." Pearson jerked at the sound of Niles' voice. "Sorry. I didn't mean to startle you. I just wanted to let you know that we worked everything out. They'll be ready to start whenever you are."

Pearson sighed. "That's great. I was starting to get a little anxious."

"I'm here."

Pearson took that to mean that he was there for her both literally and figuratively. She didn't need a drink. She had Niles. Pearson looked toward where her mother sat. She had Candice too, if just for a while longer.

"My man, my man!" Anderson greeted Niles with a hug. Giving Pearson a quick once over and approving nod, he smiled and greeted her as well. "Looking lovely as always."

"So glad you're finally here, Anderson. You scared me for a minute. I have a few things I want to run over with you before we get you up on the podium. Excuse me, Babe," Pearson said to Niles and led Anderson away. She wanted to ask about Ryan, but kept her mouth shut.

As they snaked their way through the crowded reception, Pearson thought about the fact that she had seen everyone, but Ryan, Vonnie and Mike. Based on her conversation earlier that day, she knew that there was a good chance that Vonnie and Mike wouldn't show up, but she remained hopeful. She was serious about them coming without having tickets. She was also very serious about remaining friends with Vonnie after they moved.

Within the next few minutes the Maître d announced the event would be moving into the banquet hall. Once all the guests were settled, Pearson took to the podium, offering up a moving speech about pulling the event together despite so many unanticipated occurrences in both her professional and personal life. She credited Niles, her mother, her diligent staff and the young women the organization supported for being her motivation to help her get through it all. Trying her best not to shed tears in front of her three hundred guests, she introduced Anderson, reading his bio and highlighting his most well-known films to date. The sophisticated crowd stood to their feet as he made his way to the podium. A few cat calls rang out as he stepped up, looking especially handsome in his well-fitting tuxedo.

Anderson graciously smiled, nodded and gestured for the guests to be seated. Pearson followed his line of sight and noticed Ryan seated at the table with Niles. She was happy to see that she showed up, but wished things could have turned out different for them. Vonnie and Mike were still missing.

Pearson focused her attention back on Anderson, who was effortlessly stealing the hearts of the audience. She was glad she'd asked him to be her emcee. She knew he was a great actor, but she hadn't realized just how charming he would be in this capacity. She considered the crowd captured.

Once the young girls from this year's program got up to tell their stories and talk about how the foundation impacted their lives, she was sure her guests would be impressed and be more than happy to write big checks to help G-Day continue their work.

Movement at the head table caught Pearson's attention. She peeled her eyes away from Anderson's speech and was elated to see Vonnie and Mike taking a seat with the rest of the crew. She looked over and Vonnie winked and threw her an air kiss. Everyone whom she considered essential in her life was in attendance on the most important night of the year for her.

Once the program was over and dinner was served, the electric slide, followed by a series of other popular line dances got the party started. Guests kept the dance floor filled as the band played a dynamic mix of pop, jazz and R&B from hits from the sixties to the best of what was currently gracing the airwaves.

Pearson was pleased with the outcome and enjoyed watching everyone have a great time. She also saw that Ryan and Anderson barely spoke, but she did appreciate the new air of confidence that Ryan seemed to wear.

Getting back to business, she walked around to see how the silent auctions were going. Her assistant had found the missing folders with the vendor's checks and Pearson's relief washed away her anxiety. The bids for the fur coat that Nadalia had designed and donated had reached upwards of fifteen thousand dollars. All the other bids were also going well. Pearson beamed and discretely prided herself for getting through this without a drink.

Niles had really stepped up to be by her side and help her get through, showing firm patience during the times she became weak and gave in. His love and support helped her overcome until she got to a point where she refused to take a drink for both her sake and his. She didn't want to disappoint him.

Thinking about Niles, Pearson went searching for him, spotting him at the table chatting with her mom.

"May I have this dance?" she asked, holding her hand out to him.

Niles looked at her mother and stretched his eyes. "What do you think?" he asked jokingly.

Candice pretended to think about it for a while. Pearson pursed her lips and put her hands on her hips.

Candice laughed. "Go ahead. She's kind of cute. I heard she put this whole thing together. She's probably pretty smart too."

"Brains and beauty," Niles said and nodded his approval.

Pearson took him by the hand and led him to the dance floor.

"I'm proud of you," Niles whispered in her ear as they swayed to one of his old favorites by Nina Simone.

"I couldn't have done it without you, so thank you."

Pearson closed her eyes and snuggled into Niles' shoulder, letting herself be taken away in the comfort of his arms. When Pearson looked up, she saw Nadalia heading out. Sage was still seated at the table with Candice.

"Excuse me a moment, babe."

Niles kissed her forehead before releasing her. Pearson ran through the swaying bodies and pushed through a few chairs trying to get to Nadalia.

"Nadalia! Wait!" Pearson could have sworn Nadalia started walking faster after hearing her call her name. She gestured for a gentleman to get Nadalia's attention and she continued running in her direction.

Nadalia turned back, following the man's finger as he pointed. Pearson thought she saw her sigh. Nearly out of breath, Pearson caught up with her just as she was about to exit the venue.

"You're leaving already? Where's Sage?"

"Yeah." Nadalia didn't bother responding to Pearson's second question.

"Wait." Pearson took Nadalia down a quiet corridor where the two of them could be alone. "I just wanted to make sure you were alright."

Nadalia tilted her head and smiled. "I'm fine."

Pearson pulled Nadalia into an embrace. "You call me for anything, you hear me?"

Nadalia nodded and hugged Pearson again.

"You better keep in touch. I don't want to lose you as a friend," Pearson said. "Who would I have to bicker with?"

Nadalia chuckled.

"I love you," Pearson said.

The declaration seemed to put Nadalia on pause. She closed her eyes and nodded before saying, "Believe it or not, I love you, too."

They embraced one last time before Pearson followed Nadalia to the exit, then watched her leave. She was so caught up with what Nadalia had just revealed, she never heard Niles call her name.

"Pearse! Babe! Come on!"

"Huh? What?" Pearson turned and stopped short, alarmed by the look on Niles' face. "What's going on?"

"It's your mother."

Niles took her hand and they ran back through the hall. People cleared the way as they passed by. Gripped by fear, Pearson's breathing struggled past the sudden lump in her throat.

Inside, a small crowd gathered around the table where her mother and friends sat. Pearson quickened her pace, pushing through the guests.

Candice lay on the floor, wearily lolling her head from side to side. Several people were around her, fanning her while Vonnie held her head in her lap.

"I need a towel. Get me a glass of water for her," she ordered. "Please back up a little people. Give her some air."

"Oh my goodness. Ma! What happened?" she asked frantically to no one in particular as she fell to her knees beside Candice.

Sage handed Vonnie the glass of water.

"I need you to try and take a sip for me. Okay?" Vonnie said to Candice in a cajoling voice.

Candice tried, but her head lolled and fell back into Vonnie's lap.

"Ma! Drink the water!" Pearson felt her own chest become tight. "Ma!" she cried out. "Please drink it. Please!" Holding her hand behind her head, Pearson tried to lift her up enough to get a good angle. Vonnie put the glass to her mouth, but Candice was too weak to drink. She laid her head back and let it fall to the side. "No! Mommy, please!" Pearson could no longer control her emotions and the cry that she released shook her entire body.

Pearson felt strong arms lifting her and at first thought it was Niles. Sage helped her to her feet and sat her in a chair.

"Thanks, man," Niles said and hugged Sage before lowering himself beside Pearson. "It's going to be alright, babe. An ambulance is on its way." Niles rested her head on his chest and caressed her back.

All Pearson could think of was that she wasn't ready for her mother to die.

Chapter 52

Three months later...

Pearson looked around at the few people left in her mother's home after the repast. The ones who were here now were the same ones who had been by her side for the past few months as she witnessed her mother wither away. Candice went out like a true diva, keeping her spirits up until the day she passed.

Dressed in all white, because she insisted on making an impressive entrance to the party going on upstairs, and adorned with her favorite jewels, Candice looked as glamorous and regal as she had in life. Pearson followed her instructions to the letter, ensuring that her 'going home celebration' would turn out exactly as Candice wanted it to. The intimate, but elegant ceremony seemed more like a celebratory gathering than a funeral, with no one in black—per Candice's instructions.

Pearson turned to face the person who had touched her shoulder. With glistening eyes, Walter hugged her one last time and let her know that he'd be heading home for the night.

"Call me if you need anything at all."

"I will," she said, squeezing his hand before letting it go. The sadness in his eyes made her heart break into a billion pieces all over again. "Thank you for being so good to my mother."

Walter smiled and lowered his head for a moment. "She was a wonderful person. Most people just didn't understand her like I did."

Pearson smiled because she finally came to understand the woman her mother was, too.

"I'm going to miss her," Walter said shaking his head.

"Me, too."

Walter took her hands into his and gave them a gentle squeeze before turning to leave.

"Don't be a stranger," Pearson called out to him.

Walter turned, winked, straightened his back and proceeded out the front door.

"Pearson, honey," Vonnie whispered.

"What's up?"

"The girls and I cleaned up the kitchen and packed up all the food. We left everything on the counter. If you want, we can have the men carry the pans to the car."

"Thanks, Vonnie. Don't worry about it, Niles and I can manage." Then, she added, "Don't you have a big day tomorrow? You better get home and get your beauty sleep."

"Girl, I'll be just fine."

"I'm so happy for you. We're going to have a Dr. Oz party in the conference room at the office so we can see you on the show. We're going to have popcorn and everything."

"You're kidding!"

"No, I'm not. I told them they all have to watch my friend on TV."

Vonnie laughed. "Aww Pearson. Thank you. Everything has been happening so fast. I keep getting calls for interviews. The other day, I got a call from a publisher talking about helping me write a book about the childhood obesity program that I started with my patients."

"You didn't tell me that!"

"After everything happened, the last thing I was going to do was call you about that. It seemed so trivial after…well you know," Vonnie said.

"What's going on over here?" Ryan interjected, rubbing her belly. At six months, the small baby bump made her look like she'd swallowed a soccer ball.

"I was just talking to the famous doctor about her television appearance tomorrow."

"Oh yes! I forgot." Ryan clapped. "Are you nervous?"

"Not really. I could talk about this stuff all day. I was a fat kid myself."

"Vonnie!" Ryan scolded.

"What's going down in this corner? Are you conspiring about something?" Nadalia joined the ladies in conversation.

"Who us?" Pearson feigned innocence.

"You're the main one!" Nadalia teased.

"I've turned several new leaves!"

"Yeah, right," Nadalia said.

All the girls laughed.

"Okay, I'm heading out." Vonnie gave hugs and kisses all around. "Like you said Pearson, I need to get my beauty rest so I can look good for the camera."

"How about I come with you so I can sit next to you? That will make you look even better and get me closer to that handsome Dr. Oz. Ha!" Nadalia snickered.

"If I don't get to him first! Who cares if I'm pregnant?" Ryan said and they all burst out laughing.

"Ladies, don't forget, when we meet for dinner this Friday, we need to figure out where we're going for our ladies getaway," Vonnie reminded them.

"Oh, yes! Let's lock in some dates. I want to go sometime soon," Nadalia said and then looked at Ryan. "Aw dang. I forgot about Mrs. Baby on Board over here."

Ryan pouted.

"We don't have to go far. We can do a weekend at the Gurneys in the Hamptons," Pearson said and then patted Ryan's back.

"Oh that sounds great!" Vonnie said. "I could use a quick spa vacation."

"Even we could manage that," Ryan said rubbing her stomach.

Mike walked over to where the ladies were standing and put his arm around Vonnie. "Call me if you need to," he said to Pearson.

"Yes! I know what you are dealing with," Vonnie said, referring the death of her own mother. "I'll be checking on you."

"Thanks," Pearson said, genuinely happy to have these ladies in her life. They had expanded her definition of family in the most unlikely way.

Mike patted Vonnie on the bottom. "Come on, lady. Let's hit the road. We don't live around the corner anymore." Vonnie rolled her eyes, shook her head, and gave her final goodbye kisses and hugs to the other ladies.

Ryan left next. It was weird to see her without Anderson and Nadalia without Sage. Both men had made an appearance, but left shortly after the services. Oddly enough, Ryan seemed content without Anderson. From the way she now looked and laughed, life was better for her without him.

Pearson stood in the door watching her friends leave. Feeling Niles wrap his arms around her from behind, she nestled her back into his chest.

"You okay?"

Pearson turned around to face him. "I'm fine."

"So let's go home and try to make some babies."

Pearson raised one brow. "Let's."

Not expecting her to agree, Niles eyes stretched wide. "Are you kidding me?"

Pearson grinned instead of answering. Several months ago, she would have clammed up at the idea of bringing a child into her shambolic world. She was different now and couldn't think of anything she'd rather do than start a family with Niles.

Pearson pushed the front door closed, slipped her hands under her dress and wiggled out of her lace panties, letting them drop to the floor. Niles scrunched his eyebrows and narrowed his eyes at the panties dangling around her ankles.

"Do I look like I'm kidding?" Pearson giggled.

Niles laughed—a loud and hearty one, filling the house to the rafters with the sound of his joy and then pulled Pearson into his arms and kissed her.

CPSIA information can be obtained at www.ICGtesting.com
Printed in the USA
LVOW08s0923100515

437935LV00001B/137/P